the *mystery* of the eighth deadly sin

To my sweet
great niece,
Beth

Hope your life
is as sweet
as Conci's

Love ya,
Auntie Gloria

the *mystery* of the eighth deadly sin

GLORIA D'ALESSANDRO

conci d'amato mysteries

Tate Publishing & *Enterprises*

Published by Tate Publishing & Enterprises, LLC
127 E. Trade Center Terrace | Mustang, Oklahoma 73064 USA
1.888.361.9473 | www.tatepublishing.com

Tate Publishing is committed to excellence in the publishing industry. The company reflects the philosophy established by the founders, based on Psalm 68:11,
"The Lord gave the word and great was the company of those who published it."

Book design copyright © 2009 by Tate Publishing, LLC. All rights reserved.
Cover design by Leah LeFlore
Interior design by Stephanie Woloszyn

Published in the United States of America

ISBN: 978-1-60604-693-7
1. Fiction / Christian / Suspense
2. Fiction / Mystery & Detective / General
09.01.28

table of contents

dedication

I dedicate this book to the Lord Jesus, who gave me the idea and the Holy Spirit inspiration to write this book.

I further dedicate this to Sister Mary Remegius, R.S.M., my seventh- and eighth-grade teacher at the Most Precious Blood School in Chicago, Illinois, who showed me how to live like a real Christian and how to teach children with love and mercy.

I also dedicate this book to my beloved mother, Ann Carrara Cipriano, who taught me how to cook and how to be a good mother and wife and showed me by her example that commitment and love are the glue that holds marriages together through good and bad seasons.

acknowledgments

Thanks to my husband of fifty years, Dr. Angelo D'Alessandro, who supports me and my efforts at writing and faithfully totes me to every book signing and other events. And thanks to my children, Christopher D'Alessandro and Ninette and Dr. John Ashley, Peter D'Alessandro and Cathy McClanahan, Dr. David D'Alessandro, and Angelo, Jr., and Judith D'Alessandro for their encouragement and belief in me.

A special thanks to Dennis Loane, a fellow writer and dear friend, for his blessed encouragement and patience and help in listening to the book as it evolved from an idea to a full-fledged novel. Thanks for ideas and for keeping my story making sense.

A special thanks to Linda Connors, my dear friend and beautician for thirty-six years, for all her help and encouragement and for all the time and effort she put out in publicity and promoting my books.

Thanks to my grandchildren for their love and support and for being proud of me. To Erin and Eddie Cooper and my great-grandchild, Emily Ashley Cooper, and to my other grandchildren, Laurelyn Ashley, Angelo and Wayne D'Alessandro; Karis and Kylie D'Alessandro; and Ruth Gloria and Thomas Ashley, and to my unborn grandchildren, I give Nana's heartfelt thanks.

chapter 1
the conference

It couldn't have happened at a worse time. The building was filled with not only all two thousand high school students, but also a statewide conference of teachers from all the private schools in the state. Each school sent three or four teachers to represent their school, and since there were forty-one private schools in the state and the surrounding states, there were over 120 teachers at the school.

The students had just returned from their summer break and the halls were filled with laughter and chatting as they renewed old acquaintances and made some new ones.

Suddenly a scream and then yells filled the halls, and students were running away from a certain area on the second-floor hall. It was Dr. Berger, coming from the assistant principal's office. He came out screaming and yelling with a huge long snake following him. The students and the teachers immediately ran down the stairs, but the snake was more interested in Dr. Berger and chased him until it cornered him by the window. Then the snake reared up and struck him on his face and then on his head. Dr. Berger tried to hit the thing, but it just kept coming at him.

Everyone was already out of the classrooms and down the stairs, except for the farthest room down the hall, and they would have to pass Dr. Berger and the snake in order to get out. The snake spotted them trying to get by, and they all ran into one classroom and stuffed some rags and clothing under the door to keep the snake out. Moving swiftly, it reared up and hit the door with itself several times.

"Snake, Snake!" Some of the girls began to scream, as dozens of people ran down the halls almost pushing each other aside and cascaded down the stairs and out of the building.

Screaming was causing panic, and soon, the second floor was cleared out of people. Dr. Berger lay on the floor barely breathing and then not at all, his face contorting in a hideous titanic grimace, his body convulsing as he barely breathed and then stopped altogether.

The guards stopped the students and the teachers from exiting and held them there at the bottom of the stairs until they saw one of the snakes at the top of the stairs. In the ensuing pandemonium, two thousand students trampled each other and almost killed Charlie Morton, the senior guard, as they ran out of the building, still screaming.

Finally, all the students were on the parking lot, and the building was empty, or so they thought. The teachers naturally followed the panic and left the building.

Teachers Conci D'Amato McVey, Loretta Sterns-Ryan, Mari Nelson, and Jennifer Bartnett were all representatives from their school, the Academy of Signs and Wonders and were on the spot when the panic broke out. However, they didn't actually see the snake because the conference was on the first floor. Peggy Dowling was crying almost hysterically. "It came out of Dr. Berger's office and was chasing him down the hall. Most of us got out, but I can't find Marily Thomas and Tommy DeVris, two of my students!" she screamed in a panic.

The fire department came, the police came, and the ambulance came. Dr. McMurray, the principal, was trying to get a grip on the happenings but was unable to calm the crowd. Finally, the police took charge and then had some people, experts from the serpentarium area in the zoo, come and get a description from some of the students as to what the snake looked like.

"It was long and gray or green. I don't remember, but it was so aggressive, sir. It even reared up to Dr. Berger's height and then struck him," one of the students, Hayley Studeville, said.

"I worked at the zoo last summer, and I never saw a snake like this one. I think there was another one too. We all got out of there quickly but poor Dr. Berger. The snake wouldn't let him alone, and as we ran down the stairs, we could see it cornering him and almost standing straight up and striking him in the head and face, I think. We just ran and ran. It was utter panic. I think some of my friends are still in the building," Sheila Myers, a senior, sobbed.

The people from the zoo looked at each other in alarm.

"It sounds like a black mamba, Josey."

The man, Dr. Leonard Hall, raised his eyebrows at that pronouncement.

"Yes!" she said fearfully. "How could we possibly catch it or kill it without endangering our lives, sir?" she asked her superior. He called another zoo in nearby Martindale, and soon, other experts came to their aid.

"Okay, Dr. McMurray, we need everyone to go home. Just leave whatever they have in the building, and we'll seal it up. That is one very dangerous snake, if it's the one we're thinking of." The one that appeared to be in charge commanded.

The parents had been summoned by some of the students on their cell phones and began arriving and picking up their children. It became an impossible task to keep track of who had left.

When Sgt. Jonathan Carter arrived with his wife, Marybeth, looking for their daughter, Cindy, they were unable to find her and finally cornered McMurray.

As he talked calmly to them, Hayley Thomas saw them and began to cry big time. "I think she's still in second-floor lab room."

Both parents were quite upset, and Sgt. Carter called to his superior and told him the story.

Also finding out that their children were unaccounted for, ten other parents were beside themselves. They talked on the bullhorns, trying to find the students, but no one wanted to go inside the building.

Finally, one of the teachers that was trapped in the classroom was able to get through to McMurray's phone.

"Mac, we're trapped in room 202B. We dragged the body of the dead Berger into the room with us, and we have thirteen students and four teachers here. There are snakes prowling the hallways, and we can't get out. It sounds like more than one snake now," she reported.

"Okay, Anna Lee, just hold on. I'll tell the cops right now." Dr. McMurray calmed her down.

Mike McVey, head of homicide, arrived after the call to Captain Montgomery and remembered that his wife had said something about going to the Second Chance Academy to a conference today. He looked around for his wife right away.

The whole parking lot of people was praying mightily. The cops were trying to get the students to go home if they had cars and for the parents to pick up their kids and then leave the premises. When Dr. McMurray spoke to the crowd and cautioned them about the snakes coming out onto the parking lot, most of them left.

Soon, only emergency vehicles were allowed on the parking lot.

Mike found Conci when he called her on her cell phone.

"Where are you, babe?" His voice sounded quite worried.

"We're in this crowd somewhere, Mike. Jennifer, Mari, and Loretta are here with me too," she explained. "I'll walk toward one of the police cars." That's what they all four did, and Mike finally spotted them and approached them hurriedly. He hugged Conci and held onto her tightly. She was four months pregnant much to her delight and his chagrin.

"What the heck happened?"

All four women tried to explain at one time, "This all happened about two o'clock in the afternoon as the students were changing classes."

"Okay, ladies, I want you to go home right now," Mike commanded in his best voice of authority.

Just then Dr. Mark Sondergaard spotted Conci, knowing her from her frequent visits to the serpentarium with her class. They had talked a lot about her three snakebites in Africa and how God healed her.

Conci had witnessed various types of snake-bites during her eleven years growing up in West Africa. He approached and, much to Mike's dismay, hugged Conci.

"I figured you were here, Mark. How bad is it?" she asked, getting involved in the procedures as Dr. Sondergaard pulled her into a corner to talk to the other doctors. She looked back at Mike and motioned for him to come too. He did so, if only to make sure they didn't send his wife in after the snakes. He would never permit that.

Mike pulled her away from Sondergaard and held onto her hand. They stood there, and Sondergaard introduced Conci to them. "And, of course, you know Lt. McVey, head of homicide." They all shook their heads.

"Conci here was bitten three times by snakes in West Africa, and one of the bites was a black mamba," Dr. Sondergaard explained to his colleagues. All five of the serpentarium folks looked at her with a lot more respect.

"The Lord healed me," she stated as though there would be no argument about that at all.

Mike nodded his head first, and they all followed, even the skeptics.

Conci was surprised and pleased about that. She smiled at her husband and tightened her grip on his hand.

"Okay, Conci, is there anything that you could add to our plan?" Dr. Sondergaard asked. The others just looked at him in a critical way.

Conci closed her eyes, and Mike knew she was reenacting a scene in her mind.

"One time a black mamba came into our compound. That was an unusual event, because the mambas were indigenous to East Africa rather than West. At any rate, it was looking at all of us while we were seated, eating. There were about twelve of us present. Dr. Geisman, our physician, got up quietly, trying not to make any noise. He was the closest one to the door. At first the snake just eyed all of us, slithering a little closer every few minutes. Then it spied Dr. Geisman as he reached the door. He ran out, and the snake ran quickly after him. Dr. Geisman unlatched the goat pen right outside the door to the compound and moved aside as the big snake almost ran into the compound and consumed at least six goats over the course of the day, and then the servants, the snake hunters who were quite afraid of the mambas, cut off its head. It just couldn't move. It was so engorged from eating that it couldn't bite anyone. It was a great plan, borne out of desperation," she said.

Everyone looked at her.

"How could this apply to these circumstances, Conci?" Dr. Nodderhead asked, being more interested in this interloper.

All eyes were on Conci, and she looked at Mike for help and permission to continue. He was moved by her gesture, and she moved closer to him. He nodded his head, and they all noted it, paying more respect to her and her husband.

"This is just a thought. Why not draw them out with a feast for them? We can have a temporary fence or enclosure erected in an hour or two. Then get everyone far away from the snakes coming out. As they hear the bleating of the lambs or sheep or whatever, they will be drawn outside. Of course, we have to open the doors.

The enclosure must be around the one opened door, and the others must be securely locked. We can have sharpshooters on the roof and others around the compound. Let them eat so they will slow down and then kill them. We can shoot them at this point," she said, "and no one will be in danger. Then we can get the students out. If there are more snakes than one, then we have to make sure we get them all. All of you are experts in the field and can determine if these snakes are territorial or not. Can't you?"

"Conci, if it could be as simple as shooting them, why didn't your brave Dr. Geisman get his gun and shoot the snake?" Dr. Martin Smalley, a doctor who had never met Conci, asked, sneering at her.

"At the time we were under a communist regime," she said as though that should have explained everything to them.

"So?" Dr. Smalley asked again, this time sounding surly as well. Mike turned to look at him. Dr. Smalley was from the Institute for the Study of African Snakes and was the foremost expert on the mambas. He was quite an arrogant person, a fact that all who knew him vouched for.

"The communists confiscated all the firearms. So, we had to use our machetes or other means to kill the snakes or other predators, Doctor," she said and almost smiled at him.

"Thank you, Mrs. McVey, but we have another plan," he said in his arrogant voice and dismissed her readily. The others just watched her as she shook his hand.

"If I can help you in any way, I am at your service," she said and bowed to him.

Conci was about to leave, knowing she had been dismissed by the great man, but Mike didn't like his tone at all. *Conci probably knows experientially more about these snakes than he does,* he thought stubbornly.

"Well, let's hear it, Smalley," Mike said just as rudely.

"It isn't as yet perfected, Lieutenant. We'll tell you when we're ready to execute it," he said scornfully.

Mike persisted. "Sorry, Doc, but I must know every plan and approve or disapprove of it. So you better tell me what you have planned."

"Well, Lieutenant, we will have you throw some gas grenades into the building and inundate the snakes, and they will pass out. Then we can gather them up for study."

"Wait, what about the seventeen people inside the building?" Mike asked, thinking of his nephew Mikey.

"Well, someone will have to get them some gas masks," he stated unconcernedly.

"Wait, Doc. If we could get into the room where they're holed up, we would have rescued them already, but the room they're in isn't on the window side of the building. It's across the hall and is an inside room. We can't get to them without going across the hall and endangering our people."

Just then Jed Myerson ran to where Mike was standing. His wife, Shelley, had just called his cell phone. "My wife says that they can hear the snakes in the hallway, and they're trying to get inside the room. They've stuffed coats and things under the door to keep them out," he told Mike hastily.

Back in the classroom, where the seventeen frightened people were trapped by some snakes in the hallways, Billy Sonders and Jack Randall each held a fire extinguisher, hoping that if one of the snakes got in they could immobilize it with the very cold foam from the extinguishers. At any rate, it gave them a false sense of protection and seemed to calm down the thirteen students and the other two teachers, all of whom were on the verge of hysteria as the snakes hitting against the door, trying to get in. Those that knew how began to pray.

Outside, coming up with no good alternative plan, Dr. Sondergaard sighed and took authority over the whole thing after they all conferred with Dr. McMurray, the principal who was almost overcome with the enormity of the problem.

"I think we should give some credence and study to Mrs. McVey's plan," he said, looking straight at Dr. Smalley. Mike squeezed Conci's hand and whispered something into her ear.

She nodded. "Doctors, I am but a neophyte with a degree in education, just a couple of master's, and only some credits toward a doctorate, certainly not in a league with all of you. So, if this plan is successful, I would not want my name mentioned, only that my husband, Lt. McVey, of the metropolitan police and Sgt. McAlister of the bomb squad would be mentioned as part of your team of experts who came up with this winning plan. That's all. I would be very embarrassed if I was to be mentioned. I am a team player. Yes, I definitely am."

They executed Conci's plan, and soon two mambas came out. They were clearly shocked to see that there were two of them, as the snakes went crazy eating the lambs. Some people couldn't watch, but the cops and the serpentarium people did, as did Conci.

The cops mowed them down with bullets as they ate.

Then a group of men were sent in with proper covering and found the thirteen students and four teachers and led them out to safety.

Dr. Berger's body was removed, and very few could look upon it. Mike McVey, having been a homicide cop for thirty years, took a good, long look at the poor man. An autopsy was done to make sure they knew the exact cause of death.

At the police station, Mike talked about it to his sidekick, Max, Sgt. Maxwell; Lt. Alex Melville; and Captain Montgomery, Monty to his friends. "Okay, I'm concerned because the snakes were African, and the mambas are especially fierce and deadly. So, whoever put them into the lockers must have a good knowledge of snakes and these types in particular. Perhaps they were put in when the school would be empty for a time. Then the person or persons could come into the school without any problem and without anyone knowing they were here."

They investigated every shred of evidence but could find no reason or anything incriminating about the snakes. No one saw anything or anyone putting snakes in the building.

"What a thing to happen. I'm really shocked about it all. There must be clues somewhere since it had to be difficult to bring those snakes into the office of Dr. Berger." Mike sighed, quite perplexed.

"Dr. Sondergaard from the serpentarium said they had to be heavily drugged for anyone to even handle them. But why kill a man that way? Why not shoot him or something? It's so darn strange," Melville agreed.

But try as they might, no more clues were forthcoming.

The cops found that the African black mambas must have come from the wild or from out of town because no zoos or aquariums had any missing, not anywhere in the U.S. However, there was one report of a display of dried Australian sea wasps that hung on the wall that was missing right here in the city. Everyone wondered about that. It was downright strange.

A thorough examination of the two mambas revealed that the one had no fangs at all, looking as though they'd been surgically removed, and the other one was highly dangerous and had long, intact fangs that were still filled with deadly poison as it lay dead.

Both snakes had traces of narcotics in their

tissues, indicating that they had been heavily drugged.

"So, someone breaks into the school, in the dead of night, I assume, and puts a mamba with no fangs in Dr. Berger's drawer of his desk, a heavily drugged one at that, then shuts the drawer and puts one that is deadly with fangs somewhere in his office. For what reason? Why were there two instead of one? Why put the benign one in the office at all? Why not just the dangerous one? It makes no sense to me," Mike said as he and Melville were discussing it for the third or fourth time.

Alex Melville nodded his head. He was a very laid-back individual and usually gave the impression to people that didn't know him that he was a little slow and dull witted, but that was just his innocuous appearance, for in truth he was a very astute cop, and the bad guys soon knew it and learned to fear him as much as McVey.

"Perhaps it was a warning to someone. I don't know, Mike. It makes no sense to me either."

That's all the clues they found. Hard interviews with the night guards came up with no information at all, although they did seem a little scared and nervous during the whole interview.

"Hey, what's wrong with you, Harrison?"

Melville asked the night guard, Angelo Harrison, who couldn't look him in the eyes.

"I don't know nothing. You think I'd not report it if someone broke into the school and put some deadly snake in there? You think I want to get killed myself?"

Melville thought that was a strange way of putting things.

"Did someone threaten you, Mr. Harrison?" he asked softly now, as though he were the guy's best friend.

But Harrison had dealt with the cops many times in his life and wouldn't be fooled by this guy's hayseed, friendly farmer routine.

"No way. No one threatens me. About what anyway?"

Finally they had to let him go.

The other night guard, Geraldo Ramirez, was a small, very blue-eyed man, belying his Spanish ancestry.

"No one came. I saw no one. Everyone knows that I saw no one," he kept saying.

Melville let them both go and shrugged his shoulders.

"Something strange is going on here, Mike." He sighed.

Mike thought so too.

Dr. Berger's family had him buried, and although the cops interviewed them, no one was talking. Mrs. Berger was especially nervous when interviewed—not just upset about her husband, but nervous about something else. Within two days of the funeral, the family left town, leaving their house and belongings behind.

"How odd!" Mike thought out loud. Yes, that was a real puzzle, as though they were terrified that the same fate would come upon them, and they had to get as far away as quickly as possible.

"Maybe it was meant as a warning to others, Mike," Conci ventured a guess.

Mike turned to her with a frown on his face.

"Oh? How do you figure that?"

"Well, you said that the one snake was harmless, so maybe that one was sent as a message to beware or something sinister like that. Then someone else put in the other snake, another faction altogether."

Mike just looked at her, wondering where she got her crazy ideas.

"You ought to write fiction, Conci. You're very good at imagining things," he chided her, making fun of her as usual.

"It was just a thought," she said as she walked away.

After a couple of weeks, Dr. McMurray and his board of directors decided to give the students free tuition for a month in order to get all the students back. They were successful, and the school was full again.

A couple of months passed, and the events of the first week of school were soon forgotten. The school officials stated they had to make up the money they lost, so they had a special fundraising event on their beautiful spacious grounds—a carnival.

chapter II
the carnival

The lilting refrains of the calliope, as it played the waltzes unique to it only, filled the carnival, along with the sounds of the barkers calling people in to play their games. The smells of hot dogs, hamburgers, and other highly fried foods added up to a promise of a great time.

Second Chance Academy staged the carnival on their huge grounds on the outskirts of the city. It was quite an extravaganza.

Conci McVey and her aunt, Sister Mary Concetta Rose, a missionary, slowly pushed the two-seater stroller carrying the McVeys' three-year-old twins, a boy, Sonny, and a girl, Moira. They were good children and their cheeks were all red with excitement.

There were many people in the crowd that Conci knew, as she had been a teacher in the city for over twenty years and worked at various schools during that time. She knew many of the teachers and, in fact, had seen some of them recently at the conference a short while ago. They chatted about the event, and one of her friends, Selma Noriega, greeted her, smiling and hugging Conci.

"You remember my aunt, Sister Mary Concetta Rose?"

"Oh yes. Sister, it's good to see you again."

"Are you working at the carnival then?" Conci wondered because of the apron her friend wore.

"Oh yes, the boss, Dr. McMurray, insisted that we all do our part. I'm in charge of a few booths, but especially the dunk tank, where Dr. McMurray himself is being dunked by the high school boys. He's sitting there like a drowned rat, and I'm not even sure I should rescue him," she said sardonically, looking down at the ground. Conci wondered about that.

"He's not real popular, Conci. No one really likes him, but we're all too afraid to say anything."

There was a pause in the conversation.

"Oh, I have to run. Guess who's our special guest star? You'll never guess, Conci!" she screamed. "Sonny Lopelia, the movie star. His son, Shepherd, is a student at the school and lives with his sister, Dora. I haven't met him yet, but he says he's going to get into the dunk tank this afternoon from five until seven. Isn't that fabulous? It was in the papers, so that should bring in a big crowd, don't you think?" Then she hurriedly looked at her watch.

"Oh my, almost five o'clock already. Have to run!" she said breathlessly.

Conci hugged her friend. "I hope it's a great response for your sake, sweetie. Let's get together and talk."

"Oh, Conci, I really want to do that. Let's try for next week, okay?" She sounded quite desperate, and then she ran off.

Sister raised her eyebrows at Conci.

"Your friend sounds rather disenchanted with the school, Conci. Did you get an invitation to join them?"

Conci shook her head.

"Loretta did, however, and turned them down cold. Said they wanted people with sins on their souls and would give them a second chance. But Loretta didn't buy that. She felt something else so she refused."

The babies began pushing themselves back and forth to make the stroller go, and the two women laughed and began to push them again, as they smiled.

"Look, Auntie, over there at that beautiful, tall redhead. Isn't she a famous model or something? I think I saw her face on some magazine."

Sister looked at the woman curiously as the woman walked purposely toward her car and was holding a briefcase.

Both women looked at each other, perplexed.

They walked around for a while and stopped here and there to see something and to get the children a treat to eat. The children were mesmerized by the sounds and the visual delights of the carnival.

Suddenly, everyone seemed to be running in one direction, as if a stampede were happening. Conci and Sister stood in front and back of the stroller in order to protect the children. People were shouting and screaming, and many of them appeared to be leaving the premises.

"What's going on?" Conci grabbed a hold of one of her seniors from the Academy of Signs and Wonders.

"Oh, Mrs. McVey, there's some poisonous snakes around the grounds, and one of them bit Dr. McMurray when he was in the dunk tank." Then he pushed off her hand and ran with the rest of them.

Conci and Sister both looked at each other.

"Auntie, what do you think that's all about, for heaven's sake? Maybe we should think about going." She looked at her aunt with alarm.

Sister shook her head. "We'll never get out

in this crush for the road. We'd better stay put. The whole place is almost deserted now, and the only place there are people milling around is over there. That must be where the dunk tank is located."

Conci spotted a guy who looked familiar to her.

"That looks like Lt. Fred Lawrence. He's just come on homicide, having been in narcotics for eight or more years. Mike says he's more taciturn than he is. I ask, is that possible?" Both women laughed.

The man was walking quickly away from the scene, and Conci wondered about it.

"I'm confused, Conci," Sister began. "A cop walking away from an incident like that. What's going on?"

"I wonder about that, too, Auntie. I'll ask Mike about it later."

Finally, as the crowd began to disperse, Conci saw her friend again and asked what had happened. She had been crying.

"Oh, Conci, Dr. McMuray was bitten by a poisonous snake that was in his dunk tank. It was supposed to be Sonny Lopelia in there; but he didn't show up, so Dr. McMuray went in his place. There were two snakes in the tank because the boys put a rubber one in there to tease him and play a joke on him, and he saw it and grabbed it, trying to show his mock bravery. But instead of it being the rubber snake, it was a real snake, a water moccasin, they say. It bit him right in the face. Not a good place at all. The boys hurried, and opened the door and dragged him out, and the snake slithered away. That's all I know."

"How is Dr. McMurray?"

She shook her head. "Not good."

They all three prayed about it, and then Conci and Sister got into their car and went home, discussing it all the way, as the children were sound asleep in their car seats.

They put the children into their pajamas, gave them a snack, and put them to bed. Then and only then did Sister and Conci sit down and enjoy their coffee and some pie.

Mike called.

"I'll be home late, Conci. There was an attempted murder at a carnival, of all places. Do you know Dr. McMuray from the Second Chance Academy?"

"Oh yes, Mike, we were there, Auntie and I and the twins," she said without thinking.

"What?" he yelled at her. "Are you some kind of jinx? Did you see the thing happen?"

"Oh no, Mike, we weren't even in the vicinity at the time. We just waited until the crowd dispersed, and we came straight home. We're not involved at all," she said.

"Okay, then." He was a little placated and hung up.

Conci sighed.

"I need to think before I tell him anything," she explained to her aunt.

"What's wrong with him lately, Conci? He's like a cat on a hot tin roof."

She nodded. "I know, Auntie. I know, and I don't like it. I guess it's the new baby. He hasn't been a happy camper about it at all."

They prayed about it while relaxing in the two comfortable recliners in the family room. It was seven-thirty and they were quite tired from their adventure.

About fifteen minutes later, Mike came in the door, roaring like a lion. He pulled Conci up by her arm almost pulling it out of socket.

"Mike!" she screamed, and Sister rose quickly from her chair and stood right behind Conci, making sure he wasn't going to hurt her. "You hurt me, Mike. What was that all about?"

"You were there, weren't you? What the heck were you guys doing there?"

"It was a carnival, Mike. That's why we were there, to have some fun."

He pushed her back down into the chair, and she bent over and began to cry.

"Stop the tears again, Conci. That's all you do lately is cry. I'm getting sick of it. Every time I investigate a murder, somehow you know the people involved, or you're right there in the middle of it all."

Sister just stared at Mike. She'd never seen him this angry at Conci and never witnessed any brutality ever. Now, she was stunned.

"Michael…" she began.

"Don't get me riled, Sister. Just don't interfere," he said angrily.

"We didn't see anything, just people running toward their cars or toward the dunk tank. We never went there ourselves," Conci explained, holding her arm and rubbing it.

Mike left the room and went into their bedroom and shut and locked the door. Conci got up and looked over at her aunt, who was watching her worriedly. Sister was more like Conci's mother than her aunt since she rescued her from a brutal father and brought her up in Africa on the Mission field.

"Is he like that a lot to you, honey?"

She shook her head. "No, it's only been lately that he's been so angry at times that he curses me, which is something he never did, certainly not when he's sober. I think he's having an affair, Auntie. That's what I think, and he feels guilty about it but so angry at me because I insisted on keeping the baby."

Sister looked at her, riveted to the spot.

You mean he wanted you to…?" She couldn't even finish the sentence.

Conci nodded.

As they sat down to have a late dinner, Mike came out of the bedroom, apparently detecting the odor of his favorite food; lasagna and meatballs.

He was in his stocking feet and had on his jeans and sweatshirt.

He sat down, Conci served him the lasagna and the meatballs, which he loved, and some crusty bread, and he ate with gusto and enjoyment.

"You're the best cook, baby. Yes, you're the greatest, Conci." He was obviously in a better mood and then noticed the stare that Sister gave to him. *Oh oh*, he thought, *I'm in some trouble here. I'd better apologize.* "Sorry, ladies, at my outburst. It was a great shock to me to hear that you two women and my precious children were on the site of the murder and with poisonous snakes about too. I guess I just lost it. Sorry," he said.

Conci smiled at him, but it would take more than that to appease Sister. He could see that.

She wasn't the puddle of forgiveness that Conci was. But for now that would have to do.

Mike and Sister had coffee, and Conci had the vegetable substitute that passed for the forbidden coffee since she was pregnant, and Mike asked them to tell him about the carnival.

"It was quite uneventful, Mike. We met an old friend of mine who works at Second Chance, and she told us about the dunk tank and how the senior boys were taking turns dunking Dr. McMurray, the principal, because they didn't like him. Then she also said that at five o'clock they were having a special guest, and it was advertised in the newspapers. It was to be Sonny Lopelia, the movie star, or I guess the fading movie star. At any rate, he was going to be in the dunk tank. His own son went to Second Chance, she told us."

"Yes, Mike," Sister took up the narrative.

"Who else did you see?"

"We saw that famous redheaded model; you know, the one in the magazine, Madeline something, I think. She was leaving the carnival, walking very quickly with a briefcase in her hands. We both thought that was rather odd. Then all of a sudden everyone started running out of the place. It was a real stampede."

"Yes, Mike, Conci and I put ourselves around

the twins to keep them safe, and people bumped into us too but kept on running. We finally were able to move out of the path of the runners. Some were going toward the dunk tank too."

"Then my friend came by again," Conci continued, "and she told us there had been a poisonous snake in the dunk tank that bit Dr. McMurray. We both wondered why Sonny Lopelia wasn't in the tank. That's it, Mike. Then we went home."

"That's it?"

Conci shrugged, and Sister nodded. He looked at both of them.

"Wait, Mike, I did see Lt. Lawrence; you know, Fred Lawrence. He was walking swiftly out of the place about ten minutes after the event took place. I thought that was odd for a cop to be on the scene and then leave."

Sister looked at him with her brows furrowed.

Both women agreed on the story.

"Maybe it's to my benefit that you both were on the premises since you have such good memories. Yes, it might even help me. So, I guess I have to apologize even more so. Forgive me, ladies, please. I'm under a whole lot of pressure."

Mike took a shower after Sister went to her bedroom to watch TV and pray. It was after ten o'clock. Then he got dressed, much to Conci's surprise.

"You're going out?"

He detected more than just surprise in her voice.

"Yeah, now that I have some information, I'm going back to the office to do some sleuthing and look at everyone's notes."

"Oh, does that require a shower and a shave?" she asked again, looking at him suspiciously.

"Maybe," he said, and left the house quickly, peeling away in his car.

Conci got on her knees and began to pray again.

chapter III
the investigation

Mike came home quite late that night and just dropped into bed exhausted. He was still sleeping when Conci and Sister both got up to tend to the babies and then got ready for church.

Conci left the coffee on for Mike and kissed him softly on the lips when she left. Mike felt the kiss but decided to ignore it. Conci knew that he had and just sighed. Then she and Sister gathered the babies and went off to church.

The whole church at Signs and Wonders was abuzz with the news about the snake incident at the other school's carnival. From the pulpit, the visiting preacher told the sad news that Dr. Mc-Murray was in very serious condition. Everyone went into prayer for about fifteen minutes.

After the service, Sister and Conci, while retrieving the twins from the nursery, spoke to many people about the incident. Most of them had been there at the carnival too.

"I saw the boys lurking about the dunk

tank, Conci," Loretta reported. "They sure had mischief on their faces too. I understand that the police arrested nine boys, and they denied putting a live snake into the dunk tank. They swore they put a rubber one in to just scare old McMurray, whom they never liked. The police have them all in custody still, but they deny that it was a real snake. What a mess. I'm so glad it's not at our school. We've already had our problems in the last few years. This year is going to be a good one," she said, and they hugged.

Conci called Mike on his cell phone, and he was already at the carnival again.

"Yeah, what do you want, Conci?"

"Oh, Mike, I just wanted to know if you were at home, and if so we'd come right home and make lunch. But if you're gone, we're going out to lunch with Loretta and some of the others that were at the carnival last night. Everyone has a story to tell," she said excitedly.

"I'm here at the carnival site, so do your own thing," he said and then hung up. Conci just looked at the phone. She was getting mighty tired of his bad moods again.

Conci and Sister went out with Loretta and Jennifer and Mary Elizabeth Morrison, the school nurse who had just met Sister Conci and was fascinated by this woman who looked so much like Conci and was such a fount of knowledge and wisdom. In fact, Mary Elizabeth sat next to her all afternoon. They joked and talked a mile a minute, and the twins just stared at everyone, fascinated with the high-pitched voices of some of the women.

Sister asked Mary Elizabeth some questions about her other jobs, and she told all of them about her fascinating jobs in Hollywood.

"Some of those stars were so drunk much of the time, and sometimes I tried to keep them sober and to help them with their children, who were really suffering most of the time because of the alcoholic parents. One family had two alcoholics in it; and one was a star, and his wife was a really mean but quite beautiful woman. It was horrible at times, but I did my best to help them."

Then she turned to Sister Conci. "Do you think that if someone witnessed a murder or some such heinous deed and kept quiet about it, but now is having conscience from the Lord to reveal it do you think that person should give the murderer a chance to turn him or herself in before they tell the cops themselves?"

Sister looked at her with a stern look in her eyes and then lowered them and took Mary Elizabeth's hand in hers and spoke to her so softly that the others couldn't hear very well.

"It would be a dangerous undertaking to talk to the person first. The prudent thing would be to tell the police first, for that guilty person might want to keep it quiet at all costs and quiet the one who wants to talk. Do you understand what I'm saying, child?"

She nodded her head, and everyone at the table began to talk animatedly again.

They all dispersed and went home, and Conci and Sister put the babies down for their naps and sat down tiredly themselves.

"Did you hear the conversation that Mary Elizabeth and I had, Conci?"

She nodded her head. "Yes, I did, Auntie. You gave her good advice too. I hope she's going to be all right."

"Yes, I do too." And then they prayed about it and drifted into sleep.

Sgt. Maxwell had arrived on the scene of the attempted murder almost immediately. He was an amiable guy, and everyone liked him and respected him. Max, as they called him, was forty-five and had joined the police corps when he was thirty, so he knew about life outside the ranks of the police department. He was a nice-looking guy with nappy black hair that his wife,

Risa, encouraged him to wear in dreadlocks, but he'd tried it and found them to be too tight, and he didn't look as distinguished as he liked. His own favorite was short, nappy, close-to-the-head, and easy to take care of. Risa just sighed and loved him anyway.

"You'd look like a young guy, Max, if you wore those dreadlocks again."

"Look, Risa, they pulled on my scalp too much and were difficult to wash my hair too. No, this is a cop's hairdo, now leave me alone. I never comment on your straightening your hair or whatever you do to it or color it red. I love you no matter how you look," he emphasized.

Risa just shrugged. She'd been nagging him lately for them to have another baby since her best friend, Conci McVey, was having her second pregnancy and third child and was forty-eight years old, while Risa was only forty-one.

"I'm much younger than Conci, Max, and we only have two, and they're teenagers now. I feel that empty nest creeping up on me."

Max just sighed and closed his eyes when she talked like that.

There were other police there already on the site when Max arrived. They knew that he was at homicide, and they yielded to his superior rank.

"This appears to be a very potent snakebite.

In fact, they describe it as a water moccasin. No one can find it now, sir. We've looked all over, but those snakes can hide almost anywhere. They're going to close down the carnival at any rate. We've warned those in charge to be extra careful because there might be a poisonous snake about.

"Good work, Detective." Max nodded to him.

One of the cops brought a crying Selma Noriega to Max.

"This is Mrs. Noriega, who was in charge of the dunk tank, Sergeant. She has a story to tell you."

"Yes, ma'am? I know this must be a real shock to you. Please sit down," he said kindly. Selma took a seat and looked at the sergeant with the tears still dripping down her face.

"I'm sorry, Sergeant. But it was such a shock. I was quite surprised that Dr. McMurray was in the tank at all. The movie star Sonny Lopelia was scheduled to go into the tank at five o'clock, not Dr. McMurray. I came on the scene as the boys were pulling Dr. McMurray out of the tank and actually saw the snake slithering away. We were all panicking, I'm afraid."

"Did you say that Sonny Lopelia was scheduled to be in the tank, not Dr. McMurray? What happened?"

"I wondered about that too, and when I

questioned him later on his cell phone, he said that Dr. McMurray's secretary had called him to change his time to tonight."

Mrs. Noriega looked at the sergeant, shocked.

"I then called Mrs. Lucy Benstill, and she denied ever calling Mr. Lopelia. So, that's a real mystery to me, Sergeant. Yes, it's very strange, indeed," she said, now cheering up a little at it being a mystery now that it looked as though Dr. McMurray would be recovering.

"Thank you, Mrs. Noriega. Thank you so much. I'll keep in touch with you. If you remember anything else, please let me know," he said politely.

He interviewed a few other people, but nothing much was forthcoming. Then he called in the nine boys, one at a time.

"We were only playing with him, that's all. We would never put a real snake in there. We'd be too scared to touch one, Sergeant," Tony Snyder confessed.

As it turned out, they still held the nine boys, and their parents were furious with the police.

Max called Mike and he came to the site and spoke with the parents. Since Dr. McMurray was going to make it, the charge wasn't so serious after all, and they released the boys; but they had to go before a judge in another month and would probably have to do some community service.

The next day Mike called Lt. Lawrence into his office while he was interviewing Mrs. Noriega again. He wanted Lawrence to sit in on this mystery and be a part of the investigation, since he was new to homicide and needed to learn the ropes. Mrs. Noriega did a double take when he came in, and he saw the recognition in her eyes. "You know each other?" Mike asked in his surly voice.

Selma just stared at Lawrence. "He was one of the off-duty cops that we hired for the carnival," she finally stated.

"Can I see you out in the hallway, Lieutenant?" he asked and pulled Mike out of the room.

"What the heck was that all about?"

He sighed. "We were watching the Second Chance Academy in regard to moving drugs, Mike, and this opportunity to do some off-duty work came up. I thought, *What the heck? Might as well take it and report anything fishy to the narc cops.*"

Mike just looked at him with a suspicious stare. The story sounded bogus to him.

"I thought you wanted to transfer to homicide because you were burnt out in narcotics?" Mike questioned him in a suspicious manner.

Lawrence frowned at Mike. "Yes, of course that's true, but what cop wouldn't follow through on one of his hunches and investigate this? I did need the money anyway, McVey," he said, now being a surly cop too and showing McVey that he couldn't be intimidated by him.

Mike nodded his head and then remembered that Conci had spotted him at the carnival leaving after the incident had occurred.

"Some witnesses saw you leaving the site of the snakebite, Lawrence. Why would you leave instead of holding the fort down until the other cops arrived?"

"No, they're wrong, Mike. I left after the cops had arrived. I wasn't a witness to any of it and thought I'd better get out of their way," he denied.

Mike looked at him long and hard and decided to let it go, but from that time on, he never trusted Lawrence, and Fred felt it.

What a rotten bit of luck, Fred complained to himself. *Yes, a rotten piece of luck.*

Next, they called in Sonny Lopelia. Sonny had been a major movie star for many years, but for the last ten years, he was old news, an alcoholic, and couldn't even get a job. But he did have a big following and a large fan club, and he did small gigs like state fairs and was going to help the school his son went to with their fundraising event, the carnival, by being in the dunk tank. It had been in all the newspapers too, and it brought in quite a crowd. Mike and Max both eyed him up and down, wondering what the womenfolk saw in a guy like him. He had smooth, shiny hair and was quite tall and well built but had a beer belly and really was a slick-looking kind of guy, a pretty boy that every red-blooded man wanted to punch out.

Mike shrugged off the feeling and began.

"Mr. Lopelia, Ms. Noriega said you were scheduled to be in the dunk tank at 5:00 p.m. on Saturday and didn't show up, and McMurray took your place. How was it that you weren't in the tank as scheduled?" he asked in his best cop voice.

Sonny frowned. "Someone called me and said that McMurray wanted to do it instead and that I'd be scheduled later in the evening when more people were attending."

"Who was it that called?" Mike inquired, still in his best official voice. He really didn't like this guy at all for some reason.

"She said it was Dr. McMurray's secretary, I think." He was hedging. Mike noticed and wondered about that.

"Did she identify herself further by giving her name?"

Sonny shook his head. "No, she just said she was Dr. McMurray's secretary and that I was rescheduled in the dunk tank for the evening—seven, I think she said, because there would be more people around. It didn't matter to me." He shrugged.

Mike stared at the man in front on him and then dismissed him.

An interview with the secretary of Dr. McMurray was at odds with Mr. Lopelia's testimony. She denied ever calling him at all.

"Is he lying, or is she, or did someone else call and say it was her?" Mike asked Max, who shrugged.

Dr. McMurray was still not in any shape to speak for himself. In fact, his face was still quite swollen, almost to a grotesque size and shape. The venom had eroded some of his face around his eyebrow and his cheekbone.

They would have to do some serious plastic surgery to get him looking anything normal again. He could barely talk, even though he was conscious part of the time. The board of directors wanted to speak to him badly, but neither the police nor the hospital would let them in.

Only his wife and his grown children, Charlie,

a twenty-five-year-old Marine, and Donna Mae, a nurse herself, were allowed to visit. Of course, the cops came and went at will, but even at that, only a few cops were allowed in, no one with a uniform, only the plain-clothed cops, and they had to be either Lt. McVey or Sgt. Maxwell or Lt. Melville. For some reason, Mike felt to keep Lawrence out of this case entirely. Monty wondered about that, but he never said a word. Mike was in charge of homicide, and he left it up to him.

Mike couldn't find Madeline O'Reilly, the model that so intrigued him, and wanted very badly to inquire as to why she was at the carnival that night and why she was walking to her car and what was in the briefcase. However, after a few nights, she returned.

It's true, he thought. *Her work takes her out of town a lot.*

He stopped by her house without calling, and she just stuck her head out the door, not letting him in right away. "I don't want you to come without calling, Mike. I've told you that before."

"Look, Maddy, I come as a cop in a murder investigation." Then he showed her his badge. "So open up the door and stop the nonsense," he said in his surly cop voice.

She sighed and opened the door and let him in.

He immediately grabbed her as she closed the door and kissed her passionately. She was limp as a rag.

"I'm not kidding, McVey. I told you, if we are going to do this, it's either my way or no way."

"Hey, Maddy, that's my line," he said, as he sat down and took out his little notebook.

"Okay, you were seen leaving the carnival on the grounds of the Academy of the Second Chance on the night of..." he said, and he gave the date. "You were walking briskly out of the grounds and carrying a briefcase." He looked at her with question in his eyes.

She just sat up straight as a rod.

"That's a lie, Mike. I was never there."

"Look, Maddy, I have some really reliable eyewitnesses to your being there."

"Well, it's their word against mine. I wasn't there."

"Okay, then where were you at that time?"

She closed her eyes and tried to quickly come up with something, but he'd made her nervous. She couldn't think under those circumstances.

"You make me nervous, Mike. I can't think. It will come to me."

Suddenly she looked at him in a saucy way

and came and sat on his lap, and they kissed. And he held her, and it felt so good, as though he were with Rhonda, his first wife of thirty years who had gorgeous red hair like Madeline and died too young.

Suddenly his cell phone rang, and he looked at the number. It was Monty, a call he couldn't refuse.

"Yeah, Monty," he said, trying to not sound surly to his boss.

Quickly he got up and kissed her again. "I have to leave, baby. So think about where you were, and we'll talk again," he said now in a husky voice.

She smiled at him, and he left.

A few weeks passed without any more clues, and the Second Chance Academy continued as though nothing had happened, mainly because it was thought that the murder victim intended was Sonny Opelia, not their principal. Life went on. Dr. McMurray was a long time in convalescing and never talked about the event again. Mike thought he knew a lot more than he was willing to tell.

The high school boys were let go, as they seemed to be really innocent of putting the live snake in the tank. There was a rubber snake in there too, so they were soon cleared of all charges.

But Mike was a barracuda and wouldn't let go of the investigation, knowing there had to be some connection. First, it was the death of Dr. Berger, and an investigation into his early life turned up something suspicious. His doctorate was in biology, and he had never taught or been a principal before. In the last couple of years, although he worked as an educator with a good reputation, he made little money. Then one day he was rolling in money. He said he'd received an inheritance, and he and his wife bought a brand new six thousand square-foot home for two million dollars in the best area of town in a gated community, then took three cruises during the year, while he worked at Second Chance Academy.

Mike looked into it, and just as he suspected, there was no inheritance reported at all. They got a hold of his bank records and found that huge sums of money were simply deposited periodically.

"So, Dr. Berger was getting an influx of big money from somewhere, Mike?" Melville, Max, and Monty were in Mike's office discussing both cases.

Mike nodded.

"It sure looks like some kind of business he was in or some nefarious scheme, Monty," Melville said suspiciously.

"What does his wife say?"

"She moved to Europe, for heaven's sake, Monty. We can't find her or any of the relatives that worked for him. They're all gone or dispersed or in hiding."

"But why?"

"My guess? The money was gotten illegitimately," Max offered.

"I traced the snake owners and the zoos for miles around and put out feelers in the other cities that had black mambas. There were only two places that even housed those dangerous snakes, and one of them did experiments and milked them for their very precious venom to make into antivenin. One of the places even extracted the fangs of two of their mambas, and one of them came up missing." Max looked quite pleased at the impact his information brought.

"Good work, you guys. Really good work," Mike told them, smiling. "We're finally getting somewhere. How difficult was it to steal that snake? Was it in a cage by itself?"

"Listen to this, guys. The curator of the place said that even though the snake had no fangs and the venom glands were removed, it was still mighty aggressive and would still chase a man and rear up and strike at him and bite him repeatedly with its teeth, which wouldn't give a fatal bite, but would injure him pretty badly because of the hard bites, at any rate," Max went on.

"So, then whoever put in the fangless mamba intended for the victim to be hurt but not fatally, and it would serve as what a warning?" Max continued to surmise.

"It would have been difficult for someone to break into that lab without being seen because they had a round-the-clock team working on their experiments and making medicine.

"One night, however, the doctor in charge reported to me there was a fire in the lab, and everyone was ordered to leave the building. There was a lot of smoke, etc. And when they went back into the lab, the cage with the fangless mamba was broken into, and the mamba was gone. The other ones were intact. Of course, anyone would be a fool to try to take a fully-awake mamba anywhere."

"What a story!" Mike shook his head.

"So, the thief must have had his own cage with him to transport the snake. There was a syringe on the floor, indicating to them that the person injected the snake with a tranquilizer or something powerful to make it sleep, since even a fangless mamba could be dangerous and hard to handle."

"Were all the fanged mambas still in their cages?"

"Apparently so. Also, one had to know which cages held which snakes, since it was quite smoky in the lab."

"This person knows his snakes and how to handle them too. We can bet on it," Mike thought out loud. "How about the worker?" Mike asked Max.

He smiled.

"Abraham Lohman was a little nervous about the whole interrogation and tried to get out of talking to me, but the doctor in charge, Dr. Nordham, insisted on it. Finally, he cracked after I taxed him over and over again about his story. He claimed that he was on duty and saw the smoke and that was all, but one of the other lab assistants saw him talking to a guy earlier in the day, who looked like an American guy. And they saw him giving some money to Lohman.

"He told me, 'It was a guy from the criminal element in the city. In the big city. He came and threatened me with hurting my family. Then he gave me ten thousand dollars. All I had to do was to show him which cage held the fangless mamba and give it a shot when he put the place on fire and threw in a smoke bomb. I did it and put a big red tag on the fangless cage as well as to unlock it but kept it closed. That was it. He must have taken the thing and left.

"'I don't want my Abby and my little Herman hurt. You must understand that. I was gambling, and this guy threatened to expose me to my boss. Dr. Nordham hated gambling and told us all to stay away from the city and the crap tables. I should have listened to him.'

"That was all he said so we put the guy under arrest, and he's still in the jail awaiting formal charges."

"What did the guy look like?"

"He was short and swarthy looking, with dark hair and dark beady eyes and a long gray beard and dark horn-rimmed glasses."

All three of the guys and Monty too began to laugh.

"Don't they ever come up with anything more inventive than that?"

As the men talked about it all, Mike received a call. The man Lohman was dead, killed as he left the jail after someone paid the ten thousand dollar bail.

All the men sighed.

Mike took out his bottle of booze and four

glasses and gave them all a glass of scotch and called Dora, his secretary, to get some ice for them.

Monty just stared at the three cops in the room. They were certainly his best, and they worked together quite well.

So where did the dangerous mamba come from? they all four wondered, as they sipped on their scotch and water.

After a few minutes of drinking and meditation, Monty chimed in, "Any luck in tracing the snake from the dunk tank?"

"The aquarium in Austin is missing a water moccasin, as of two weeks ago, and then suddenly it appeared a few days ago," Mike reported.

"How difficult would it be to kidnap a water moccasin? I know it's not as aggressive as a mamba and its bite isn't as lethal, but why bring it back? That's what gets me. Why even bother to bring it back?" Melville shook his head.

All four men looked at each other with puzzlement on their faces.

"I talked to the zoo; and they had a water moccasin, and so did the aquarium. Apparently they are stock in trade at these underwater expositions. So, why snake-nap one from Austin when there were a few right here in town?"

"McMurray was quite hurt by the thing too.

I wonder who wanted Lopelia out of the way. What is the real story behind this? I talked to Lopelia, and he's upset about it all, feeling that he was the target.

"'So many of my colleagues are jealous of me and want to take all my fame and fortune away from me,' he told me, guys. He is so darn arrogant; I feel I'd like to punch him in the nose. Does anyone else feel like that?" Mike asked, feeling a little sheepish if no one else came forth.

"Yeah," Melville agreed.

"He's very arrogant, and yet my wife says he's like some little lost boy; poignant is how she describes him."

The other guys just wrinkled their noses.

"The fact remains that it was McMurray who was bitten by the snake, not Lopelia, and the first murder involved the associate principal. McMurray is the head principal. If Lopelia wasn't scheduled that afternoon, I'd think the attack was meant for McMurray," Mike also confessed.

Monty just looked at him.

"If you feel that way, McVey, then go for it. I've never known you to be far wrong," Monty said, and all the guys smiled.

"That's true, Mike. That is true," Max concurred.

"Come on, guys," Melville teased. "Let's not

get our own Sonny Lopelia thing going here. Mike's been wrong a time or two." The others laughed at that.

"Melville's right, guys. The other way puts too much pressure on me," Mike concurred.

chapter IV
the p i

Palmer Mortenson peeked around the corner, trying to keep the woman he was following in his view. It was no easy job. She was a former cop, a policewoman for over twenty years. He was a good private investigator himself, not finishing the police academy many years ago and really disdaining the training. *A bunch of egotistical morons,* he thought. *Yes, they were arrogant and unprincipled sometimes worse than the vermin they arrested.*

In the ensuing years, observing both good and bad cops come and go still did not change his poor opinion of them as a whole.

He tailed the woman as she came around the corner, but instead of continuing, she turned and looked directly into his eyes.

"Okay, who sent you? Who hired you?" she asked angrily and with the surly tones of a big-city cop.

Palmer stood there transfixed. No one had

ever detected his shadowing before. He just stared at her. Suddenly, she took out a gun and put it right under his chin and put her face right against his.

"Okay, buster, who are you?" she asked, pushing the gun right up to his neck. Palmer wasn't anyone to bluff with, however. He knew she wouldn't shoot and kill him right here in the street with other people around. So, he pushed her hand away from his neck and shoved her aside and walked away.

Cici DeMarco was a big-city cop for most of her life, but now at age fifty she was in search of some answers. Red haired and tall, five foot nine in stockinged feet, she was still a lovely looking woman even now. Her ambition caused her to become a police captain at the tender age of thirty-five, and now she was police commissioner, but even that wasn't enough for her. She was grooming herself for bigger and better things; a run for the governor's office most people thought that was next on her agenda. Her many contacts and so-called friends were encouraging her to be a candidate in this next election, which was still a year away. But Cici had her eyes on a bigger prize: the U.S. Senate. An election would happen in eight months, and she was determined to be the one to grab the seat. She already had a lot of political pull and clout as police commissioner in a big city.

Who the heck is having me followed? She wondered furiously.

Cici usually played a lone hand, preferring to do things by herself and without any accomplices. When she accosted the PI, she took his wallet out of his pocket without his knowing it. She just smiled at her quick hand. She could pick pockets with the best of them but seldom used her expertise in this matter. One Ronnie Carsons, a felon she made a deal with, taught her the fine art of pick pocketing, and she did it just for her own amusement with friends and once in a while for a serious thing when she wanted to know what her cops had in their wallets. It really amused her and sometimes even shocked her. No one else knew she had this talent.

Now she got into her car and drove to a quaint coffee shop on the edge of town. She loved to go there because it was so quiet, and they knew and respected her there. The proprietor, Sam McGinnis, was a former cop whom she dated for a couple of months long ago.

There was no magic between them, but they remained good friends nonetheless.

Cici opened the wallet while she waited for her coffee and cheese omelet to arrive. It tickled her to look at the pictures, and the contents of the wallet told a lot about the owner. This guy was a PI for many years, and she recognized his name. Yes, they'd used him many times in the police department. Sometimes the PIs could solicit information from a suspect better than the cops because people weren't suspicious or scared of them.

He had over a thousand dollars in cash and several major credit cards, a driver's license, his private investigator's license, and some letters from various clients. Yes, that's just what she thought. The present senator, Majelle Collins Brown, was the office that hired him. Oh, it may not have been her directly, and one of her cronies or her employees who would swear that she had nothing to do with it.

Surprisingly, there was picture of him with what appeared to be a wife and four children. The picture looked old, and according to his license he was fifty-one now, so the children would probably be grown. Then there were pictures of two women, signing "to daddy with love," and two pictures of men, not signed at all. One of them looked just like the PI, and she assumed they were his grown children.

There was another picture of a lovely blond woman about forty, and it was signed "To my darling, Palmer, love always, Majelle." Staring back at Cici was a woman she was familiar with, the present senator who was up for reelection.

"Yes," she said under her breath. "This is a prize of the highest order. This may actually buy me not only the nomination of my party, but also the senator's seat, replacing the present Majelle, who seems to have a boyfriend." She just laughed at her own good fortune. Things had always gone her way in her life, and if they didn't she made them do so.

Cici ate her repast and settled back to have a cigarette, a habit she had no intention of stopping. She really enjoyed her ten cigarettes a day, and that was that.

Cici went home and thought about her early life. She had always been a loner, but did like the guys a lot and has married a couple of times along the way. Currently, she was in a twenty-year marriage to a very wealthy, politically well-connected man, a retired general. Now she was famous because of the unique way she treated her staff, or maybe it was because of a famous serial killer that she captured singlehandedly. "I just showed my cops how to do it, that's all," she said with a real heart of pride. The newspapers picked it all up. This was such an unusual commissioner of police, who tracked criminals herself, unbeknownst to her other cops. They even made a TV show about her.

She was certainly the most famous of police commissioners in the U.S. When she was a cop she had a few relationships that wouldn't bear close scrutiny. A couple of them were passionate and of long term. She thought about Johnny Cartellini with a little smile on her face. He was now a lieutenant of the eastside division and still flirted with her when he met her, which really annoyed her to no end. He gave her a long seductive look when he thought no one else was watching. She'd have to deal with him. That much was for sure. *He had been a married man too and wanted to divorce his wife for me,* she thought. *Yes, he really did love me. But I knew he was a skirt chaser, and we parted on good terms, though. And he promised to never mention our affair.*

Then she thought about Johnny Mastropetro, who was a tall dark and handsome guy, ten years younger than her and very much in love with her. Now, however, he was a U.S. Senator from another state and knew how to keep his own secrets. To reveal something between himself and Cici would be the death knell of his own political aspirations. So, her secrets were safe with him.

One in particular she still had a passion for, a certain police lieutenant, head of homicide.

There had even been talk of love and marriage, but he was already married and reluctant to leave his wife of many years. Cici had even gotten pregnant and pushed for marriage, but he insisted that she get an abortion and she did so. That was long ago and now he was remarried and had some children, which surprised her. Her own marriage didn't stop her from playing house with someone else now and then which brought her to her present dilemma.

Yes, she had to clean up her past a little in order to be able to field questions and be able to have her past put under a magnifying glass. So, she'd have to talk with all three of these guys and see if he told anyone else about their affair.

But she had other issues to attend to at this time. Her husband, General Morty DeMarco, retired Army two-star general, who was her husband for over twenty years, was about to leave her. Somehow he got wind of some past indiscretions and her desire to run for U.S. Senate and was livid with rage against her.

"Why are you wanting to be a U.S. senator, Cici? You have no experience toward that end? Who would vote for you anyway? It's all about power, isn't it? Or is it fame? Yes, that's it; you want to be famous and powerful both. It can't be the money, because I give you a lot more than you could ever make as the senator. You almost make the amount a U.S. senator would makes in your job as commissioner anyway. I don't get it." He sighed and frowned at her. "How much power do you need, Cici? You've got the whole police force in your hand and the mayor and even the governor. They've written stories and plays and books and screenplays about your infamous exploits. Not all of which are true, I might add. Then you set yourself up as a model of family values and have this sordid past yourself.

How much fame is enough for you, woman?"

But in the end, they talked more calmly; and he did love her, and they reconciled. Cici knew she had to keep this marriage intact if she was going to run for Senator. Divorce was out of the question. Widowhood, on the other hand was not. She stopped, wondering at her own thoughts and stared ahead.

A month later Cici made her bid for the U.S. Senate. The party chiefs were delighted to have a woman of her caliber on their team. She was everything they needed and wanted: good looking, but not sexually threatening to the women, a good speaker, a very brave woman with many medals and a successful person, in fact very famous because of her exploits when she was younger and being immortalized in the movies and a TV series about her. So, everyone would know her and liked her. She would get a lot of votes; that much was for sure. She had only the one husband and was faithful and devoted to him and at his side. At least that's the way it appeared. She was a churchgoing Christian and did charity work and helped the poor. She had good family values and wanted to focus on what she called eliminating ignoring the needs of the poor. She would change all that. That was her promise. She ran a dual platform; she would work toward ending poverty and fight for family values, which she always lived herself.

In the meantime, Conci McVey was aware of this woman's past with her husband, Lt. Mike McVey, head of homicide. He told her all about it once when he was drunk and upset with Conci.

"I've had better women than you, babe, believe me. Even the commissioner will tell you what a great lover I am and how she even got pregnant and had an abortion because she loved me. You're nothing, Conci. Believe me," he said over and over again. Conci just slapped his face.

However, that was a long time ago, at least three or more years, certainly in the early part of their five-year marriage. Now they got along better, except for this new baby on the way, which annoyed her husband.

Cici kept an eye on Mike McVey off and on throughout the years, as he tried to be a good friend to Cici and not a lover. Their relationship was platonic for a number of years, and Mike felt proud to be helping the police commissioner.

Lately though, since she had announced her run for the U.S. Senate, she called Mike into her office more often, and they talked more about his personal life than his police work, which stymied him, wondering about her motive.

Cici wanted to get close to Conci for some reason, and it became plainer to Conci after Cici invited her to lunch one day.

"She asked me a strange question at lunchtime, getting chummy, Mike. It really perplexed me." Conci stopped and took a good long look at her husband.

"What was that?"

"She wanted to know if you had ever talked to me about your past. 'Did you know that Mike and I were old friends from a long time ago?' Then she talked about your first wife, Rhonda, and how sad it was that you lost her when you both fell in love again. 'I was a captain at that time and noted that she ran around on Mike, but he was running around some himself. Did he ever tell you about that time in his life, Conci?' she asked me so pointedly that I wondered what she was getting at. Then it dawned on me. She wanted to know if you told me about your relationship with her and the baby she had aborted. I just looked at her innocently and with a perplexed look on my face. 'Mike and I decided that the past was just that, the past, Cici. We never discussed any of our past achievements or our sins. Besides, Mike told me he was clean when Rhonda and he were married, and I for one believe him. He'd never lie to me,' I said militantly and with my best sneer. I know she believed me, sweetheart. But why would she care if I knew about your little tryst with her? But, of course, she wants to make a run for the Senate. She needs to be clean. Somehow I felt a real threat if I had answered her honestly, Mike. Then it also occurred to me that perhaps she had some other involvements in her life too, and how is she going to handle all that?"

Conci looked at Mike, who was watching her with his mouth opened, staring at her and then began to frown.

"What the heck does that mean, Conci. You accusing me of being a big mouth, a gossip?" Mike got really angry at Conci and left the house pondering their conversation, slamming the door. The sound of his car peeling off filled the neighborhood.

Mike thought about all this and remembered the day he was called to Cici's office, about a month previously. He wondered what it was all about. They had been on friendly terms but certainly not intimate friends or anything.

So, Mike went to her office that day, and she smiled when he came in. He looked her up and down. She was still a good-looking woman, but much harder than she used to be.

"Am I in trouble?" he asked rather tongue in cheek.

"No way, McVey. I just wanted to touch bases with you. I'm going to put my cards on the table. I'm seriously thinking of running for the Senate in a few months, and I have a good record of standing on family values. So, I just wanted to know that the past was buried so deep that no one could ever dig it up," she said and looked at him with a threatening look on her face.

Mike just stared at her. He didn't like this at all. *Is she threatening me about our old affair? That was must have been twenty years ago,* he thought. *Yes, a long time ago, but she was really good.* And he smiled.

Cici misinterpreted his smile and stood up. He got up too out of courtesy.

"Are you going to give me a hard time, McVey?"

He just shook his head.

"No way, ma'am. I was just reminiscing, thinking about…things. That's all. I would never do anything to hurt you, Cici. No, never. My memories of you are very precious to me and very private. No one ever knew then, and no one will ever know now," he said adamantly and softly.

She crossed over and put her arms around him, and they began to kiss passionately.

"There's never been anyone like you, Mike. No, never. Many is the time I wished that you would divorce your wife for me. Yes, I really wanted that," she confessed, and they made love right there in her office. Mike was astonished that she still had a thing for him.

Later, when his head cleared he was upset at himself for getting involved with Cici again, hoping his wife Conci wouldn't somehow find out. Their marriage was an up and down affair and mostly due to his propensity for redheads and his fondness for extra-marital affairs, which he indulged in every now and then. No matter how careful he was, somehow Conci always seemed to know. He just shook his head.

Please, Lord, don't let this lead to a permanent situation.

But he needn't have worried, the commissioner just wanted to reaffirm her hold on McVey and was satisfied that she could have him any time and any place. Little did she know that Mike was finished with her.

Soon, it was time for Cici to make her move toward the Senate seat. Her fans were delighted that she would be their representative in the Congress of the United States. The newspapers and the other party began their systematic search into her background and found that she was pure as the driven snow as the saying goes. It made Mike McVey smile a little. If only they knew about her scarlet past, but that was his own little secret that he hadn't shared with anyone else, he thought. However, one time when he was quite drunk, he blabbed it not only to his wife but to a significant paramour that he cared for, a cop by the name of April.

chapter V
a bible class

At the Academy of Signs and Wonders, one of the high school teachers, Agnes Dooley, was teaching her Bible class. They were reading about and discussing the Seven Deadly Sins as they were perceived down through the ages.

"Not all the lists are the same, Mrs. Dooley," Timmy Wiley, who was Mike McVey's nephew, pointed out. "One encyclopedia lists them one way, and the Catholic pope who maybe thought up the list put different things on the list."

"Okay, then let's compare the lists," she decided.

So they did, finding that all of them seemed to agree on most of the sins but called them different names.

"For instance: greed is sometimes called covetousness or avarice," Mrs. Dooley informed them. "Now let's list all of them and study their meanings."

"Lust!" one of the students called out.

"Yeah, that's a really good one," another boy yelled.

"Okay, boys, one at a time, and let's do it decently and in order, please," she restrained them.

"Greed," another called out.

"Sloth," then…

"Envy!"

"Wrath!"

"Pride!"

"Gluttony!"

"Okay, that completes the list. Let's go over the meaning they had for the early church and the meaning they have now."

The bell rang, so they couldn't finish the discussion.

"Next week we'll do more discussing. For your homework, study these names and try to think of an eighth deadly sin that wouldn't be covered by these seven. It would probably be one that encompassed all of these others," she said and smiled at them. *This class loved a challenge, and the whole study intrigued them.*

Timmy really got into the study of those sins— he did his research on the Internet and found some interesting facts.

At the next week's Bible class, he presented his findings.

The teacher was quite impressed.

He went to the chalkboard and began by writing the list on the board and discussing them as he went on.

"Lust—you all know about that one. Let's see what Pope Gregory the Great in the sixth century AD said about lust."

"'Lust or Lechery is usually thought of as involving obsessive or excessive thoughts or desires of a sexual nature. Unfulfilled lusts sometimes lead to sexual or sociological compulsions and/or transgressions including (but obviously not limited to) sexual addiction, adultery, rape, and incest.'"

He looked up at his audience.

"That's pretty self explanatory," he said, and they all laughed.

"Greed," he went on, "or avarice, covetousness on some lists, is, according to Pope Gregory, like lust and gluttony, a sin of excess. Greedy behavior can result in lying, stealing, cheating, taking something from someone who has nothing, or withholding all your goods from those that are starving. It may even cause you to commit murder, to take something away from someone else that you are obsessed with having."

"Gluttony—over-indulgence and over-con-sumption of anything to the point of waste, excessive desire for food, or withholding food from the needy."

Maryellen Foster raised her hand.

"I never thought of it in that context at all, Timmy. Imagine withholding food from the needy. That's one that is probably committed right now during modern days."

Others threw out a comment or two, and Timmy carried on.

"Sloth—it was first called the sin of sadness. It was what now would be described as melancholy, apathy, depression, joylessness—a refusal to enjoy the goodness of God and the world he created. It involves a spiritual apathy that affects the faithful by discouraging them from their religious work. Sadness describes a feeling of dissatisfaction or discontent, which caused unhappiness with one's current situation, as described by St. Thomas Aquinas. Dante described sloth as being the failure to love God with all one's heart, all one's mind, and all one's soul. Modern conception of this sin more simply is an unwillingness to care, a sin of laziness or indifference. We can be indifferent to the suffering of our fellow man too." Timmy stopped there, as he really had the attention of his audience.

"That definition really surprised me. It was something I'd never thought about. I guess we watered down that sin in recent times, but I like the description of Gregory the Great and Thomas Aquinas. It really makes me think."

"Wrath—or anger—it has been described as inordinate and uncontrolled feelings of hatred and anger, revenge, and generally wishing to do harm or evil to someone else. The transgressions borne of vengeance are among the most serious, including murder, assault, and others. Of course murder can be motivated by any of these other sins as well."

"Any questions about these sins so far?"

He looked over at his audience whom he held in the palm of his hand. Timmy was a very charismatic speaker and always did well in these oral presentations. There being no questions, he went on.

"Envy, like greed, is an insatiable desire. They differ according to Pope Gregory for two main reasons. First, greed is largely associated with material goods or wealth, whereas envy may apply more generally. Second, those who commit the sin of envy desire something that someone else has that they perceive themselves as lacking. It is to delight themselves in the misfortune of others. Thomas Aquinas described envy as 'Sorrow for another's good.'"

"Pride—in every list pride, or vanity, is

considered the original and the most serious of the seven deadly sins, and some say it is the ultimate source from which the other sins arise. It is identified with Lucifer and his fall from heaven and his resultant transformation into Satan. Vanity and narcissism are prime examples of this sin."

Everyone was very quiet while Timmy continued explaining the theory behind the seven deadly sins.

"Thank you, Timmy. That was excellent," Mrs. Dooley congratulated him. "Okay, folks, what do you think? Are seven enough? Does that cover everything? Can you think of an eighth deadly sin?"

Many hands were raised.

"Okay, Charlie." The teacher pointed to Charlie Harris.

"How about ignoring the needs of the poor? That would be a good one."

The teacher wrote it on the chalkboard. "That seems to have been covered by the one called gluttony," she ventured. Then she looked around.

"Annabelle." She pointed to Annabelle Sargent.

"How come murder isn't one of the deadly sins? It seems to me that it should be number one. My cousins Janey and Jonathan Grant go to the Second Chance Academy, and they had a murder and an attempted murder just a little while ago. What kind of sin was it for the person who did the committing?"

The teacher looked at Timmy for the answer.

"Any insights, Timmy?"

"Yeah, all and any of these can cause a person to murder, so it doesn't have to have its own category. That's what I think."

Everyone seemed to agree.

Just then the bell rang.

"Okay, students, see you on Monday. Have a blessed weekend."

Everyone moved to the door, but before he could leave the room, Mrs. Dooley grabbed Timmy.

"Great job, Timmy. Isn't your uncle head of homicide at the police department?" she asked sweetly.

"Yes, he is."

"Well, why don't you ask him if he thinks murder is one of the deadly sins. His answer should be interesting."

"Yeah, thanks, I will." Timmy was excited at the prospect of interviewing his uncle on anything, really.

First, however, he stopped in his Aunt Conci's

room to talk to her after school. As usual, she was grading papers.

"Don't you get tired of doing that?" he asked compassionately.

"Oh hi, Timmy. Yes, this is the part I dislike most about teaching, grading the papers. Oh once in a while it's okay, but every day and then so many of them is a real chore."

She looked up and smiled at him.

"We're discussing the Seven Deadly Sins in Bible class, and I did a short study of them and found it interesting. Then the teacher asked us to think about what we would consider an eighth deadly sin. What do you think?"

He looked at her with a question on his face. Many times when he was stuck with something, especially Bible stuff, he asked Aunt Conci. She was a fount of information and really knew her Bible.

"The Bible doesn't exactly list those seven. You know that if you did a study on them, but the early church did believe that these would cause other sins to follow. In the book of Galatians, Paul has another list in Galatians 6:19–21. That list reads," Conci had opened her Bible to the proper verse and read out loud:

"Now the works of the flesh are manifest, which are these; adultery, fornication, unclean-

ness, lasciviousness, idolatry, witchcraft, hatred, variance, emulations, wrath, strife, seditions, heresies, envyings, murders, drunkenness, revellings, and such like; of the which I tell you before, as I also have told you in time past, that they which do such things shall not inherit the kingdom of God.'"

"Wow! That's a lot of them," he said and smiled. "Well, wrath is mentioned and envying. Gluttony would be drunkenness and revellings. Greed is part of selfish ambitions. I think pride is implied in all of these too, don't you?" he asked her furrowing his brows.

"I think you're right, Timmy. Sounds like you did a great research on this."

"The teacher suggested that I ask Uncle Mike if he thought murder was one of the deadly sins and what ones did he think were, since he was around those kinds of sins all the time. She had wondered how he can keep himself clean with all that sin that surrounds him all the time." Mikey frowned at her, suddenly having an insight into one aspect of his Uncle Mike's life that he really hated, cheating on Aunt Conci. It's not that the adults talked about it; but he saw it himself once when he was at a ballgame with his church group, and there at the ballgame was Uncle Mike hugging and kissing a redheaded woman, sitting only two rows in front of him.

He never saw me, but I wondered about him ever since. Then I heard this and that around my own house and listened especially to hear about that. One time I heard Mom raking Uncle Mike over the coals, saying 'A real man wouldn't cheat on his wife. What's wrong with you, Michael?' she chastised him for these actions. So apparently he did this regularly or at least once in a while. But if he was around sin all the time, it might very well rub off on him too.

Timmy's thoughts were almost an open book, and Conci stared at him and his depth of spiritual insight. Neither of them spoke about it, but he left soon afterward and went home, thinking about all these things.

chapter VI
the fundraiser

So it was that Cici DeMarco announced her drive to the U.S. Senate seat. Toward that end, there was a huge fundraiser for her at the Capto De Leon Hotel, newly renovated and had the largest banquet hall in the area.

It was a lovely night, and the huge banquet room was crowded. There was an air of anticipation as everyone sat at their appointed table. Soon, the person of honor came in, and they all stood and gave her an overwhelming ovation.

Cici DeMarco came in dressed in a beautiful silk poi de soi gown in emerald green, which highlighted her thick glossy red hair, short and sassy, just like her. Actually she wasn't very short: five foot eight or nine in her stocking feet. On her arm was her husband, retired General Morty DeMarco. On one side of her sat Sonny Lopelia, the movie star. On the other side of her sat Governor Terry Lomas Hughes, an old friend and one of her main supporters, with his wife,

Margo. There was the mayor, Lillian Lancaster, and her new husband, Buddy Scoffield, and the chief of police, Gerald Selmon, and his wife, Lola. On the other side next to General Masters sat U.S. Representative Lorna Sadusky.

The MC who was seated on the other side of her was the Reverend Johnny Bob Connors and his wife, Lara, a lovely looking redhead in her forties. Johnny Bob was deemed the best-known evangelist in the world. He was on hundreds of TV stations, radio, had his own newspaper, traveled all over the world, and had many edifices named after him.

All those present were ardent followers and focused supporters of Cici in her run for the U.S. Senate.

Seated all around the banquet room were the large round tables that seated ten people. The closer to the stage of course denoted the degree of importance of the guests. However, the commissioner honored and thanked her volunteers by having them seated closest to the stage so she could see them and they could be her cheering squad.

The chief of police, who was seated at the head table facing the crowd, surveyed the group that was in the front table with curiosity. The Stoner Rislings were owners of the major newspaper in the city and great supporters of Cici. They could make or break a candidate, and they both liked Cici a lot since she cracked the case of the drug dealer that sold to their son who had died of an overdose. They were eternally grateful to her and got on her bandwagon right away.

Okay then, he thought. The chief continued to reflect on this. *Sergeant April Conover, now that's an enigma to me. The note I received from Cici last month really perplexed me. Imagine her wanting someone to be promoted. In all those years she's been commissioner, she never requested anything like that at all, leaving those things to us. What the heck prompted this? Said it had to do with her loyalty to herself and to the force and how she did Cici a favor. I don't buy it, nor does Monty. No, it was downright strange. But Monty was right to give it to her and not ask questions. Cici could be a formidable enemy. Don't we all know that first hand?* The chief took a deep breath. *Now the other woman, by herself, someone told me she was a nurse. So, why is she at the table?* The chief continued his perusal of the guests at table number one.

First the MC proposed a toast to Cici, and everyone held up their glass of champagne and toasted to her winning campaign.

Prior to the food being served, the MC, the Reverend Johnny Bob had everyone bow their heads, and he said the blessing of the food. Then the food was served. It was a prime rib or lobster, a choice that had to be ordered two days in advance, with the dessert being cheesecake or chocolate fudge cake. Soon, everyone was served.

After the dinner was eaten, the coffee and teas were served, along with the fragrant Italian cookie trays, filled with such delicacies as biscotti, fig cookies, pizzelles, pignolis, and Italian creampuffs that Cici had ordered herself.

"Give this small plateful with the Italian cream puffs to Mary Elizabeth Morrison and tell her it's a special tray from Cici." She told one of the waiters then thought better of it and got up herself.

"Never mind, I'll bring them to her myself," she decided, taking the small paper plate with two cream puffs on it. She approached the table and sat down at the seat that had been vacated temporarily by one of the women.

"Hello, you must be Mary Elizabeth Morrison. I've heard so many good reports about you and how diligently you've been working in my campaign. I also heard that you love these Italian cream puffs. Please eat these two as a small tribute for you generosity." Then she hugged Mary Elizabeth who was looking at her with big, staring eyes.

"Thank you," Mary Elizabeth said and immediately began to eat one of the cream puffs. The others at the table had been diverted by bathroom breaks or had gotten up just to walk around and get some exercise. Only a few others were at the table at the time, and they were talking animatedly to each other.

Cici got up and left the table and returned to the stage where the head table was placed and took her seat.

The huge platters of the cookies and pastries were put on each individual table, and several were placed and then passed around the head table. While most of the guests were partaking of the delicacies, the MC, Rev. Johnny Bob got up and told about his early encounters with Cici and how she came out to the missions with him and helped him in his revivals.

"This is an once-in-a-lifetime person, a real lady, and the next U.S. Senator from this lovely state." The crowd went wild with applause.

Then he introduced Sonny Lopelia, who told about Cici being in one of his pictures and how she helped him…

Another speaker was the chief of police, who went over her impeccable police record, and then he held up her badge. Then they all laughed, as he realized it was upside down and turned it right side up again. He appeared embarrassed.

"Who would ever have thought that this badge number 606 would someday be the commissioner of police and then the U.S. Senator?" It was amazing how rowdy the crowd became.

Everyone at the first table stood with the singular exception of Mary Elizabeth Morrison. She simply sat there with a stunned look on her face. Cici noted it right away and wondered about it, as the person next to Mary Elizabeth nudged her to stand. She did and clapped like everyone else.

The next speaker, of course, was the honorable Cici DeMarco, who gave a rousing speech that satisfied both the men and the women. She paid tribute to the cops, the mayor, the governor, the chief of police, and others of her vast acquaintance.

Mary Elizabeth was focused on the badge that the chief held up, and her mind was thrown back to more than twenty years before. It was during a big snowstorm in the city, and she was on surgery duty that week, and an emergency came in, a shooting. A little boy was killed by a man escaping from a jewelry robber as he was being pursued by a lady cop, who shot and killed him. A bystander trying to help was also shot by the robber.

The lady cop, a young one, was quite upset about the whole thing and insisted on being in the emergency room with the very injured bystander, who was going in and out of consciousness. Finally though, they had to evict her from the surgery suite and called her boss to talk with her.

Mary Elizabeth had not been in the emergency room but was in the surgery suite when the man was wheeled in with the officer insisting on coming in. Finally, the guards took her out.

Mary Elizabeth thought it was rather strange that the cop was so adamant about being with the man.

"What if he says something that's important?" she asked militantly.

"Oh, he won't even regain consciousness, ma'am," the doctor assured her. She calmed down and sat in the waiting room but not speaking to anyone.

However, just before they gave him the anesthetic, he did awaken and looked at Mary Elizabeth and spoke quickly and softly, almost in a whisper. "Badge number. She killed the kid accidentally and then shot the robber, and then when she saw I was going to the child's aid, she shot me too. Badge something zero something," he said again. "Nine," he said aloud, "nine."

"Oh, he must be a German or something, saying, 'No, no,'" Mary Elizabeth said in explanation to herself. He was whispering it to Mary Elizabeth, and no one else heard it. She just looked up and shrugged at the other nurses and the doctors in the surgical suite. They were all busily preparing for the surgery. The poor man died right there and then.

She saw the lady cop again leaving the hospital well after the surgery. She turned around suddenly and saw Mary Elizabeth staring at her and wondered about it.

The next day Mary Elizabeth was in a car accident when another driver just plowed into her and drove off. No one could identify the hit and run driver, and Mary was in the hospital for almost two months. As time went by, she forgot about the incident at the hospital.

Now, Mary Elizabeth looked around and knew she'd seen someone familiar earlier and found her with her eyes and stared at her. It surprised and shocked her. She sat down and made plans to just sneak out as soon as the opportunity presented itself.

After the speeches there was to be dancing if anyone so desired. It was meant to be a fun night, and they had all paid dearly for the privilege, except for the few who were graced with a free dinner, compliments of the city. Namely, the cops who attended. If they did double duty as guards of the would-be senator, or were highly placed cops then they were free at the dinner.

That was how Lt. Mike McVey and his wife, Conci, happened to be at the fundraiser sitting with the Captain Montgomery and his wife, Colleen, and Captain Billy Ryan and his wife Loretta who was a dear and close friend of Conci McVey's. In fact they both taught at the Academy of Signs and Wonders. Conci was four months pregnant with their third child, a fact that did not thrill Mike McVey. They already had three-year - old twins, a boy and a girl, and he was crazy about them, but felt a noose being tightened around his neck with this third child's birth pending. *Here I'm fifty-four years old, and she in her late forties, and we're still having babies,* he thought disgustedly. However, the guys at work thought he was some macho guy to impregnate a gal at age fifty-four, and so he really did have mixed feelings about it some of the time.

Sitting at the table with the McVeys was Conci's aunt, Sister Mary Concetta Rose, who was not only the aunt who raised Conci from the time she was five and was her godmother and her mother's twin sister, but was also a teacher in her early years as a nun and had taught Sonny Lopelia when he was a boy and many years later helped him with his daughter, Isabella, after her mother's murder. So, Sonny asked Cici if he could invite her, and Cici jumped on it. Cici liked that Sister was a missionary, Conci McVey's aunt and having her on her team gave some real credence to the religious Christians in the city. She immediately okayed the plan.

Sister was neither surprised nor expected this so-called honor. She was very inquisitive, just like Conci, and thought herself a bit of a sleuth. So, it was with pleasure that she accepted the invitation.

Everyone was talking and visiting waiting for the orchestra to begin the dance.

Suddenly all heads turned as a hush fell on the room, and everyone watched in awe as a drop-dead gorgeous redhead, with a long willowy model's figure walked in on the arm of Phillips Bastriani, supposedly a clean member of the infamous crime family. She was, of course, the famous model, Madeline O'Reilly. No one spoke as they hesitated at the door, looking over the crowd for their seats.

Quickly Cici nodded her head to the main usher, who went on the stage, and she whispered something to him. He quickly put two chairs at the head table and got their food for them, ushering the two latecomers to their seats. Rev. Connor was a little flustered and frowned at the new arrivals.

Conci McVey took notice that Mike was almost mesmerized by the latecomers. His attention was riveted on the beautiful redhead who smiled at him and nodded. He nodded back. Conci wondered what that was about. She snuck a peek at her aunt, who was looking at them too with a strange expression upon her face. Colleen nudged Conci and whispered something in her ear. Conci had to laugh.

Everyone at the table suspected that McVey was fooling around, even the chief and his wife, Lola. Now, Lola stared at McVey too, as her husband nudged her, frowning at McVey.

Mike felt everyone's eyes on him and looked at the people across the table from him. He put his eyes down when Monty stared at him with a question in his eyes. Then Mike took his wife's hand and kissed it, and she smiled at him.

Conci leaned over and said something to auntie. She agreed. "What was that all about?" Mike asked almost angrily. He hated to be out of any loop.

"Auntie feels that there's something strange going on here," she hesitated, "and so do I."

"Yeah, the Bastriani thug being here is very odd." He thought that was what they were talking about.

Mike couldn't get his eyes off the gorgeous Madeline. He decided to take things into his own hands and approached her at the head table. Bastriani had gone somewhere to talk to some guys.

"Hello, Maddy. It's a real surprise to see you here, baby. What's with you and Bastriani? Do you know what his family does? Maddy, it's not pretty. I thought you were my girl?" Mike asked with a teasing look in his eyes. She smiled and touched his cheek.

"I'm his girl, Mike. Yes, I like to live a dangerous life. But, this guy isn't bogged down by a pregnant wife and children. You talk a good game, McVey, but you haven't delivered yet." *How wonderfully strange it would be to have a boyfriend who is a top cop and then one who is a top crime family person,* she thought to herself. Outwardly, she just looked at him with a dare in her eyes.

Mike wasn't in the mood to be teased, and angrily, his eyes became black slits in his face as he whispered saucily to her. "I don't share my women, Madeline. It's either him or me. It's either be safe or be in bondage all your life," he said with a little smile. Things had not gone far with Madeline yet, but he was tempted almost beyond his capacity for resisting. Not only was she beautiful, she seemed to be interested in him right away when they met during a murder investigation of another model. They had a few dates and some kisses, but the intimacies had gone no further. Mike wanted to stay clean for his wife and his marriage and had done so for a few years now, but Conci's pregnancy threw him into a really rebellious state.

Madeline seemed to be teasing him. She liked that he was so jealous he could barely think straight. Little did he know that Philly had encouraged her to go after him. "This one might help us, chookie," he said to her sweetly. (That was his pet name for her, "Chookie," and then he'd say, "rhymes with cookie.") And she'd laugh.

Madeline liked Philly although there was no love there, but he was very instrumental in getting her career on superstar status. She owed him and owed him big, and she thought maybe marriage to McVey would get her away from the criminal element and give her control of her life back. That's the only reason she went along with Philly's request to vamp Lt. Mike McVey, head of homicide. Also, although she would admit it to no one; she had a passion for him.

She was used to high-end things and places, however. So, Mike reluctantly shelled out some big bucks to take her to the nicest places, but he always felt out of place.

They necked, and he was intrigued by her long willowy body and her beautiful face, but especially her gorgeous thick curly red hair, just like his first wife, Rhonda's. He and Rhonda had been married for thirty years, most of them unhappily. They separated for a time and then they got back together the year she came home, to die. He was bereaved when she died and blamed God for it. That was, of course, before he met the beautiful, compassionate Conci, whom he later married.

Now he was discouraged and unhappy at home because of Conci being pregnant again, although Mike was an excellent father to his three-year-old twins, Moira and Sonny, whom he adored.

Madeline was going too fast for him, though. He liked to romance the women he dated. Yes, he liked to go slowly and feel the romance part and the special feeling when they first made love. These romances only lasted about a month or so and sometimes even a week or less. In fact, Mike had been a very good and faithful husband for a long time now and seldom got tempted, but this woman was exceptional and looked so much like his wife Rhonda, whom he'd loved so devoutly.

Abruptly ending the conversation without another word, Mike left the table and joined his wife.

Cici saw the interchange and wondered about it. She purposely took a couple of cream puffs, placed them on a little dish, and brought it over to Madeline. "Hello, I'm Cici DeMarco, and I've been wanting to meet you, Miss O'Reilly. I've heard a lot about you and read some too. It's an honor to meet you," she said so humbly that Madeline turned and looked at her with astonishment.

"Oh, Commissioner, I'm so delighted to be here at your fundraiser. I can assure you that both Philly and I are great supporters of yours," she gushed. They talked for a while, and then Cici gave her the dish of cream puffs.

"These are Italian delicacies that are difficult to find here in the city. The chef made them especially for this dinner. Please try them, as they're my favorites," she urged.

Madeline took one and put it into her mouth, and the cream ran down the sides of her mouth; and she laughed and Cici wiped it for her.

"These are truly delicious," she said and ate

the whole one and began to devour the other one when Phillip came back to the table. Cici got up, shook hands with each of them, and thanked them for being there.

"Here, Philly, Cici brought these over just for me. They're specially made by her private chef, and she wanted to share them with me. Here, eat the second one. They're delicious." He smiled at her and let her shove the cream puff into his mouth.

Cici motioned for Mike to come up to the stage, and he did so, bringing his drink. She was smiling at him.

She proudly introduced him to the governor.

"Governor, this is *our* best cop. No, Lt. Mike McVey is probably the best cop in the nation. He's a bulldog and has received many well-earned awards." Mike tried to look humble but failed.

"Glad to meet you, Lt. McVey. It's a pleasure to meet a real cop, a man who puts his life on the line all the time." They chatted for a while, and Cici had the waiter bring the drinks to toast to the table.

Mike took his toast too, although he really hated champagne.

"Don't drink it all yet, Mike. We're all going to have a toast in a few minutes," Cici exclaimed.

Finally, after a few minutes, he went back to

his table. Conci and Mary Elizabeth were talking to the chief's wife, Lola.

"Mike, have you met Mary Elizabeth Conover? She used to be our nurse at Signs and Wonders. Now, she's working for the commissioner." Mike just nodded, then sat down and looked around as the girls continued talking.

Cici then had everyone have a toast of the champagne, and they came to Mike's table. He motioned that he already had some. Then came the big toast.

This time it was Sonny Lopelia who proposed the toast. "To our next U.S. Senator, Cici DeMarco." And she stood up and bowed to everyone as they all raised their glasses and drank. Mike saw that neither Mary Elizabeth nor Conci had the wine, and he gave his to Conci.

"Thanks, honey, you know I never drink the stuff." And she smiled at him. Mike got up and went to circulate some more, and Conci gave her wine to Mary Elizabeth. Then the waiter had already brought them some wine to use as a toast. Mary Elizabeth had two glasses and felt quite giddy. Conci gave her the other three on the table. She just smiled.

Finally, the music began, and since it was so crowded and so many were on the dance floor, Mike decided to just cool it and drink instead of dance. He was still disgusted with his wife and Madeline too but tried to hide his negative feelings toward Conci anyway, not wanting anyone else to know how he felt about her pregnancy.

Conci accepted the uneasy peace between them and danced with the chief, who loved to dance, and with U.S. Senator Johnny Mastropetro, who used to be a member of the board of the Academy of Signs and Wonders. He always had a little crush on Conci and liked her a lot, thinking she was a really classy lady, especially since she'd been a missionary and grown up on the mission field.

They laughed and got caught up on their lives; and suddenly, as they were dancing, Sonny Lopelia cut in, and they laughed about that, too. Johnny graciously sat down and watched the two of them dancing. Sonny was quite tall, hovering over six foot five. Conci was only five foot four, but he enjoyed dancing with her so much.

They talked and laughed too, and he danced her all around the dance floor, almost to a dizzying spot.

As the night progressed, everyone was dancing with everyone else, and it was almost chaotic. Sonny Lopelia was dancing with Cici and accidentally bumped into Mary Elizabeth who was dancing with Rev. Connors, and Sonny hugged her as though he knew her well. Within minutes, as they danced to the other side of the ballroom, Mary Elizabeth collapsed. Everyone flocked around her. There were some medical doctors on the scene, and they moved the people aside. Mike was on the case immediately too and took a look at her. She was having convulsions, and her back was arched in a terrible way. After a time, she opened her eyes. Conci was right beside her, as she tried to tell them something, "To budge, ta budge, six zero, wrong way, budge…nine, oh, the killer," too, and Mike moved her bodily out of the way.

"Tabaudge, the budge," she gasped. It sounded like cabbage to him. Was she allergic to cabbage? They did have some stuffed cabbages as their appetizer course.

The ambulance came within minutes, but she was already unconscious. Mike got on the microphone and cautioned everyone to be seated and not leave the room.

Then almost immediately about twenty cops came pouring into the building. Names were taken. The commissioner took charge then and pushed Mike out of the way. She was, of course, the commissioner *and* a cop. She would take any credit that was forthcoming.

Mike just raised his eyebrows at her and

moved aside graciously. Monty caught his eye and nodded to him. He just shrugged. The chief too nodded his head. The women at the table almost laughed about their so-called subtle signals.

Mike came over and kissed Conci on the cheek and hugged Sister.

"Go home with someone else, baby. I need to stay here now. You can see that," he ordered.

"How is she, Mike? She's trying to tell us something, Mike, having to do with a number. I knew her from school, Mike," Conci continued telling him.

"I'll let you know later, honey. Please go," he asked sweetly but firmly. Conci nodded and kissed him softly on the lips and talked to Colleen, who was glad to give her and Sister a lift since Monty was busy on this incident too.

The three of them talked unceasingly during the ride to Conci's house. Colleen felt a little spooked herself, and Sister insisted that she stay overnight with them. "The men won't be home for many hours, maybe even late tomorrow," Sister explained. Colleen concurred, and Conci found a nightgown and robe and some underclothes for Colleen. Sister even had a new pair of slippers for her. She was enchanted and decided to stay.

They stayed up half the night and talked about things, and she loved to hear both Conci and Sister's speculation. She smiled, and then called Monty on his cell phone.

"Yeah, Colleen, are you home?"

"I was feeling a little spooked, Monty, and when I drove Sister and Conci home they insisted, especially Sister did, that I stay the night. So that's where I am until tomorrow, just so you know."

He paused. "That's a great idea, honey. Then I don't have to worry about you, and Mike won't have to worry about his women, either. Thank Sister and Conci for me," he said, and they hung up.

Colleen nodded her head. "I'm glad he wasn't in a surly mood," she commented. "Sometimes it's better to just get their voice message and leave one yourself," she said, and Conci raised her eyebrows.

"Yes, I sure agree with that one." And they all three laughed.

Sister took the bull by the horns and called the hospital. She sighed sadly and turned to the ladies, holding onto the bottom of the phone to hide her voice. "She died an hour or so ago. They don't know what caused it yet, but they're going to do an autopsy since it was so strange and so sudden. It really looked like she was poisoned, Conci. Don't you think?" she said and hung up.

"That's too bad," Conci commented. "She was a nice person when she was at the school."

The children were sleeping soundly, and the women got into their nightclothes and made some coffee and tea and began to speculate. It was two o'clock in the morning before they were finally exhausted and said their goodnights.

As predicted, Monty didn't go to Conci's and claim his wife until noon the next day.

He had a cup of coffee, and Conci made him some breakfast, then they left.

Mike, however, didn't come home until late that night, around eleven o'clock when the children were already in bed and Conci and Sister had made preparations for school the following day. Sister was going to Maureen's in the morning for a little excursion they were taking into the country and antiquing, which both of them loved, so Sister was in bed sleeping and Conci was about to get into bed when her husband came home. He almost fell into her arms.

"What a night, baby. What a mystery too," he said, as she gave him some coffee and some meatballs and crusty bread. He ate three of the meatballs, two pieces of bread, and then had some more coffee and sat in his recliner and fell asleep. He didn't give her any explanations, and she didn't ask any questions either.

Conci took the children to school but for some reason didn't want to go to school herself, wanting to spend some time with her husband. It bothered her more than she liked to admit that he was talking to the model the other night. *Why would she even be interested in a guy like Mike McVey, especially since she was dating the Bastriani guy? Auntie sure looked askew at him, remembering some things, I guess. She didn't want to talk about it though.*

chapter VII
confrontation

Mike was up and having his coffee that Conci left for him when she came in the door.

"Hey, what the heck are you doing home, Conci? You ditching school?" he laughed at his little joke. Mike used to ditch school a lot and get some of his many girlfriends to cover for him. Conci laughed too and kissed him on the lips softly.

"I just wanted to see you for a while, Mike. The whole incident of the other night really bothered me."

"Yeah? Well the autopsy showed that Mary Elizabeth died of some kind of rare poison. Very potent. It sure smells funny to me."

"To me too," Conci concurred.

"Oh?" he said angrily and got up out of the chair and went into the bedroom, slamming the door.

Conci followed him. "What's going on, Mike, between you and that red-haired model? Why would she want to be with you anyway? You're certainly not in her league, especially if she's dating a crook like Bastriani?" Conci confronted him, although she knew better.

"Get off my back, Conci. Who could blame me for fooling around when I live with a fat walrus who's nothing but a baby machine. If you listened to me, we wouldn't be shackled by another kid. Yeah, I'm flirting with her, and she seems to be going after me too. But I'm a faithful man now and won't fall, but if you stay on my back, I'll leave you anyway. Do you get it?" His face was all furled up in a nasty looking frown.

Conci took a step back. "There's the door, McVey. I can't live worrying about who you're playing house with anymore. Either be nice to me or get out. I've had it with you anyway," she shouted at him, something he'd seldom heard from his soft-spoken sweet wife.

"I'll leave when I say so, woman. Not when you say. Get it? I'm the boss of me and not you." He walked away, which ended the conversation, took his shower, and when he got dressed, he returned into the kitchen for another cup of coffee. Conci was gone. He sat down and held his head. He did have a bad headache, something that had been happening to him lately even if he didn't drink. Sometimes he'd see some red lines in his eyes and would just take some aspirin and ignore it for the most part. But he was so very tired today, more so than he'd ever felt. *Why do I berate her when she's so sweet and good to me? I'm a real cad. I know that, but I have to get out of this house and away from this baby machine,* he thought and sighed, packed his bag, and got into his car and drove off. *Little does Conci know that it isn't just Madeline that she has to worry about but also Cici DeMarco, who wanted to start an affair with me,* Mike thought. *Satan must be after me big time with two broads chasing me like that.*

Conci went and did her grocery shopping and did some shopping at the mall. It was good to get out without the babies and be by herself. She stopped and had an ice cream and then a cup of cocoa. Unfortunately, she was not allowed to drink her beloved coffee while pregnant.

Sister was out doing some antiquing with Maureen Wiley, Mike's sister, so Conci picked up the children, who were all full of vim and vigor and chatted to her about their very exciting day at preschool.

Mike stayed gone for three days, staying in Madeline's apartment although she was out of town. They didn't talk together much while she was gone, but they did talk that first night.

"I'm here in your apartment, Maddy. Conci

and I had a real fight. She suspects that we're together. I wish you were back in town."

Madeline seemed a little upset that McVey took upon himself to use her apartment. "I don't like that idea, Mike. I don't like anyone in my apartment while I'm gone. Are you doing some detective spying on me?" she asked harshly.

Mike got quite insulted. "What the heck are you talking about? I thought you cared for me, Maddy. Why are you insulting me like that? Believe me, I'll leave, and you can find yourself another fool."

He hung up angrily, and she soon realized she'd made a mistake with him. He didn't talk to her after that for a long while.

That night after talking with the coroner, Mike went home and shared the information with Conci. "Mary Elizabeth died of some kind of poison that's in a sea wasp. Now isn't that strange?"

Conci raised her eyebrows and stared at him, "That seems so odd doesn't it?"

"That's what the doc said. He's still not sure how it got into her system. It must have been with her drink or wine or something like that."

Conci's eyes got very big, "How was the stuff

administered? Surely no one in their right mind would take something like that."

"The stuff had been ground up, but the stingers were still lethal even like that. The coroner sent the tissue to a marine biology lab for further analysis," Mike explained.

Mike had his dinner and took a much-needed nap. Lately he'd felt not completely well. His head hurt him most of the time, and there were those pesky red lines again in his eyes. He'd have to go to an eye doctor, he assumed. He had stopped drinking too since his head hurt him all the time. Drink just exacerbated it and made him sick on top of it. Coffee, however, did seem to help. Now he was taking some potent headache medicine he'd gotten from John Wiley, his brother-in-law, a doctor, for migraines they assumed. The medicine did help somewhat. Mike did feel better when he was in his own home and lying down and Conci was around. Yes, she was his strength. He realized it before and knew it again. She did soothe him, although at the moment she was upset with him. They had an uneasy peace in the household, but Conci let him come and go as he pleased for the moment.

chapter VIII
reverend johnny
bob connors

Everyone that came in contact with Mary Elizabeth Morrison was questioned carefully. There were a lot of people though only some of them were in close proximity with her during the time that the poison was introduced.

The Reverend Johnny Bob Connors tried to get out of having any interrogation because he had some appointments out of town and was going on a crusade to Kenya. The police stopped him, however, and detained him for questioning.

Johnny Bob bristled at the treatment of the police. "Do you know who I am, Officer?" he asked Melville angrily.

"Yes, sir, I know that you were the person dancing with Mary Elizabeth Morrison a little before she died. That's who you are to me, sir," he said pointedly.

Johnny Bob sat down. "Okay, shoot, Lieutenant. I will be cooperative," he promised.

"How did you know Ms. Morrison?"

He just shrugged. "I met her years ago in Africa when I was doing missions. That was over twenty years ago, Lieutenant."

"Did you keep up a friendship with her, then? Is that how you happened to be talking to her and dancing with her at the banquet?"

"She came up to me and told me who she was. I was surprised because she looked so different, but twenty years really takes a toll on the womenfolk," he insisted.

"What did you conversation consist of, Reverend?" Melville doggedly pursued this angle.

"Look, Lieutenant. She said she was Mary Elizabeth and reminded me of our time in Africa. If you want to know the truth, Lieutenant, she pursued a relationship with me when we were on the same mission team. I rebuffed her.

That's all," he said and started to get up.

"All right, Reverend, but you cannot leave the city, much less the country, for at least a week."

"What? I have things to do and places to go and preach the Word of God," he pleaded.

He continued pleading, but his words fell on deaf ears. Melville had heard some things about the reverend that the reverend didn't know about, and his admission of innocence didn't ring true. But, for now, he'd let him go and pursue this further.

"Just don't leave, Reverend, or you will be in a lot of trouble," he warned him.

Johnny Bob got up, and when Lt. Melville proffered his hand, he ignored it and slammed the door after him. Melville just shook his head.

Johnny Bob Connors sat in the expensive hotel suite, the penthouse one to be exact, and thought about the death of Mary Elizabeth Morrison. He also thought about himself, which he always liked to do. He knew he had a special talent, and he nurtured it and nursed it his whole life. His position was quite fragile, he knew, and so he took great care of it.

He had known the Lord since he was seven years old. Now, he was on the TV circuit. He was able to reach more people this way than he had ministering in Africa. Yes, he'd enjoyed that thought. *It was a very nice time though,* he thought lovingly as he reminisced over the many years he'd been ministering.

Yes, Mary Elizabeth did want a relationship with him while they both were there in a mission house, but he had already fallen in love in West Africa with a beautiful young girl who ministered alongside her aunt. He wondered many times how and where Concetta D'Amato was and how she'd turned out. That was over thirty years ago, and there was a lot of water under his bridge. However, he saw her at the banquet, and it brought back some beautiful memories of the time when he was young and innocent himself and on fire for the Lord. He'd been married now for twenty five years to Lara Timbers, the daughter of a famous minister. Johnny Bob had craved that kind of attention too, and marrying Lara Timbers was a real step up, or so he thought. Actually, she'd been married when he met her, but in the middle of a divorce, so she told him. Until that time he'd just been known in parts of Africa and then in his local community in the United States, but when he joined forces with Lara, his whole perspective about life and the Lord changed.

First of all, he still ministered to hundreds of thousands of people and brought them Jesus, but it was only just so much words to him now. He and Lara were having trouble in their marriage almost from the first day. She was spoiled and had her own ministry and was not above faking a few incidents to mesmerize the crowd. She wanted to be on top of the ministry field and well known, and suddenly that same spirit caught on with him too.

Their first assignment was in the children's ministry of her father's well-known ministry on the East Coast of the United States. There was another pastor in place already who was ordained by the Lord, and they all knew he was the one that God had chosen for the job, but when Johnny Bob and Lara came on the scene, they humbly worked under this minister for about six months and then took over, citing him for some kind of hidden sin that he swore he hadn't committed or rather committed before he was saved. Then he was ousted from the ministry, and Johnny Bob and Lara took over. This was none of Johnny Bob's doings, but he knew his wife was involved and felt badly but not badly enough to confront her on it or to refuse the position.

From there it was all uphill. The assistant pastorship came open after there was an accident to the assistant, and Johnny Bob and Lara took over, even over the protests of her father, the senior minister. But Lara insisted and even held something over her father's head. The family dynamics were changed from that time forward.

The whole thing broke the pastor, and soon Johnny Bob and Lara were the pastors of one of the largest church in Christianity in the United States. They traveled all over the country and were on TV, and soon he was the most celebrated minister in the world. He got accolades from many churches and many countries. To their benefit, they did give big tithes, but lived very high off the hog because they preached the message of prosperity and lived it even more than they preached it. They had palatial homes in California; in Florida; in Venice, Italy; and in the Caribbean, even owning their own island.

Johnny Bob enjoyed the fruits of his labors, but sometimes he sat back and wondered how things would have gone had he stayed around and pursued the sweet missionary girl he'd fallen in love with. He and Lara had both grown very far apart in their hearts, but had stayed together.

Johnny Bob and Lara were certainly the most famous ministers of the gospel on the TV circuit. They made great friends with politicians and movie stars, and everyone that was anyone knew about Johnny Bob and Lara and desired to have them officiate at their wedding or whatever and even big events in Washington. They were entertained by the president and his wife in a small private dinner.

The interview with Mrs. Lara Connors was much better, and she was a striking woman with a lot of sex appeal, which surprised Max, who was a devout Christian himself and met many pastors' wives and women who were either co-pastors or pastors themselves. Although they might be beautiful women, or attractive at any rate, none of them radiated the sex appeal that emanated from Lara Connors. She always looked at him straight in the eyes and with a feminine and flirty look. Max was uncomfortable under her gaze.

"Did you ever meet Ms. Mary Elizabeth Morrison?" he asked politely, looking everywhere but in her eyes.

"No, I'd never met her until tonight, but really, not even then. We just bowed to each other as Johnny Bob talked with her. I guess he knew her slightly from ministering in West Africa as a young man. Afterward, he told me how shocked he was at how she'd changed in the ensuing years. I pointed out to him that there was a vast difference in a young woman at eighteen and a middle-aged woman of forty-eight."

"Did your husband have any negative dealings with her either during that time or afterward?" he probed.

"Well, of course not, but how would I know anyway? He and I didn't meet and get married for several years after that."

That was all he could get out of her.

They checked all champagne glasses at the table and didn't find anything in any of them. When they checked the fingerprints, though, there were two glasses with her prints on them, but no poison in either of them.

All the people at the table had glasses with their fingerprints on them except Mrs. McVey.

"Well, she's a teetotaler," Lt. Melville said. Mike turned to him, remembering that he'd given her his glass of wine. Melville saw the look. Afterward, he taxed him on it.

"What was it, Mike?" he asked.

Mike paused for a moment. "I gave my glass of champagne that Cici gave me at the head table to Conci. So, she should have had a glass with her fingerprints on it."

"Hm…that is strange."

"But Mary Elizabeth did have a couple of Italian creampuffs; everyone agrees. In fact, the commissioner herself brought her a small tray with some on it according to witnesses," Mike continued.

Mike immediately went to school to talk to Conci, knowing it was a zoo trying to get her on the phone during school hours.

She was busily reading something to her students, and they seemed to enjoy it.

Mike just waltzed into the room and confronted her. "I need to see you promptly out in the hallway."

She just stared at him but knew she'd better not refuse. "Okay, class, finish reading this silently, please. Nora, you're the monitor," she said threateningly.

Once out in the hallway, she looked at him perplexed. "What is it, honey?"

"I gave my glass of champagne to you at the table, and what happened to it after that? No one can find it." He said it like the big cop he was: surly, but in charge and ready to pounce on the unsuspecting guilty party.

Conci just stared at him, thinking all the time. "Why, I told you I was a teetotaler, and I gave the glass to Mary Elizabeth. What did you say? You mean you can't find the glass?" she said, suddenly getting the impact of his question.

"Yes, and it looks amazingly like you did something with the glass."

"No way, McVey. No way. I told you I gave the glass to Mary Elizabeth."

He just sighed. "Well, the darn thing is missing, Conci. We're not sure how the poison was administered, and we're checking all angles. Come down to the station after school, and I'll get your statement."

"What shall I do with the children?"

"That's your problem, not mine," he said in his surliest voice and left her standing there with a worried expression on her face.

During lunchtime, Conci talked to Halperan,

and they prayed about it. She was released for the afternoon and first went upstairs to the chapel and prayed and then went to the police department. Mike wasn't there, but she talked to Alex Melville.

"That is very strange, Conci. What do you think happened to it?" he wondered.

"I have no idea, Al. It could have been a number of things," she said and gave her statement. Conci drove on home then and had a little time for herself and enjoyed putzing around without the children or Mike around.

Soon, though, he called her. "I told you to come after school. Why did you come so early, Conci? I wanted to talk to you myself. Don't you ever listen to me?" he asked in an agitated voice.

Coni just sighed. Nothing she did ever satisfied him completely, especially lately. "I'm sorry, honey, but Leo gave me the afternoon off. I wanted to get it over with so I could do some things in the house and relax without our precious children around, chattering to me," she said it tiredly, but in a joyful way.

Mike relented. "Okay, I can see that. All right. Did you tell him everything?"

"I did my best, honey."

"Okay, then. I must have just missed you. Did you see me rounding the corner? We almost bumped into each other," he said and sighed. *She didn't sound angry or upset, so she must not have seen me with Madeline. I have to be more careful,* he scolded himself.

chapter IX
sister talks about
sonny lopelia

Mike and Alex were putting their heads together. "So, one of the people that came into close contact with Mary Elizabeth was Sonny Lopelia. He certainly hugged her a few times and then actually danced with her," Mike suggested.

"What do we really know about him, Mike, except that he's a movie star, though maybe a has-been movie star at that?" Melville answered with another question.

Sonny had been interviewed by Sgt. Maxwell and swore to his innocence. "You obviously knew Ms. Morrison, Mr. Lopelia. When and how did you meet her?"

He just sighed, telling himself internally that this was just another role he had to play: the innocent victim of both his ex-wife and of anyone else. "Sergeant, I never met the woman until that night. I never met her except at the banquet when she came up to me and introduced herself. She'd been a big fan of mine for years, she told me," he said with an arrogant smug look on his face.

"You hugged her and kissed her on the cheek and danced with her, Mr. Lopelia. Isn't that kind of intimate for a woman you've never met before?"

"Not really, Sergeant. That's the way we do it in Hollywood. I often have to kiss and hug and say wonderful things to people I've never met. They are usually my fans, you understand. After all, I am Sonny Lopelia," he said with great arrogance, leaning back in his chair.

"All right, Mr. Lopelia, please don't leave the city until we clear up some things."

Sonny started to balk, but then decided to be cooperative. "Don't worry, Sergeant. My son Shepherd is a student in a school here in town, and I can take the time to really re-bond with him again," Sonny said, smiling at the prospect.

"Good, then. Thank you for your cooperation, Mr. Lopelia. Oh, by the way, my wife, Risa, is a great fan of yours."

They left it that way, but Max was dissatisfied with the whole interview.

Later that day, all the cops working on the murders conferred in Monty's office. A chance remark made by Conci one day about Sister knowing Sonny Lopelia and his history made Mike think now that she could help him. Mike was there and insisted that Sister Mary Concetta Rose be interviewed about Sonny Lopelia.

"Please don't let her know any of the facts of our investigation, or she'll bug me to death. It would be better if you called her, Al," Mike suggested. "They're upset with me for the moment," he said, looking down at his desk unhappily.

Monty just shook his head. "You at it again, McVey? What does it take for you to come to your sense and love that woman the way she loves you?"

"Well, for your information, Monty, as you know, she's pregnant again, and I don't even have a say about whether we have the baby or not. There, does that shock you?"

"Nothing you do shocks me, McVey," he grumbled.

"Oh? Did she catch you with the lovely Madeline?" Max suggested, rather tongue in cheek. He knew darn well that Mike was staying at his office for the last couple of days.

"Enough of my personal life, which seems to be of such interest to you guys," Mike said, glaring at all three men in the office.

Monty sighed and changed the subject.

"Okay, so, Melville, will you call Sister Conci and get her statement about Sonny Lopelia?"

Melville hesitated to call Conci about Sister coming to the police station. "I'd like to go to your house, Mike, and visit with Sister and take down the information she'll give us," he said pleasantly.

Mike looked long and hard at Melville. Obviously he had a plan. "Yeah, go ahead, I'll stay here and try to get some more information about the reverend."

Al nodded his head, and later in the afternoon, he went over to see Sister who was delighted with Al's suggestion. She really liked this man.

Of course, Conci and Sister regaled Alex Melville with his favorite, a sandwich of Conci's meatballs and crusty bread followed by lemon meringue pie.

After being gastronomically satisfied, Melville took out his little notebooks and began his interrogation. "Okay, Sister, Conci said you knew a lot about Sonny Lopelia. I'm all ears."

Sister took a sip of her coffee and settled into the recliner across from Melville and began her story. "I was assisting and observing Sister Gertrude Manning at the time after I decided to become a nun and was doing my student teaching, and my path seldom crossed with Sonny, who was a student, except during the recess time, when I, as the teacher with the least clout, was assigned a permanent lunch and recess duty. But, I always noticed how he would hang back when he was alone and appeared to be almost frightened of meeting friends or speaking to the girls and even the teachers. That puzzled me at the time, but years later I understood that he was very shy, despite his desire to be in show business. There was something always so poignant about Sonny that tugged at my heart. His sisters who disliked him and always picked on him, were the apples of his eyes. He was in eighth grade, and I had Patricia in my seventh-grade class. And Paulina was in seventh grade too, having been held back twice. At the time, we knew very little about learning disabilities, but she would definitely fit the pattern. Sonny tried to get their attention in all kinds of ways that only boys could imagine.

"I was at the school for only ten months and then went on to the mission field. I tried to follow Sonny's career as best I could over the years. He was in many plays and some minor roles in movies, and then he hit it big in Las Vegas. He was primarily a nightclub singer and became very popular. By this time his handsomeness showed through, but he always stayed a really nice guy, despite the rumors that he was gay. Nothing could be further from the truth, though. He was actually quite promiscuous with the ladies, getting three of them pregnant. Two of them had abortions, which at that time was against the law. Sonny was quite upset about that, even though he refused to marry the women. I found this out through reading his autobiography, so the story could had been skewed in his favor.

"Finally though, with the last one he fell in love. He married Iris Donnegan, a minor movie star he met and played house with for three years. She was pregnant at the time, but unfortunately, about three weeks after the wedding, she lost the baby. He was really upset. His sisters disdained him this time too. One of them became a nun and took the name Sister Lisa Lorraine and just stopped talking to her brother and began a lifelong habit of constant prayer and fasting for her brother's soul. The other sister got married and was left taking care of their elderly parents, whom Sonny tried to ignore.

"Eventually his older sister took him to court, and it was in all the papers. Trying to salvage his reputation of being such a nice guy and a family man, Sonny began to support them and even bought a house for them. Of course it was in all the papers and the magazines. Sonny, the family philanthropist. From that time on, he went with his own feelings, which I sincerely believe, truly was to help people." Sister paused then looked at the lieutenant to make sure he was listening. He nodded his head.

"Unfortunately, along with his big heartedness, he also had an ego as big as New York City, to use the hyperbole that my creative writing students used," she continued. "He knew he was special and tried to be humble about it all, but that wasn't Sonny. No, Sonny felt God had put him in a unique situation to help others. That sounded so spiritual and noble, but the fact was that Sonny only helped those who could get his name in the papers. He never gave a dime to his church or to any other church. He did give to his favorite charity, an obscure one that no one else famous knew about. And every time he gave a dime, he took a picture with them, and it was in some newspaper or magazine.

"There were all kinds of offers since his popularity in Las Vegas and New York for a movie deal. He fell for it and began to make some really big bucks. And then his wife had another miscarriage, and their relationship began to crumble. She had affairs, unbeknownst to him, so the biography stated. He began to drink, and soon his star, which had risen to superstar status, began to decline. He was drunk for engagements, showed up late or not at all, became completely impotent because of the heavy drinking, and soon, he and Iris were in the divorce courts.

"Sonny begged her to reconcile, but she had enough of his split personality: sweet and considerate when he was sober and brutal and insulting when he was drunk. They parted bitter enemies.

"According to Iris' reports, which were substantiated by his own family, Sonny was always a star, no matter what he did with the family or friends or whatever. It was always about himself. Yes, he was generous, but instant adulation had to come from that or he'd get very depressed. He was also prone to dark moments of depression, where he wouldn't even bathe or interact with anyone, just sit in his bedroom and lock the door.

"Time passed, and he was on the rise again, taking some big TV parts and then being able to get the same part on the movie screen. He dated many women and fell in love with Felicia Dorsett, a body builder and that year's female bodybuilder of the year. She was Miss Body of the U.S., quite a stunning looking woman. While not really pretty, she had a great body and winning smile and could be very attractive. They were a love match at first, since they lived in different types of worlds. They were fascinated with each other.

"Felicia was twenty-eight and had never been married, although she'd lived with one guy that she was engaged to for four years. They broke up just a short while before she met Sonny. She was almost six feet tall, just a few inches shorter than Sonny, and had golden blond hair that she wore in a short, manly hairdo.

"After a brief courtship, they got married, and almost immediately they both realized their big mistake. Within two months they got an annulment and went their own way, parting as friends of a sort. In Sonny's autobiography he put the blame for their breakup on himself. 'I really had no idea that my wife would get up at 4:00 a.m. every morning and run five miles and then lift weights when all I wanted to do was lounge around in my robe, have a great breakfast and make love. We were completely incompatible and neither of us wanted to change.' That was as good an explanation as any, most people thought.

"Five years later he met Sally Carter, who was a singer on the rise. She was quite beautiful, and it was instant love between them. They got married within two months, and in another two months Sally was pregnant. They appeared to be quite happy. His career was doing very well, and she decided to give up singing and concentrate on his career and really to manage it from behind the scenes. Sally had won a Fulbright scholarship to college and was really a brilliant girl academically. Her IQ was in the 160s. According to her autobiography, this caused some problems with Sonny. He wanted to be the star in the family and no one else, and he had a hard time accepting her comments about his career choices, although nine times out of ten, she was right.

"Soon, he began to trust her more and lean on her good sense and her brilliant mind. She was to be the beautiful, adoring wife. He insisted that she get some breast implants as soon as the baby was born and that she get some nose jobs. Nothing about her was perfect enough for him. Little by little, her own manic depressive tendencies came to the fore. She was hateful to him and his family and insisted on doing things her way. They fought almost constantly and cursed a blue streak at each other. His father, Salvatore, Sr., Sal to his friends and family, commented one time that the children's first word was the F-word. Soon, though, they both calmed down and had two more children: one a little girl with Downs Syndrome and a little boy who was the apple of his mother's eye.

"Still they fought, but now Sonny knew he'd made the mistake of his life. The woman he thought was so sweet and innocent had many affairs to get ahead in Hollywood and wasn't the hayseed she tried to make herself out to be. Little by little they grew far apart, but to the public they appeared to be great lovers.

"His last movie failed at the box office, and he began to drink heavily again, going in and out of sanitariums and drug rehabilitation. She, in frustration, began having affairs. He had an inkling but hated to confront her lest the rumors be true. Sonny tried to kill himself by shooting himself in the head, but his hands were shaking so hard that the bullet just nicked him in the skull, taking a little cartilage and some flesh. It was painful but not fatal by any means. The newspapers viewed this feeble attempt at suicide as a real ploy to get more newspaper coverage.

"Seeing her husband's agony, Sally settled down and tried to help him. Finally, it came to a head when their little daughter, Angelina, who had Downs, was struck by a car. She was only eleven years old, and she soon died of her injuries. Sonny was quite distressed, favoring this child over the other two because of her disability. The child was crazy about him, too. She was in a special school and had everything a child could want. His son, Shepherd, was his mother's favorite, and their oldest child, Isabella, went her own way most of the time. She tried to be sexy like her mother, and they let her have a breast implant at age fourteen and had her nose done. She was quite a beautiful girl. She had some minor roles in her father's movies and began to drink a lot too. By the time she was sixteen, the die was cast. She was an alcoholic and a drug addict. No one in the family paid much attention to her anyway, only her aunt, the nun, who got her into drug rehab, and then took her out to Africa with her on missions for a year. The parents acted like they were sacrificing their time with their daughter to let her have this chance with Sister whoever and do God's works. It would help her a lot. Actually, everyone that knew the couple agreed that they were glad she was gone.

"That's where I entered the story. I was in Africa at the mission house, teaching the children English at the time. That's where I met Isabella Lopelia. The first day at the mission when her aunt brought her from the train, she wore very short shorts and see-through peasant type blouse with no bra on. She was quite provocative looking. However, after about four hours of the intense heat and the constant buzz of the insects trying to get a bite out of her, she began to wear the long sleeves and long jeans and boots worn by everyone except the nuns, who wore their long-sleeved habits though they wore boots too.

"Isabella tried to run away after the first week after realizing that the nuns expected her to do some work. This caused the first encounter with a poisonous snake. She left early in the morning and took some of the food that was always in short supply out there in the boondocks. She had only gone a little distance when we heard some screams. Dr. Geisman had a vehicle of sorts; and I got into the dilapidated truck with him, and we raced in the direction of the screams that kept on and on.

"In minutes we were at Isabella's side. She'd been bitten by a poisonous snake and was almost comatose when we reached her. The doctor did some quick action and gave her a shot of antivenin. It was my job to locate the snake and see what kind it was. Fortunately it wasn't a mamba. He gave her the proper antivenin and brought her back to camp. I stayed with her for a couple of days, and she bonded with me. It was the beginning of a great friendship and a mentor relationship.

"She told me about the hectic crazy household in which she lived with her two angry, impetuous parents. Little by little, we prayed, and she became saved and a great helper. By that time, Sonny caught his wife being unfaithful, and she even bragged to him about her other guys; and he left her and filed for divorce.

"It was a good thing that Isabella was out of the line of fire that whole year, because it was a horrible year for everyone involved. Sally just wouldn't let him go without a big fight. She fought him at every turn. Their story was in the paper almost every day. Amazingly, he was being a gentleman in most ways and soon his star began to rise again.

"He pursued fame like someone would pursue eating if they were starving. He took everything that came along, and soon he was on top. Finally, the divorce was over, and they split the many millions he'd earned. But he hated her for it, and she hated him for trying to keep her from it. She got custody of the son, and he got custody of the daughter.

"Sonny took a trip to West Africa to see his daughter, and that's where I saw him again. In fact I was the one who met him, along with his daughter Isabella at the train station. It must have been a shock to him to see the terrible situation of the people, although he always bragged in that humble way of his that he walked among the poor in India and Africa and drove a truck with supplies to aid the natives and gave them food and solace. No one believed him, because even if he did give out these items generously and even wept openly for these people, when he slept at night, it was in a palatial room at the very best hotels.

"Sonny Lopelia got off the train. He looked tired and exhausted. When he saw Isabella looking so beautiful and happy as she ran up to him, he held her close to him. They both began to cry. Neither of them gave any notice to me, but that was all right.

"I ushered them to the old truck that I was driving, and both of them sat in the front seat with me.

"I introduced myself to him. 'Hi, I'm Sister Mary Concetta Rose,' I said in my most amiable and friendly voice. He just stared at me and took my hand and shook it.

"'You look so familiar to me, Sister. Have I met you before?' he asked innocently.

"Isabella looked at him and laughed. 'Sister is the nun in charge out here, Dad. So be nice to her. She's my best friend,' Isabella said proudly and beaming.

"Sonny looked at me with a puzzle in his eyes and raised his eyebrows.

"'Your daughter Isabella is a wonderful, spiritual, and very talented person, Mr. Lopelia. We're blessed to have her here with us.'

"Sonny kept looking at me, and I felt that perhaps he saw some similarity to the very young teacher that I used to be.

"Finally, he just shook his head. 'You look so familiar to me, but I see so many people. Do I know you?' he asked.

"'When you were in St. Bonadventures school in eighth grade, I taught you English Literature for one semester, but it was so long ago, Mr. Lopelia, that I certainly don't expect you to remember me.'

"He just stared at me. 'Really? Did I have you for any other classes?'

"'No, I was working with Sister Claudia Lillian, teaching literature and creative writing. But I did have your sister Pauline also in my classes. I know that now she's a nun, and I see her every once in a while,' I said happily.

"He just stared at me. I noticed that he had very green, green eyes now and thought it was because of contact lenses. In his earlier years the green was toned down by the grayness in his eyes. He looked rugged, but very, very tired and older than I expected.

"The drive was uneventful, except that the route took us through a few of the African towns. In one of them I was well known, well, really infamous rather than well known, and was not supposed to go through it at all, but I had no choice. The bridge was washed out in the other route, and this was the only way to camp.

"As we drove to the compound, he kept staring at me. 'You certainly don't look old enough to have taught me, Sister.'

"I wanted to say that I'd had an easier life, but that was so incongruous that I wondered why I even thought it for a moment. This was a millionaire, maybe a billionaire, who always traveled first class and always had the first spot at the table in the restaurant and went ahead of everyone else. Isabella told me stories about stores closing to other customers when he came in so he could have the stores exclusively for himself and restaurants that also closed their doors to other customers. Yes, he lived a very privileged life. He had everything material and fame too. Everyone loved him except maybe his wives. I shook my head. He was just staring at me.

"Sonny stayed for two weeks and bonded with his daughter nicely. She showed him all the jobs that she did, and the all of us nuns were so satisfied with her. It was quite hot during that time, and Sonny really suffered.

"Sonny was so helpful to us and drove one of our trucks for us when Sister Hilda Angelo Michael had trouble with the clutch. He seemed to relax the whole time he was visiting with us. He was a perfect gentleman and so charming and quite amusing as well. He regaled us with stories about Hollywood that filled us with wonder and made us laugh.

"He even stayed an extra week when we offered to pray for him every night. Finally, though, his commitments called to him. Isabella saw the change in him and decided to go back with him and see if things had really changed. We hugged, and I knew I'd miss her a lot and she me. That was two years ago.

"So, there I was one morning about a year ago reading the papers about Sonny Lopelia's ex-wife being murdered. They thought it was a burglar, a prowler, because some of her valuable jewelry was stolen.

"First thing I did was to call Isabella, and we talked for a while. She was, of course, quite upset about the whole thing. Regardless of how her mother was, Isabella loved her and prayed for her to change back into the sweet loving mother she used to be before the bad times and dope and the drinking messed up her mind. She was staying at her grandparents' house, and her father was almost a basket case about it all.

"'He's still drinking and going up and down,

and this really has unhinged him, Sister. He always loved my mother so very much.'

"I remembered Sister Mary Claudine Fortunata's words to the Lopelias about the terrible life they were training their son to live. By now, they were old people and very regretful about their son's problems. He took such good care of them now, but still they were alone. He had them living in a palatial house with many servants and with anything they wanted. They had lived a life high off the hog due to Sonny's largess, but eventually they came to see it as Sonny's life, not theirs. They had wasted their whole life, hanging onto their son, living their life vicariously, instead of striking out on their own, as Iris's family did.

"I got that story secondhand from Isabella. Now I wondered about the last time she saw her mother. She was slightly incoherent and muddled so I directed her.

"'Start with the murder first, Isabella. Start the day of the murder.' I encouraged her. 'Where were you, and when did you see your mother last?

"She paused, not knowing which question to answer.

"'Just tell me when the last time was you saw your mother alive.

"'About a week before her murder, I went over

to her house and had breakfast with her. She was so darn stoned on those prescription drugs she took. Her pupils were so dilated, it was amazing. I hugged her and she hugged me back. I hoped she knew who I was. "How are you, Mom?" I asked her, and she just stared at me.

""I'm beautiful, honey. I'm the most beautiful woman in the world. I've had two breast implants, two tummy tucks, liposuction on everything but my brain, three nose jobs, a little bit here and little bit there on the face. I have false nails, a butt implant, and special attachments for my hair. That makes me the perfect woman. Yes, even your daddy would love me now. I'm more beautiful than any woman he's ever met. He told me that every day," she lamented. Really, Sister, she was in bad shape, and so doped up and ready to either kiss me or kill me. I went over and hugged her and made sure she ate something. She was getting so thin and looked so full of pain. I'd even hired a nurse to take care of her, and Mama liked the nurse at least and let her do things for her.

"'Mom, are you all right?' I asked, very upset.

""I'm the most beautiful all right you'll ever see, ugly sister. You aren't even as good looking as me." I just hugged her and made her a sandwich and brought her a cup of coffee and left. She just dozed on the couch as I went out the door.

That's the last time I saw her alive, if you can call it that,' she said bitterly, and I could hear the tears in her voice. Well, we prayed, and I called her every couple of months to check on her. She was doing amazingly well. Her father had come through for her and straightened up himself, and he and her brother, Shepherd, were living with him and enjoying it.

"'We're really a family now, Sister,' she told me."

Sister sighed, took a deep breath, and then drank a good gulp of her coffee, which had gotten cold. She looked at Conci askew, and instantly Conci was up to refresh Sister's cup and looked at Al with a question on her face, and he nodded too.

"Thank you," he said and smiled at her. "That's quite a story, Sister. I'm glad that I came here today." Alex had listened intently and wide-eyed the entire time. *Both Sister and Conci could weave a story so well*, he thought with admiration. "So how long ago was it that his ex-wife was killed, and how was it done?"

"Oh, about two years ago, Al. She was shot right in the head, and it was made to look like suicide. But the police were a little unhappy about it all, but eventually it all died down, I guess, when Sonny had a chance to go through her things and noticed that the very expensive diamonds and gold that he gave her were missing. Friends speculated that she might have sold some of it, but he was adamant that it must have been stolen. So, they had to go with that, Al," Sister finished, sounding uncertain about it all herself.

Al Melville stared at Sister for a long time and she never flinched. *So, she had a hunch about his ex-wife's death. Yes, she felt that Sonny had killed her or had it done. Was that it?* But Al just shrugged himself and centered his thought now onto Conci.

"Do you have anything to add to that, Conci?"

She just smiled and laughed. "I'm afraid not, Al. I never met him until the night of the fundraiser. This is Auntie's experience, not mine," she said with a lilt in her voice. "I'm so glad too, Al. At least for once I'm out of the mainstream of information." She just sighed.

He looked at her askew. "I'll bet not," he teased, and even Sister had to laugh at that.

During this whole time, Conci just sat there quietly and looked at Sister while she talked, sneaking a peek at Melville every now and then. He too stole a look at her occasionally.

"Do you have *anything* to add to that, Conci?" he repeated, feeling she had something to say.

She shook her head. "I didn't meet him until the night of the banquet when Sister introduced me to him. He was certainly a man full of charm," she noted, smiling.

"What did you do when Mary Elizabeth fell over, Conci?" Melville asked in his best police voice.

Conci almost smiled. "I was dancing with the chief, I think, Al. Yes, I was dancing with him," she said and smiled at the memory.

"Okay, then, did Mary Elizabeth drink out of the glass?"

"I really don't know. She had three champagne glasses full in front of her. People kept giving us champagne glasses full of champagne. We also had some Italian pastries on her plate: a cannoli. A cream puff and a biscotti, I believe," Conci commented.

chapter X
mary elizabeth

"Well, ladies, thank you for your time."

"Wait, Al, don't you want to know about Mary Elizabeth? I have some things to tell you," she said, perplexed at his brevity of interviewing her.

Al sighed and sat down. "Okay," he said in a disinterested voice, "go on." Al just looked at her with a stare that said, "Hurry up with this story." Conci got very nervous.

Alex Melville always marveled at the information that Conci McVey had in her curly black head, but he was tired after hearing Sister Conci's very long version of Sonny Lopelia.

"Okay, Conci, but your information would be about Mary Elizabeth Morrison, whom you said you worked with for the last six months. Tell me about her."

Conci closed her eyes. She could see everything as though it was just happening, like a motion picture.

"She came to Signs and Wonders at the beginning of this school year. The former nurse had to leave because of personal reasons, and Mary Elizabeth came on board. She was lovely person, having had a lot of experience in the world. She had just received the Lord about a month before she came to work for us. That in fact was what tipped the scale for Leo in hiring her over other nurses.

"We hit if off right away, and she would give us extra help with our children, for instance if there was some kind of physical check that had to be done with whole classes. She'd tell me to leave my class and she'd bring them back to me, thus giving me a much-needed hour-long break. It was a real friendly thing to do, Al, and I appreciated it a lot. So, we began to go to lunch with Mary Elizabeth, Jennifer, and Loretta and once in a while Mari. She was a very serious person and was so hungry for the Word of God. We taught her, and she entertained us with stories about some of her private patients. At one time, I believe, she even worked out in Hollywood and took care of a big star's drunken wife."

Al turned quickly. "Who? Lopelia's?"

Conci shrugged. "She never said, but it certainly sounded like that family. But it could have been any number of Hollywood families that had that same problem," she continued.

"Go on!" he commanded.

"Well, she had a boyfriend whom she was trying to cool it with. Not break up but just stop...you know...being so intimate with now that she worked at Signs and Wonders. She was always afraid that Halperan would find out. We all prayed for her and we all fasted, and still she had a problem now with getting rid of him. She'd decided she didn't love him at all, and he was quite enraged at her," Conci said.

Al raised his eyebrows. "So, do you know him or where he is?"

Conci just shrugged. "She never told me his name."

"What about his business. What did he do? Where did the both of them live together?"

"I'll give you the address, but she soon left that place and got another one by herself. At least that's what she told me, Al. She did say that he had to go on duty one night and that he worked nights and that his job was dangerous. Then as we fasted and prayed with her, she got more and more upset about something.

Then one day Auntie and I were with her and she unburdened herself to us.

"'If you know that someone committed a crime and you never said a word about it to anyone and now you're beginning to get told about it from the

Lord, should you tell him you're going to reveal it and give him a chance to redeem himself first?' she asked directing her question to auntie.

"No," Sister counseled her, "No, if that hypothetical person told the one who committed the sin or committed a crime they might not want to confess and would possibly hurt the other person. So, I would go to the police right away and tell them, and they would take care of you.'

"'It's not me, Sister,' she said and left the room angrily."

"You ladies are always so astute," Melville said and tried to make up for his earlier abruptness.

"When the Chief got up and said all those wonderful things about Cici and then he mentioned the badge number," Conci continued, "I looked over at Mary Elizabeth, and she was just staring at her while sitting down. Finally, someone had to nudge her to make her stand up. Then she applauded. I looked over at Cici, and she was staring with a puzzled look on her face at Mary Elizabeth."

Conci stopped and looked over at Alex Melville. He was frowning at her.

"It was only an impression, Al, but when Mary Elizabeth collapsed I was one of the ones nearest to her, and she said something about a budge or a badge and the number. It sounded like nine o something." Conci stared at Al Melville.

"So? That was the upside down number of the commissioner's badge, and everyone at the dinner knew it by now, especially since the chief held it upside down at first."

Conci nodded.

"I know that, Al. And it was just a strange thing, and I know you cops want to know about any 'strange or unusual things,'" Conci quoted her husband word for word.

Al nodded his head.

"Thank you for all your help, both of you ladies. Now, can I have another piece of pie?" He smiled at them, and hurriedly Auntie and Conci scurried about to fulfill the lieutenant's wishes, bringing him pie and coffee.

They made small talk then Melville thanked them and left.

chapter XI
a question

Timmy Wiley made an appointment at the police station to see his Uncle Mike, citing his research in his Bible class. They had been studying the Seven Deadly Sins for over two weeks now, but since their Bible class only met twice a week, for forty-five minutes, they didn't have much time to discuss it at great length.

Mike McVey was amused at his nephew's insistence on seeing him at the police station.

"This is a professional visit, Uncle Mike. I'm interviewing you for one of my classes," he stated. So, he sat in Mike's office and took out his notebooks and explained his interest to Uncle Mike.

"We're studying the Seven Deadly Sins in class, and since you're a big cop and in charge of homicide, the teacher wanted to know what your opinion is of murder? Is it one of the Seven Deadly Sins?" Then Timmy began to recite the seven, "They're lust, greed, pride, gluttony, sloth, envy, and wrath. So there's not one that's especially for murder, but do you think murder is part of one of these or one deadly sin on its own?" he asked as though his uncle would know the answer to this.

Mike McVey just stared at his nephew, wondering how he should answer this. He was out of his realm of expertise in relating these crimes to sin.

"Did you talk to Aunt Conci about this?" he hedged, hoping Conci said something he could agree with.

"Yeah, I did, and she thought it was a good idea to interview you."

Mike just sighed.

"The early church thought that murder was the result of one of these sins, not the deadly sin itself," Timmy went on, warming to his subject.

"How do you mean?" Mike was getting a little interested despite himself. He'd taken courses on the philosophy of crime and reasons for murders and psychological debates about it all, so he really did have some knowledge on the subject.

"Well, for instance wrath would cause a person to murder someone else, wanting someone else's goods, as greed would motivate someone to kill a person for their goods or their wife or their position or something like that."

Mike raised his eyebrows.

"All I can tell you is this, Timmy. I've seen hundreds of murders in the thirty years I've been on the police force. Some of them have been caused by jealousy, anger, meanness, hatred, to save one's hide. I guess pride would be the one for that, for money, for power, for revenge. So, I guess what the early church people felt would be how I feel too. Is murder a deadly sin in itself? Yes, I think it is. To think about killing someone is not a crime. But to do it and actually kill someone is a crime, so I imagine it would work like that with a sin too. So in answer to your question, I think yes, murder should be one of the deadly sins in itself." He stopped and looked at Timmy, satisfied with his answer.

"So, then you're saying to lust after someone in your heart is not a sin, but to act on that lust and have an affair or be unfaithful would be a sin?" he asked, staring right into his uncle's eyes.

Mike looked back at Timmy with surprise and shock and pushed back in his chair. "Yes," he whispered. "Yes, I guess it would be a sin," he said as much to himself as to Timmy.

"Thanks, Uncle Mike. I knew you were a really intelligent cop and could answer my questions. Thanks a lot. Mrs. Dooley will be pleased."

Mike just leaned back in his chair and shook his head. "Out of the mouths of babes. . ." he said quietly and closed his eyes.

chapter XII
reconciliation

Mike knew he had to get back in his wife's good graces again and assure her of his fidelity even though it was lie. *For heaven's sakes even my nephew somehow knew or suspected that I was committing adultery.* He felt that his life was starting to go down the drain again, and although he disdained his wife for wanting to have this baby, he knew she was the only one keeping him from going downhill. He did love her on some level. He was just upset with her.

Once that was settled in his mind, he could see things more clearly, especially since Madeline was gone again doing her modeling. So toward that end, he bought some gardenias and made a reservation in one of the best restaurants in the city for the next night, which was a Saturday. His brother-in-law, Dr. John Wiley, mentioned to him a few days ago that Conci was having another ultrasound to make sure the baby was all right, and this time they would know the sex for sure. The last time it was unclear. He thought it was today; in the afternoon, John said.

So, he called Conci at home first, not knowing if she'd be in school or not. No answer, so he called the school.

"This is Lt. McVey. I need to talk to my wife immediately. It's very important."

Sunflower Bodine, the school secretary, just smiled to herself. "Of course, Lieutenant. I'll get her right away."

A few minutes later, Conci was on the phone. "Hello," she said her soft, sweet. lilting voice. He loved to hear her voice and especially her laughter.

"Honey, what time is your ultrasound? I'll come by and pick you up and go with you," he said as though they'd already discussed it.

Conci was quite surprised. "It's at twelve thirty, Mike." Then she paused. "That would be very nice, Mike. I'd like that," she said softly.

He breathed a sigh of relief. "Okay, I'll pick you up at twelve. Are you taking off the rest of the day?"

"Yes, I am."

"Good, then we can spend some time together."

Conci just shrugged and hung up. "See you then. Thanks, Mike," she said and hung up.

Mike said a little prayer. "Lord, please don't let me goof this up."

So, he went with Conci to the doctor and had the ultrasound. He stayed in the room with her, and the doctor was quite pleased. Dr. Oliver was a friend of the family and had been Conci's OB and Gynecologist for a long time and had delivered the twins.

"Look, Mike," he said, and Mike could feel his excitement. "It's a little girl. Can you see that?"

Mike smiled at him and then at Conci.

"Another little girl who will love her daddy forever," Conci said, and Mike held her hand and kissed it in the open palm. *Lord, I don't know what's happening, but please let it be a true repentance,* Conci prayed silently.

Afterward, he took her out to lunch. "Where to, honey?" He was on his best behavior and being the exemplary gentleman that he could be.

They talked about the baby and the children and the investigation. Finally, he gave her the box of gardenias.

"Oh Mike, thank you so much. They're lovely." Then she looked at him perplexed.

"I want to be on good terms with you, Conci. Please don't jump to conclusions about my fidelity. There was nothing between Madeline and me, nothing serious. Satan has been assaulting me with temptations for a long time now, and I almost fell. But I decided that I love you and no one else and I want to be married to you. I'll be faithful. In fact, I have been faithful," he lied, and she knew it was a lie.

"Are you going to be upset about the baby still?" she asked him, which surprised him. He thought she'd want to know how far his relationship with Madeline had gone, but instead it was purely domestic issues that interested her right now.

"I'm all right with it now, Conci. Honestly. I won't disdain you, and you don't hold it against me that I said the A-word. Okay?"

They both agreed on that.

"Did you get it all out of your system, Mike?" she finally asked almost in a whisper.

Mike grabbed her hand and held it against his cheek. "There was nothing to get out of my system, baby. I overcame the temptation, that's what. I feel proud of myself for it," he said, and she knew that was only a partial lie.

"No more running around or even dating other women, Mike. That's the only way you can come back. Can you promise me that?" she continued.

He nodded his head. "Yes, I don't want to stray, baby, believe me. I want to be a good boy for you and for God and for myself too," Mike said sincerely.

They talked about the murders for a while.

"You have any ideas?"

"Well, of course, Mike. Don't I always?" And she started to laugh at herself. He joined her and then got into her side of the booth and held onto her and began to kiss her.

"Want to go home and have some dessert?" Conci asked him in her best saucy manner.

He jumped on it. "Oh yes, honey. Yes."

That day they reconciled. Conci was singing in the house again, and Mike was smiling at her ample frame as she danced and cavorted about the house. The children too were full of joy and tried to sing with their mommy. Mike sat back in his chair on the nights that he did come home and drifted off to a really peaceful sleep after playing with his children and kissing his wife. He was really trying to be a better husband and father. Conci appreciated it.

Mike redoubled his efforts to find the killer of Mary Elizabeth. No one wanted to undertake the interrogation of the commissioner. Mary Elizabeth was reported to be her greatest supporter and carried signs and did other things to promote the commissioner. She had never personally met her, until the night of the fundraiser, but her campaign office touted her as their best worker.

Mike took Conci out to dinner at least twice a week now and romanced her as best he could. One night during dinner, he reached over and took her hand. "I've been a bad husband, Conci. I know that. I don't deserve someone like you. I don't deserve you. That's the whole thing. I'm a moody old crab sometimes, but I really don't mean anything by it. It's just my initial reaction, and you should be used to it by now. You know how I get when you're in trouble or if I even perceive some danger to you. Can't you just let it roll of your back? We're back together again. Please don't leave me on the basis of this alone. I want to be with you and be a better husband. I'm going to try harder, Conci," he insisted. He just sighed, knowing this was an uphill battle.

Conci decided to ride it out. She wasn't in any shape to get a separation anyway. The problem with Mike was that when he was good, he was very very good, and when he was bad, he was horrid, kind of like that little girl in the nursery rhyme. That did make her smile.

Things were great with the McVeys, and

Mike became so loving and caring with his wife and brought home the case for her to read and discussed it with her. Even the twins were delighted with their daddy being home more, and Moira especially hung around him a lot. Sonny was always so busy taking things apart and then surprisingly putting them together again, but when he was tired, he sought out both his mommy and his daddy. Sister was so pleased with Mike's apparent trying to be a good husband and father. If she had any thoughts otherwise or discerned something else, she kept it between herself and the Lord.

Conci, however, detected an undercurrent that she could not identify in the last few weeks. It was as though she was watching a movie or a play and things weren't the way they seemed. But she shook off her negative feelings and went with her heart.

chapter XIII
a hurt so deep

A few weeks later there was a party and banquet to honor the chief, really a roast of sorts, put on by his buddies. They had invited not only Mike and Conci but also Sister Conci whom the chief and Lola just loved.

"I can't go tonight, baby," Mike complained. "I called the chief and gave our regrets. Sorry, honey, my work comes first." Conci just looked at him with that deep searching gaze, and he hurriedly left the house. However, after Mike left, Lola called Conci and said she wanted her and her aunt to come anyway. In fact, she insisted on it. Auntie agreed and Conci tried to get a hold of Mike, but his phones wouldn't answer.

Thus, that night, Conci drove them. When they arrived, Monty motioned for them to come to their table, which they did.

"Where's Big Mike?" Monty asked, rather worried about it, hoping that Mike was coming too. Otherwise it would look strange them being here. He was quite surprised at Conci's moxie coming alone with her aunt.

"Oh, he can't come, Monty. He has to do some detective work. You know how committed he is." Conci smiled at Monty. "We called in our regrets, but Lola called me today and really encouraged Auntie and I to come alone if that was the only way we could come," she said and smiled at him.

Monty closed his eyes and gave a little shove with his knee to his wife, Colleen. She looked at him perplexed.

"You two seem to be making it this time, Conci," Colleen said with love and affection.

She nodded happily to him.

"We're doing so well, Colleen. This time it's for good, he tells me." She sat down next to Colleen, and they hugged and so did Sister.

Everything went well as the Maxwells arrived and sat at their table and the Melvilles and the Ryans.

The women talked over the men, and they laughed and joked. And Sister was a big help.

"You look absolutely great, Conci," Joey, who had just arrived with Jennifer, commented.

Jennifer nodded her head. "You do, Conci."

So, there were ten of them, and the table held twelve. The meal came and went and then the toasts and then the funny speeches as they roasted the chief. Everyone had great time.

Then suddenly it was all over as all eyes turned toward the door as Mike McVey came into the room. On his arm was the lovely Madeline O'Reilly. She had her very pretty nose upturned toward the ceiling in an arrogant pose.

They quietly waited at the entrance as a huge hush fell over the crowd. The chief quickly called one of the waiters and instructed him to put them at the table in front.

Mike and Madeline walked to the table, quite surprised and even shocked that Mike's wife and mother-in-law were sitting there. Conci just stared at him.

"I think you all know Madeline O'Reilly, the famous model?" he said briefly and couldn't look at either his wife or at Sister Conci.

The tears ran down Conci's cheeks as she just stared at him, in utter disbelief that he'd embarrass her right in front of all their friends and dozens of people they didn't even know.

Sister looked at her niece with alarm and touched her gently on the lap. Colleen too felt Conci's tremendous, almost overwhelming hurt. It was so strong that everyone in the room felt something terrible had happened. A hush fell over the crowd, and people only spoke in whispers.

Still, the tears ran copiously from Conci's eyes and landed on the table and all over her dress, making stains that even a talented dry cleaner could not remove.

"Oh Conci!" Jennifer sighed out loud. "Oh, honey, I'm so sorry," she said and looked at her husband. Joey was staring at McVey with an angry face.

Monty was overwhelmed at this action of Mike's. As if someone said something, everyone got up and moved over so that Mike and Madeline were sitting by Sister and Conci, with Conci sitting next to Mike. She just kept looking at him. He felt her shock and her deep sadness and felt it inside himself. He looked at her, and she stared at him with those big eyes.

"Conci," he said and then dropped his eyes. "I'm sorry," he whispered. "I had no idea you'd be here."

She never spoke a word, just kept staring at him, then spoke softly,

"How could you do this to me, Mike? How?"

Madeline felt something sad too and wondered about it. She felt bereft and wanted to cry about something and wasn't sure what it was.

Suddenly the scene changed, and Mike was standing with a whip in his hand that had glass chards on the end of it, and Conci was hanging from a rope that had her hands tied as Mike was whipping Conci's body over and over again. She just sighed and screamed and cried and begged him to stop.

"Please kill me, Mike. I cannot bear this agony anymore," she said, and then Madeline took the whip and beat her, laughing all the time.

Just as suddenly they were back at the banquet, and Mike was sitting next to Conci and saw her face and felt that terrible hurt inside of her. It was physically making him sick. The whole table just stared at Conci and then at each other. They had all seen the vision, and it startled them. Madeline got up from the table. "No, I'd never do that to anyone. No, not ever. It's a big lie." And she ran out of the room. Mike went after her, and that was the last they saw of him that night. Suddenly everything was back to normal, except for the people at the table who came up and hugged Conci and held her close to them.

Finally, Monty spoke. "What happened?" he asked Sister.

She just nodded her head. "For a few moments we were all allowed to see what Mike and Madeline were doing to Conci. Yes, her pain was so strong that we all felt and saw it," she said and hugged her niece as she just sighed, and all of them got up from the table.

"I guess we need to go," Conci said as the chief came over to her table.

What they all didn't know was that everyone in the room saw inside of Conci's soul that night and saw and felt her hurt. The Chief grabbed Conci and just held her, and Lola joined them. Soon everyone was praying for Mike and Conci and rebuking his relationship with Madeline.

As if a signal was given, everyone got up from their seats and left the place, quietly with no one talking.

How strange this all is, the Chief thought as he and Lola walked out of the banquet hall. *I feel as though I've been privileged to see inside the spirit tonight.*

Everyone said a hushed goodnight, and the party was over, much to the pleasure of the chief, who hated parties anyway.

Mike immediately ran after her. "Hold on, Maddy," he yelled in alarm. He grabbed her arm and pulled her back to him, and then he walked beside her and steered her out of the banquet hall and into his car. Once safely ensconced in the car, he breathed a sigh of relief.

"Okay, McVey, what the heck was that all about?" she asked in a scared voice.

"Look, honey, all I know is that once in a while I can see into Conci's thoughts and she into mine, but it's never been this kind of thing. I think she hypnotized us all at the table. That's what I think."

"Yeah, did you see the looks on the faces of the others at the table? They looked at me as though I was some kind of murderer, Mike. I don't like that at all. I'm a good person," she said rather insincerely.

Mike put his arms around her and hugged her tightly before driving off to a penthouse hotel room he'd reserved for the night. He wanted to show her that he had some class too and was willing to spend some serious money on her.

"This is definitely much better, Mike. Yes, I think I'll stay with you," she said and began to vamp him. Unfortunately, the trauma of the night hurt both of their libidos, and after a few futile attempts, they both just gave up and went to sleep.

Both of them had very strange dreams. Madeline saw herself on a fashion runway, wearing some old torn rags, and the audience began to boo her off the stage. She was shocked and looked down at her garment, not realizing until that moment that they were dirty and all in tatters.

"Oh no, what happened here?" She couldn't believe it all. Then she awoke shivering, and Mike was already up and watching TV in the living room part of the suite. Madeline got up quickly and went to him and sat on his lap. "I had a horrible dream." She began to relate it to him.

He held her close to him. "I too had a disturbing dream." But he didn't tell her the dream, nor did she ask.

Mike thought that was so odd. Conci would have probed until he finally told her, and then she'd make him feel better. But Maddy was involved with herself more than anyone else. *She's the perfect self-centered hedonist.* Then Mike shook himself, wondering why he'd thought that.

Neither of them felt very good that morning and were reluctant to go back to sleep, so they got their showers and dressed and went out for breakfast. While Mike was showering, he thought about his dream. He and Conci were traveling someplace with the twins, and Conci was still pregnant, but very large now. The children were chatting the way that they do. Mike just smiled at his little family, and looked long and hard at Conci's stomach. She wasn't sitting in the front seat with him, but rather in the back with the children. Somehow he knew that he'd told her to get in the backseat, that he couldn't stand the sight of her. They had to stop at a railroad crossing, as a train was in the distance. Mike thought this was his chance to get rid of Conci and the children so he could go with Madeline.

So, he parked the car on the railroad tracks, breaking the wooden gates that came down to stop the cars, and he tried to get out. But he was stuck in his seat, and he saw the train barreling down on all four of them. And he screamed and screamed, while Conci and the children prayed out loud. Mike awoke with a start and got up and went into the living room area of the hotel room and made some coffee. He was mightily upset.

"Oh Lord, I'd never do that to my wife and children. I would never hurt them like that. How selfish could I possibly be?" He prayed over and over again, shivering from the thought that these ideas were even somewhere in the dark recesses of his mind. Mike thought all about this as he and Maddy dressed to go down to breakfast. She had a big frown on her face too, and he watched her face closely. Indeed, she was a beautiful woman on the surface, but she was very wrapped up in herself and not him. Why did he find her so maddeningly attractive that he was willing to give up his wife and children for her? They quietly went down to breakfast and ate very little, but drank copious amounts of coffee.

Mike was reluctant to go home and face Conci, so he waited until she went to school and then went in and got his clothes and some other stuff. He left her a note.

I'm sorry, Conci. Really and truly, you deserve someone better than me.

Mike.

Just then, as he put the note on the dresser, Conci came in. She saw his car in front of the house and had already decided to go to see Sam Morris, her attorney.

"What are you doing here, Conci? I was just leaving you a note."

"What's wrong with you, McVey? How could you do this to me, to yourself, to your children?" she chided him. "Then you were so deceptive to me. You broke my heart, Michael McVey, Jr. Yes, you broke my heart. I don't think it will ever heal again." And she began to cry almost uncontrollably.

Mike put his arms around her and explained. "Madeline came back, Conci, and I realized how much I loved her. And I want to get married to Madeline, Conci. Don't you understand? I don't love you anymore, honey. Not in that way, but I do love you like a friend and a sister or something, but not a lover. Please be reasonable. I love this one so much; she's just like Rhonda."

"Really? You mean she cheats on you and treats you badly? Well, I guess she is just like Rhonda, but how can you marry her, Mike, when she's still married to Philly Bastriani?" Conci confronted him.

Mike got up and glared at her. "Where do you get your information from, Conci? She's not married. I would know it if she was."

"Well, she is, Mike, and all you need to do is to go to an Internet site in England to find the marriage license. And no divorce papers have ever been filed. What a fool you are, letting her make such a fool of you. Don't you even have a clue that you're being set up?" she shouted back at him, even surprising herself with outburst.

Refusing to listen, Mike left the room, slammed out the door, and peeled away. He drove and drove without saying a word. Finally, he stopped along the road and turned around. He went back into the house and found Conci sitting at the dinning room table.

"All right, now tell me where you got this information?" He said in a more reasonable tone.

"I looked up the marriage records in England, Mike. That's where they got married."

"How did you know to do that and to look there?"

"Because she spent a lot of time in England about ten years ago when she was first getting started."

"Oh, so she married Bastriani, and he furthered her career. So that's what you want me to know?"

She nodded her head. "Yes, and also that there's not record of a divorce any place, certainly not one recognized in the U.S. But the marriage was recognized, to answer your next question," Conci said softly.

Mike wondered about this wife of his, wanting him to leave, but not giving him a divorce, still wanting to hold onto him.

"I was just wanting you to stop and realize what a mistake this was for you, Mike."

"Did you think it would make me come back to you?"

She shrugged. "I don't know and don't care, because I'm not going to take you back anyway. This is it for me, Mike. Yes, this is it, but I don't want you to go down the drain either. On the other hand, maybe a turn in the sewer would wake you up to your irresponsibility and sophomoric actions," she stated softly.

He just looked at her and sighed. "Do you still love me?" he asked softly, looking directly at her deep inside her eyes.

She turned from him. "Yes, I'm afraid I do," she said and got up from the table. He pulled her back down.

"I'm really sorry, Conci. I can't help myself. I have to be with her. Please understand. At first I thought you and I could make it. Then Madeline came back, and I didn't want to lose you or hurt you until I knew that she was definitely wanting to be with me. Can you imagine that beautiful woman, so perfect and so much like Rhonda, wants me, Mike McVey, a man twenty years her senior?"

Conci just stared at him. He was really deceived, and it was sad to her but didn't hurt her, not nearly as much as the other night. Conci got up added more hot coffee to his cup and flung it in his face and then tossed hers and ran into the bedroom and threw herself on the bed and cried her eyes out. "This is too much. No, he'd done it this time," she wailed.

Mike sat there at the kitchen table wiping off the hot coffee, his face painful and burning and cleaning up the floor, as well as himself. It really surprised him that Conci had such deep feelings for him. He really didn't want to hurt her and knew he had some love for her, but it wasn't as strong as his love for Rhonda. *No, wait, not Rhonda. Madeline. Madeline.* He shook his head at himself and remembered the dream he had of trying to kill his wife and children and how he was stuck to the seat of the car too. In light of this, he couldn't leave her like that, so he went into the bedroom and lay on the bed with her and held her in his arms. Reluctantly, she let him.

"Forgive me, Conci. Please forgive me and let me go. I never had this kind of woman to love me. Please, Conci, let me go and tell me you'll be waiting for me like always," he said and then wondered why he'd said it like that.

"No, Mike, if you leave, it will be forever. Yes, you've hurt me so badly this time I may never recover," she said and pushed him away from her.

Mike got up, left the house, and drove off. Conci sighed in relief. Suddenly it seemed to be a really good idea to get away from Mike McVey. She called her aunt, who was distressed at Mike's behavior toward Conci. "Oh, darling, I'll be out there in a few days. I can't stay away from you when you're hurting this badly."

"It made me see how really misguided he is.

And really, Auntie, he's not a faithful man, and I don't know if he will ever be unless there is an intervention from the Lord himself," she stated. Auntie concurred with that.

"Thanks, Auntie," she said and then heard a cry and hung up and tended to her children.

Mike went right to Madeline's opulent condo and barged in using his own key. She was surprised and shocked to see him and so angry as well.

"Okay, Maddy, what kind of game are you playing with me? I understand that you're still married to Bastriani, and you never told me that at all. What's wrong with you to marry that big crook?" he asked, almost livid with rage.

"Now calm down, Mikey. I asked him for a divorce, and he got very upset with me. Then, suddenly someone turned state's evidence against him for some murder he committed years ago, and now he's in jail, probably going to go to prison for a long time. What a wonderful coincidence for me, sweetheart, because now I can file for divorce and get one within six months. Then you and I can get married. Isn't that grand how everything in life works out for my benefit?" she gushed and became very flirtatious with him.

Mike calmed down and wondered about this

feeling he had for her. It was almost like a sickness, more than a passion, close to an obsession. He quickly pushed the feelings from his mind and embraced her.

chapter XIV
separation

The next day Conci was in the office of her lawyer, Sam Morris, who was also her accountant, figuring out some financial things. They froze the accounts right that day and put all the cash in Conci's account across town, and she cancelled all their charge accounts except for the one in her name only. Now, the only asset they could both use was the checking account.

Mike was furious when he tried to get into their bank box. Then to find that the charge cards were reported lost or stolen was too much for him. He was furious. He almost broke the door when he entered the house that afternoon. Conci knew better than to be at home alone. Loretta and Billy were there, and so was Colleen Montgomery. Mike was surprised to see them.

"Hello, folks, I hope you don't mind, but I need to talk to my wife privately."

Conci wouldn't budge from her chair. "No,

Mike, my friends know all about our trouble. Please speak freely," she said reasonably.

He sat down and had some coffee. He was really steamed. "How dare you tie up my assets?" Everyone just stared at him, embarrassed, but knew Conci wanted and needed them to stay.

"You told me that you weren't going to support us anymore, Mike. I got scared and knew I had to protect the children and myself. I will have three children to raise by myself when you leave, and I need money to do it properly. Now, sit down and let's talk about this in a calm way. You've ignored the children, and they feel your absence."

"What about the charge cards? How dare you cancel my cards?"

"I didn't cancel your card, Mike, only the ones in both our names. I left your card alone. I couldn't cancel it anyway; only you could," she said reasonably.

He just sighed. "Okay, then, I needed a couple of those cards because mine is maxed out."

"Sorry, Mike, you'll just have to get some more cards in just your own name. I've started proceedings to get a legal separation, and then you can go your own way. But you have to support your children, Mike. I talked to the chief today, and he said that the policy book says that you have to support your family, and if not, then they will automatically take out what the court orders before you even get the paycheck. So you have to support the children whether you like it or not," she said adamantly.

He got up and put his face right up next to hers in a threatening way. She moved back, and Billy got up and stood behind her.

"Sit down, Billy. I won't hurt her," he said angrily. "Do you mean that you called the chief and told him about our problems?"

"Well, not all of them, but certainly about the financial thing. Yes, I did. He's the only one that would know for sure about the policy. Besides I wanted to get some advice from him," she explained.

Mike closed his eyes. For a person he thought was a doormat, she certainly had a lot of backbone.

"How could you leave me for a woman with such a scarlet past, Mike?" she asked angrily.

"What past? She was married once, and that didn't work out. She's as clean as the driven snow," he defended her.

"She's still married to Bastriani, Mike, and you know that for a fact. Are you two going to commit bigamy? Are you going to jail for her and ruin your whole life and your profession?" Conci tried to get him to see his foolishness.

"Well, she's getting a divorce from Bastriani," he said and took a deep breath and looked at her frowning.

"Oh, you think he'll sit still for that?"

"He's in jail, Conci, and going to prison for murder. He will have no choice in the matter," Mike said adamantly.

"Oh, Mike, you act as though he doesn't have a dangerous family for you and her to contend with. For heaven's sakes, what about the other Bastrianis? Do you think they'll just sit back and take it? You know better than that. Well, it's your life, but it better not affect the children or me in any way," she said in a threatening voice.

Mike just looked at her. He hadn't thought about his children in this scenario at all. Now, he wondered. *Darn,* he thought, *that's the problem with a family; you always have to watch out for them. It's no longer just me; now there are three more little people that are part of me.*

"Okay, now let's go over finances and then child custody," Conci continued, but she didn't get a chance to finish.

"You can have the kids. I want to be free from you and the children, Conci," he said angrily.

Conci just stared at him. "I hope that I didn't hear you correctly," she said. He put his head the mystery of the eighth deadly sin

down, suddenly aware that three people were witnessing his outburst.

"I love them, Conci, but they're so darn little and so much trouble. I'll support you, but I don't want the children. You know I never wanted the little one anyway," he said grouchily.

"Please go, Mike. You're making me so darn upset," she said, and he got up and left angrily, slamming the door and speeding away.

"I wouldn't have believed it if I hadn't been here, Conci," Billy commented. "I would have believed you, but to hear him is another matter." They prayed the rest of the afternoon.

Mike went to Madeline's apartment. She was in a bad mood, having heard from her manager that she'd lost one of the biggest contracts for modeling of her life. "What's wrong with you, Maddy? Can't you see that my life is in turmoil? And here you're barking at me. I just talked to my wife about you and me getting together and getting married, and she had a fit. So why are you so angry at me?"

She just frowned at him. "I lost the biggest opportunity of my life, Mike. That's what. You're always so concerned about your own problems that you can't see mine. I need to move to New

York in order to schmooze these magazine guys," she stated to him in no uncertain terms.

"But what about us and our love for each other? I thought you wanted us to get married? I already broke it off with my wife, and now you're wanting to go somewhere away from me. What's up, Maddy?"

"That's on the back burner, Mike. I need to establish myself again. I was the biggest and most desired model until I started going with you. And then Philly got upset, and he's the one who brought me this far. And he told me he could make me or break me, and he started some rumors about me being on drugs and alcohol and not being reliable. Can you imagine that? The dirty rat."

"He's in a Phoenix jail awaiting trial on murder charges, Maddy. I checked it all out. How can he hurt you now?"

She screamed and cried and threw dishes at the wall and broke every lamp in her house as Mike watched her in astonishment. *She's just like me,* he thought. *My gosh. She's like a female McVey. Very moody.*

"I've never seen this mood of yours, Maddy, and I must say I really don't like it."

Mike wouldn't stay much with Maddy after her angry outburst to him. On one hand a small part of him did want to stay with Conci and ride out any bumpy part of his marriage. Monty told him that marriage had seasons.

"Look, Mike, there are seasons in a marriage. Sometimes you're on a perpetual honeymoon, and sometimes you're both bogged down with children and diapers and debt. Sometimes I love my wife with an overwhelming love and we're so passionate and on fire for each other, and then sometimes we're like siblings, arguing over every little thing and I wonder what I ever saw in her. But you ride out the bad seasons until you get into another good one. Commitment is the glue that holds the marriage together when there's a bad season. That's what causes you to stay and wait for another season to arrive. That's what commitment is all about, Mike. By golly, I made a promise to her, and I'm a big man, a promise keeper, a really macho guy, a commitment man."

Mike thought a lot about what Monty said. After all, he and Colleen had been married for almost thirty years, and she was a much bigger pain in the neck than Conci ever was. Mike just sighed with it all. But regardless, he stayed mostly in the office and slept on a small two-seater sofa in his own office and bathed in the jail. *Conci probably won't take me back at any rate after the way I shamed her,* he thought glumly.

He was very busy anyway, because of investigating the death and the attempted murder. It interested Melville, who related it to Mike when he interviewed Auntie that she seemed to feel that it was Sonny who killed his wife, not some stranger as reported. He didn't press her on it, because he knew she would clam up entirely. But it did give him something to think about.

In the meantime, Madeline went out of town without McVey on a modeling tour, *or whatever,* he thought. It made him angry that she didn't want him to accompany her.

Mike was finally doing his usual excellent work and staying out to all hours following leads and crooks, and Monty commented on it.

"This last month you're the old McVey, a bulldog, and so focused on your work. Glad to have you back, Mike. I hope this McVey stays," he commented and slapped him on the back and shook his hand. Mike sighed. *Yes, I've let a lot of things slide because of my obsession with satisfying Madeline.*

Finally, she came back, and he waited for her to call him. All the three weeks she was gone she never got in touch with him at all. That infuriated him and hurt his feelings too. He had no way to get a hold of her, and that also bothered him.

Finally, she did call him one night a week after she returned.

"Hi, sweetheart," she said in her most sultry voice. Mike just caved.

"Maddy, why didn't you write to me or call me when you were gone?" He wondered, showing her he was a little perturbed.

"Oh, Mikey, you know how it is in Europe. It's hard to make a phone call sometimes, and my cell phone didn't work out there."

They chatted for a while and made arrangements that he'd take her out to dinner that evening. It was now two p.m.

As Mike returned to the office, Monty cornered him. "Got something important to talk to you about, McVey. Right now, please," he said tersely. Mike sighed and thought dejectedly, *what now?*

"Are you ready for this, Mike?" Monty asked as they both sat in Monty's office. He tried to show some compassion, knowing that Mike was a fool about redheaded women and his wife was about to throw in the towel forever. Everyone that knew her felt it was imminent. Colleen told him Conci had already filed for the separate maintenance, and it was just a matter of a few months until it became legal.

"Yeah, go ahead." Mike closed his eyes and

put his hands together at the palms, waiting for the worst.

"Last month when Madeline went to Europe, to Paris, she met another guy there, and they stayed together for a couple of weeks, touring Europe."

Mike just took in a deep breath. "Who was it?"

"A guy that calls himself Baron Ziegfried Von Molltovich, a real poser and a con man, according to our information. In fact he spent three years in a French jail for counterfeiting."

"Were they together in one room, or how did they travel?" he asked, hoping that these guys didn't know.

"We really don't know, Mike, but thought it was worth telling you."

"Yeah, thanks, guys. She does know a lot of titled people, even at that, and I guess she may have been duped by this guy. So, you're saying that we're not sure if they were just traveling companions and not sure if they were lovers?"

Monty just shrugged. "We don't know that for sure, Mike."

"I guess you think I'm some kind of fool, Monty. Maybe I am or maybe not," Mike said mysteriously, as he got up, shook Monty's hand, and thanked him, and walked out of the office.

chapter XV
the wake

It really wasn't a very sorrowful wake at all, much to the surprise of most of the visitors. Sgt. Johnny Cartellini had died unexpectedly, the doctors calling it a coronary. He was forty-three years old and divorced with one child, Candace, aged thirteen, along with his own four brothers and two sisters and a few aunts and uncles and many, many cousins and nieces and nephews.

The Italian music piped into the funeral home was lively and an apt accompaniment to the two huge tables in the back of the room, heavily laden with the Italian delicacies that his family cooked for this occasion. People went up to see the body, paid their respects, then offered their condolences to the ex-wife and the child and Johnny's many siblings and then hit the fabulous buffet and got themselves a plate, some wine or beer that was offered, and sat down in back and shot the breeze with the other cops or family members, friends, and relatives of the deceased.

To some of the guests it seemed more a party than a wake. The music wasn't especially somber as it usually was in a funeral chapel. In fact it was lively, and a few of the old aunts actually danced to the tarantella. Adding to the festive atmosphere was the good-natured banter of Johnny's four brothers, all priests, with their two uncles, Zio Giovanni and Zio Pietro, both union men. The arguments seemed to be purely political and heated up as the night went on.

The women in the family, the Cartellini girls, Sara and Anna, were very pretty women in their thirties, both nurses, married to doctors. They each had five children who were running around the chapel as though they were at a wedding, not a funeral. No one seemed to care one way or the other whether they behaved or not. The adults just moved out of their way.

The whole atmosphere changed when Rev. Johnny Bob Connor and his wife, Lara, came into the room. Reverend Connors had been a good friend with Cartellini when he ministered at Cartellini's church. They became friends and visited with their families every so often. Lara was mesmerized with the handsome, curly-haired Italian who loved to laugh and joke and to sing opera.

"Let's all join hands and pray," Rev. Connors said somberly, and they prayed the "Our Father."

And then Johnny Bob told about his friendship with Johnny Cartellini and had everyone, if not laughing, at least smiling. It picked up the mood considerably again.

Lt. Mike McVey, head of homicide, sat with his estranged wife, Conci, who was holding the hand of Cartellini's ex-wife, Millie, who divorced Johnny several years ago when their child was only four. After the divorce, they had enjoyed joint custody of their only child, who just stared ahead, sitting next to her mother.

Mike just watched everyone suspiciously and wondered why he had this strong feeling that Johnny was murdered. He couldn't put his finger on it at all. The circumstances of his death seemed to be okay and aboveboard.

The strange thing was that it came close on the heels of Johnny's meeting with Mike the day before his death. He'd come into Mike's office, and they had a drink together. Mike knew he had something on his mind. These visits with Cartellini were rare, although they were poker buddies but in different divisions: Mike in homicide and Johnny in bunco.

"Some odd things have been happening lately, Mike, perhaps concerning that model you've been drooling over, Madeline something?" he asked looking straight at Mike.

"Yeah, so what?" Mike was getting hot under the collar already.

"I don't care what you do with your private life, Mike. I just need to tell you that I saw something that puzzled me, and I wanted to share it with you."

"Go on," Mike growled.

"We have uncovered some kind of counterfeiting ring, and it pointed to some models smuggling in plates for counterfeiting. You know it's hard to get things through the security, but they apparently put parts of them in their equipment. And then some of the models have received awards, and the parts of the plates were in the plaques and statuettes they received. It was a great smuggling operation. We caught about three models, but one got away. We don't know her identity, but we have a good description of her: tall, very slim with long shapely legs and thick dark auburn hair and gray eyes and an upturned nose. She also has a tattoo on her upper left leg, but we couldn't see the picture clearly."

Mike's heart almost skipped a beat. "And?"

"We think it's the supermodel Madeline O'Reilly." He stopped and looked at Mike, then looked down.

"Have you ever gotten close enough to see if

she has a tattoo on her upper left leg?" Johnny asked him boldly.

"I haven't been intimate with her, Cartellini, and that's the truth," he lied. There was a long pause.

"Why do you think it's Madeline?"

"Well, she's been hanging around the Bastriani family for a long time now. There are rumors that she is actually married to Philly Bastriani and he helped her career and now she's famous partly due to him. This operation that we've almost uncovered has to have some big money and muscle behind it. We believe it's being done right here in the city, Mike, and the plates and special paper were brought in by these models. They were so popular with the customs and security officials that they were barely screened at all anymore.

"I heard that you investigated that shooting that took place at the models' show recently. Do you think it has anything to do with this smuggling and counterfeiting operation?" Cartellini looked at Mike with a question on his face.

Mike shrugged. "I have no idea, but that does put another spin on the motive at any rate. I'll sure look into it closer, and see if there's anything suspicious of that nature involved. But, I'm curious, Johnny, who told you that I was dating the model Madeline O'Reilly?"

Cartellini laughed, showing some very straight white teeth, thanks to his cousin Bruno, a dentist. "Cici DeMarco told me. Yes, the commissioner seemed to be quite upset about it, Mike." With that parting shot, Cartellini left the office.

Mike thought about that now as he perused the crowd carefully, nodding here and there to some of the cops that he knew. Cartellini died that night or about four or five o'clock the next morning. Mike thought long and hard about this. *Was it cause and effect?* Now he just watched everyone as they ate their food and circulated. *You'd think this was some kind of party, a celebration instead of the end of a man's life,* Mike thought soberly.

He looked over at his wife who was talking animatedly with someone and seeming to enjoy this. He tugged on her hand. She turned surprised. "What's wrong, Mike?"

He gestured with his head. "This whole thing is upside down. A man is dead, and everyone's eating and singing and some are even dancing, for heaven's sakes, Conci. It's quite disgusting," he stated, talking almost too loud.

"Why? The man is gone, Mike. He had a lot of friends and relatives and a daughter who loved him and many girlfriends, I see, and they're celebrating his life, not his death. I think it's beautiful, and at any rate it's certainly ethnic and quite Italian. I noticed they have some homemade biscotti and the great cannoli that you like," she said in a helpful way. He just looked at her with a sneer and moved away, got up and walked around a bit, eyeing the commissioner, Cici DeMarco, as she made her rounds of the cops that were there and spoke to each and every cop and spouse.

She looked up suddenly and realized that Mike McVey was watching her closely, and she smiled at him, a long sultry smile. Conci McVey saw the gesture too and wondered about it. But Mike turned away disgusted, so she removed the thought from her mind.

Sgt. April Conover spotted Mike and went over to him and offered him a bite of her cannoli. "This is great food, Mike. Have some," she invited. He just stared at her.

"I heard you made sergeant, April. Congratulations."

"Thank you. Did you hear that the commissioner is going to run for the U.S. Senate. Isn't that a gas? Her, running on family values? That should be a revelation, Mike. Really, what a thing," she said and laughed almost too much.

"Why is that so surprising to you?" he countered.

"Well, what with your affair with her and the

abortion, really, Mike. That is too, too much." Mike reared back and stared at her and then frowned.

"Where did you get that bit of misinformation, April?" His voice was hard like granite now.

"You told me, Mike, when we were going together, one night when you were drunk out of your skull. You're really quite a gossip when you're drunk, sweetie. But it got me a good promotion anyway." With that she walked away from him rather arrogantly. Mike just stared after her wondering if he'd really told that to her. *It's true,* he thought, *I did have a short affair with her, and she wasn't even a redhead. But I was so upset at Rhonda running around on me. I was a really mixed-up guy then.* His wife Conci always said that he was a big mouth when he was drunk and even bragged about his exploits with other women.

Monty, Captain Montgomery, Mike's boss, was watching Mike more than usual, knowing he and Conci were separated because he was running around with the model Madeline O'Reilly, whom Monty didn't trust at all. *What a fool he is, astute in the cop world, but quite gullible when it involves a long-legged redhead,* he thought in disgust.

Millie Cartellini, Johnny's ex-wife caught up with Mike. "I need to talk to you later, Mike. Can you come over to the house after this is over? Candace told me something last night that puzzled me, and I want her to share it with you. It sounds so suspicious to me."

Mike looked at her puzzled and surprised. "Yes, I'll take Conci home and come back later. Thanks."

Mike wondered about that. It would appear that Sgt. Cartellini's teenage daughter was spending the night with her father but never said anything about a stranger or a visitor in the wee hours of the night.

Mike was a guy who never left anything to chance. Even the smallest possible clue got his full attention, and this one did also.

After the wake was over around ten o'clock and everyone had left, Mike took Conci home. For some strange reason he insisted that she go with him and not by herself to the wake.

"I'd rather go alone, Mike," she protested, still upset with him. But, just before it was time for her leave her house, he turned up, and she was too disturbed to refuse him. Now, he was looking quite frazzled and upset.

"Are you all right, Michael?" she asked him, noticing his frown.

He looked over at her and her pregnant body that annoyed and irritated him. *This baby is one too many as far as I'm concerned, but Conci is in some kind of lala land loving having babies. And here she is forty-eight, for corn's sakes, and I'm fifty-four,* he thought and frowned even more.

"Yeah, my life is a bowl of cherries," he spat out at her. Conci just sighed and made a promise to herself to refuse to be with him alone ever again. They hadn't been separated very long and she had initiated separate maintenance proceedings, but Mike seemed to be upset by all of it, not just the money part.

After he dropped off Conci, he went over to Cartellini's house and talked to the teenager. She was quiet and wouldn't talk much at all. He encouraged her and noticed that when he mentioned a woman visitor she just looked at the floor and put her hands in her lap and twisted her Kleenex over and over again until it was just a ball of fluff.

"Please, Candace, this could probably help your dad if you can tell us anything. Did you hear voices?" her mother probed her.

Mike continued to gently question her and was gratified that the mother was with him and was quite agreeable to the interrogation as long as it was gentle.

The girl nodded her head. "It was a white lady, Mom," she said as she turned to her mother.

The former Mrs. Cartellini, Johnny's ex-wife, was a beautiful African American woman; however, the sergeant himself was Caucasian. Candace was a beautiful mixture and held the promise of being a real beauty when she grew up.

"Do you know who it was, honey?" her mother asked her holding onto her hand.

She shook her head.

"But she had a nice voice, and Daddy seemed upset to see her. That's all I know." She began to cry. "I was scared. I was really scared!" she said and really began to bawl like a small child, not like the almost woman she was turning into.

Mike looked at the mother, perplexed.

"Why were you afraid, sweetie?" he asked in his most gentle voice, putting his arms around her.

"She was so angry at Daddy about something, and he said, 'No, no, I didn't do that.' Then there was silence, and I guessed that he was being sweet to her. Then I was embarrassed because he said, 'Well, let's go to bed and settle this,' and both of them laughed." She looked down at the floor and couldn't look at either Mike or her mother.

"Okay, sweetie, that's very good," her mother told her.

Lt. McVey nodded his head. "You've helped me more than you know, Candace. Thank you. If you remember anything else, please tell your mom." She nodded her head.

Mike left more perplexed than before. As he approached the door, Millie Cartellini, agreed. "I'll call you, Mike, if she says anything else. Thanks for being so kind to her."

"Thank you, Millie for being so helpful."

As he got into his car, Millie ran outside and flagged him down. "Just one other little thing, Mike. I don't know if it means anything or not. When I took Johnny's mother's jewelry for Carla, I found an ankle bracelet on the floor, way under the bed that I doubt was his mother's, but I took it anyway and wondered who it belonged to. Then I decided to put it back into the top drawer. It had some initials on it. I didn't even look at them, just threw it back into the drawer."

"Thanks, Millie."

Mike hurriedly drove over to Cartellini's apartment and looked through the top drawer. Sure enough there was a beautiful eighteen-carat gold ankle bracelet with initials. They were very tiny initials, and being carefully not to put his fingerprints on the bracelet, he used a tissue from beside the bed and put the bracelet into a little plastic bag that he never left the house without.

Then he looked around to see where Johnny had the heart attack. *I have no grounds for suspicion at all, except that Johnny was only forty-three and in good health, as far as anyone could see. Yet I feel something that my instinct tells me is wrong with this scene.*

When Mike returned to the office, he put the ankle bracelet under a magnifying glass and saw the inscription clearly. *To my darling Cici, Love Johnny,* and the date was 12–26, dated ten years before. Mike just held it and whistled. He held a hot potato in his hand and didn't like it at all.

Conci was still up when he rang the doorbell. It was after one o'clock in the morning, and she was reading her Bible. Cautiously she looked out of the window. The locks had been changed as soon as Mike left to go with Madeline or wherever he went. Monty told her he was at the police station sleeping there most of the nights. That confused her even more.

"What do you want, Mike?" she asked with the chain across the door.

"Hey, Conci. You all right?" he asked trying to get on the good side of her.

"Yeah, McVey. Why are you here?" she asked as she unlatched the chain.

He breathed a sigh of relief.

"Are you drunk, Mike? Is that why you're here so late? I have a writ keeping you out of the house, so please don't make trouble or upset me," she said in a threatening voice. Halfheartedly, she let him in.

He got some of the coffee she'd hurriedly made for him and sat down with her in his own recliner.

"I'm beat too, babe. What did you think of that wake, for heaven's sakes? Don't do me that way, please. Just cremate me and bury my ashes next to Rhonda. That's all." Then he realized what he said. "Or next to my parents, yeah, maybe that's better," he suggested and drank his coffee silently for a while.

"I was thinking that it would be more apropos to have all the women you slept with as your pall bearers, Mike," Conci said, rather tongue in cheek.

Mike turned to look at her quickly and saw that she was teasing him.

"There wouldn't be enough to hold up the casket, babe. You seem to think that I've had a lot of women. That simply isn't true," he insisted. After three cups of coffee, he fell asleep on the recliner. Conci looked at him with disgust.

"Did his precious bimbo throw him out?" she wondered out loud and went to bed and locked her door, not wanting to be with him at all. Conci really had it this time. *Nothing hurt me as much as him bringing Madeline to the banquet after he'd romanced me even up to the night before. Just like Satan, a big deceiver,* she said to herself, suddenly realizing that Mike was not only an inconsiderate, mean guy, but evil too. At least that's how she thought of him at that exact moment.

chapter XVI
sgt. april conover

April had to smile at herself after talking with Mike McVey at the wake. She was on the top of her game today, thirty-six years old, single, and now a sergeant, a promotion she was sure she deserved long ago.

She thought back to two months ago when she heard via the grapevine that the Commissioner Cici DeMarco intended to run for the U.S. Senate. It was really laughable that she would be running on a platform of family values when April knew some things about her that Mike McVey, whom she dated awhile, had revealed to her in his drunken state.

April could still smell the liquor on McVey's breath as he weaved back and forth, yelling at her and blaming her for his own inadequacies in the intimacy arena. "You're just a lowly detective, and I'm the guy in charge, you bimbo," he shouted, looking at her bleary-eyed.

"Shut up, McVey, and go home, you broken down bum," she retorted angrily.

"Yeah, bimbo, I've had better than you. Even the commissioner, Cici DeMarco loved me and wanted to have my baby, but I said no, cause I'm the boss. She got an abortion because I said so. She loved me so much. I've had better than you, see?" he shouted and then finally, walked to the door but didn't get far, as he passed out right in front of the door.

Now, however, it seemed like a real benefit to her to know this information. *This is a good time to get some much-needed and earned promotions,* she said to herself, and smiled. *Yes, this was a great opportunity.*

The next day, April approached the commissioner, who was surprised and a little leery of inviting Officer Conover into her private chamber. *What on earth did she want?* The message that she got said that April wanted to join her campaign and had some interesting things to tell her about her opponent.

Once warmly ensconced in the office, April hinted to the commissioner about her knowledge, telling her she thought it was about time for her to have a really big promotion.

The commissioner looked at her and wondered what she was hinting at. "Oh? What is it that makes you feel this way, April?" she asked with her syrupy sweet voice.

April just smiled at her. "I'm a person that is trustworthy and knows how to hold onto a secret, and I'm very discreet. Oh, by the way, did you know that I used to date Mike McVey off and on for about a year? He was married to his second wife at the time, but unhappy because she was having twin babies. He's a real mess but seems to have turned over a new leaf. However, he's a guy that keeps his counsel, unless that is of course, he's really drunk. Then, he becomes the biggest-mouthed gossip, especially about his private life. But me, I'm the perfect picture of discretion. I feel that my discretion should be rewarded at any rate.

"I think this puts me in the front as one of your big campaign managers or perhaps as one of your assistants even today. Or, I'm still a detective and would like to be at least a sergeant. What do you think, Cici?" she asked using her first name in a stance of familiarity that was unwarranted.

Cici just stared at her. "I really don't know what you're talking about, April. I wish you'd be more open and aboveboard and bold about what you're trying to tell me," she said in an irritated voice.

April just shrugged. "I just thought I'd come in

and give you a vote of confidence, commissioner. Good luck in your race for the Senate."

She went to the door as the commissioner just stared at her. Then, April turned around with her hand on the door handle.

"Oh, by the way, I too had an abortion, but no one cares in my case," she said and quickly left the office.

Cici stood up, but through the window, April saw her face filled with rage.

Now, bringing her thoughts back to the wake, April saw the commissioner looking at her with a piercing glance, and she smiled at her, like the cat that swallowed the canary. *She can't do a thing to me, and she knows it,* April gloated and went looking for another cannoli. She just loved those Italian pastries.

Cici came up to her. "Nice to see you, April. I noticed that you really like these pastries. Which ones do you favor?"

"Oh Cici, I just love the cannoli, and it's difficult to get them here." She smiled at Cici, who took the one cannoli she had left on her little paper plate and gave it to her. "Here, I haven't touched it. I already had one too." And they laughed together.

Cici's husband was right at her side in a minute

and offered to find a fresh one for April. "Please don't bother. This is really fine," she insisted.

April's eyes viewed the whole crowd, and then she stopped, stunned. Someone looked very familiar to her. April was busily getting her master's in police investigation and was doing her master's thesis on some cold case files that she uncovered just a few weeks ago. One in particular caught her eye, and she did a lot of investigation and discovered what to her looked like an accidental killing and then a purposeful murder to keep a witness quiet. It had never been investigated at any length before, and the cop involved was exonerated. April wondered about that. Now, she was looking right into the face of that person.

"Hello," the person approached April, and they introduced themselves. "I don't believe I've ever met you. Were you a close friend of Johnny's?" the person asked with a sympathetic voice.

"This food is fabulous, though, isn't it? I especially love the cannoli's, and I see that you love them, too." April tried to be civil, and suddenly, it occurred to her that she'd found the golden goose.

That night, for some reason, April was very tired, and she fell right into bed. *However, sleep eluded her as she thought about the interesting conversations of the night.*

Oh, she thought, *I need to take my medicine or I won't be able to sleep for more than four hours at a stretch.* She hurriedly got her purse from atop the dresser and remembered how she'd lost it for a while or mislaid it or someone took it by mistake at the wake but later she found it under one of the tables. After opening the bottle and finding only two of the six capsules inside, she looked at it puzzled. Had she dropped the bottle or was there indeed only two in there? She just shrugged and obediently took the two capsules that the doctor made up for her containing a strong sleeping potion and went back to bed.

She slept so soundly.

Her partner, Maria Santos Philippe, was annoyed because April didn't call in to say she'd be late or absent. Finally, after her not answering her phone, Maria went over to her house and rang the bell and still no answer, so she found the extra key in the doghouse in the backyard and opened the door herself.

"April, you still in bed?" she yelled and then saw the absence of movement and felt her pulse. April was dead!

Monty was surprised and shocked that April was gone. *She was so alive and well last night,* he thought. "Was it foul play?" he asked the coroner.

"Well, we'll see. She seems very peaceful in her death as though she just went to sleep and never woke up, but we'll see," he said in his usual sardonic voice. Then they hung up.

Monty called Mike immediately "Mike, come in here," he ordered.

Mike raised his eyebrows and obediently entered Monty's office.

"Close the door. April Conover is dead. Died in her sleep last night apparently. No sign of any foul play, but it's mighty strange. Two of our cops dying so young. Yes, it's very strange, indeed. But the coroner will give us his results as soon as possible."

Mike looked at him, shocked. "I had a great conversation with her last night as she was stuffing her face with a cannoli, Monty."

They tossed it around for a while, and then they parted. Mike thought about it a lot, though, especially since she said something about getting her promotion by holding something over on Cici's head. That just didn't sound very good at all.

Mike went over to April's apartment and

looked around but saw no signs of any break-ins or any sickness on her part. He looked at the pills she had taken and saw that she was on an anti-depressant and an empty bottle of some kind of sleeping aid but that was about all. However, he still procedurally took samples of all of them, as well as the vitamins, and bagged them for the lab. He looked around some more and went through her drawers and found a couple of folders in her desk marked personal and private.

Mike sat down and read through the first one, which contained the information about Cici DeMarco and their talk in Cici's office and April's promotion to sergeant.

The rest of the folder contained a diary of sorts relating her everyday life as a Sergeant. The second folder was her folder on school things. She was studying for her master's on criminal investigation and this folder was full of notes and newspaper articles. Mike took the two folders with him and left her apartment.

That same morning Mike called Cici right away and made plans to meet her at a restaurant they used to go to way outside the city, about fifty miles. They would meet in two hours. Mike said a silent prayer about the whole meeting, knowing Cici could make his life miserable.

When she arrived he stood and helped her

into the booth across from him. They looked at the menu and then ordered. "Okay, McVey, what's up?" she asked in a professional way.

"Cici, I need to talk to you about the death of Johnny Cartellini." He approached her carefully, couching his words in niceties.

"So? Yes, he died of heart attack." She eyed him in an unfriendly manner.

"There was a bracelet that was found among his possessions, an ankle bracelet, quite pricey too. It is eighteen-carat gold and has some writing on it."

"Oh?" she looked at him directly into his eyes trying to intimidate him.

But no one, man or woman, intimidated Mike McVey, a hard-nosed cop for over thirty years and on top of his game.

"The inscription is: *To my darling Cici, Love Johnny,* and it's dated 12–26." And he gave the date as ten years before.

Cici closed her eyes. "I knew him a long time ago, before you, Mike, and he fell in love with me. You know how easily that can happen," she explained arrogantly, and Mike marveled at her opinion of herself. "We had an argument a long time ago, and I gave him back the bracelet. That's all. He must have kept it for old time's sakes. That's it, Mike. Don't make something out of nothing," she warned him.

Deep down he knew she was lying. "When was the last time you saw the bracelet, Cici?" his eyes burning into hers, and she lowered hers. *My gosh, he's good,* she thought professionally. *His eyes are almost hypnotic.*

"Look Cici, I think someone is trying to frame you, and I'd like to help you. This bracelet was actually on the floor under the bed with the latch opened as though someone lost it."

"Frame me for what? Causing him to have a heart attack? I'm good, McVey, but not that good," she said tongue in cheek.

"I have a hunch that his death wasn't accidental. And there was a woman seen visiting him in the middle of the night, and he died a few hours later."

"So? Johnny was a real stud, if you know what I mean, Mike. I think you're barking up the wrong tree. Don't ever come over here and accuse me of anything unless you have the proof in your hands," she warned him. "How much does your captain know?" she asked, eyeing him again.

Mike stared at her. "I've not done my report yet." He danced around the question, metaphorically speaking.

Cici got up and pulled Mike up from the booth and searched him, much to his amusement.

"Okay, you're clean. Just had to be sure, Mike,

that this conversation wasn't recorded." She sat down and so did he. "Okay, so I had the bracelet in my jewelry box, I guess. I never looked at it in a long while. In fact, I may even have put it into a garage sale we had last year for the department."

"Oh by the way, Cici, April Conover died sometime last night; the coroner is doing an autopsy at the Captain's request. Isn't that strange, first Cartellini, then April?" He just shook his head as she looked at him quite shocked.

She was really frowning now, and Mike wanted to get out of there without any problems. So, without another word he got up, paid the bill, and left.

Cici wondered about McVey. Did he really not make his report as yet? That would be so unlike a devoted cop like McVey. She sat back into her booth seat and thought for a while, and a plan began to formulate in her mind.

When she arrived home, her husband was very confrontational with her. "I'm tired of all these deaths happening, Cici. They seem to be to your benefit too. Surely you're not making them happen in your insane quest for more fame, are you? You're talking to your constituents about one of the deadly sins being ignoring your brethren, and you've committed all seven of the other deadly sins to get where you are now, woman.

You miserable hypocrite," he shouted at her as he packed his clothes, preparing to leave for the fourth time in their twenty-year marriage.

However, the general wasn't finished. "Pride? You've got enough of that for ten people. Gluttony? Nothing is ever enough for you you have to have and have and have. Sloth? You're so energetic and such a go getter in every arena except our marriage. Then you're so slothful it's pathetic, too lazy to even try to meet me halfway or be nice to me. Envy? You envy everyone that's got more than you or is more popular or has more power than you. Lust? I see you looking over the new young male recruits and even some of the old ones, like Mastropetro and McVey. I know what goes on in your office, Cici. For a smart cop you're not too smart are you? I have pictures and films of you and McVey, and that is recently. Anger? I've seen you so angry that you almost beat our dog to death. Yes, you are easily enraged and very mean. Covetousness? Yes, you covet your neighbor's husband, more than one of them. And you covet the U.S. Senator's seat, and you covet her goods. You're a greedy person, Cici. Yes, you are so greedy and want everything that everyone else has. Nothing is ever enough for you."

He stopped, looking at her with hatred in his eyes. "Don't think you're going to get much money from me, either. The money you earned is yours, but nothing else. We had a prenuptial agreement, and I'm sticking to it," he said as he slammed the door behind him and drove off.

Cici had seen him enraged before and knew he had a thing for her and would be back.

A few days afterward, Mike was following some evidence that someone had phoned in, a clue that a neighbor saw a woman dressed in black with black hair that might have been a wig going into Johnny's house the night before his death. She had no car apparently but was on foot. The neighbor could not even identify her but felt he would report it at some time, but he had a heart attack the next day himself and was getting out of the hospital when someone told him about the sergeant's death of a heart attack.

"It was a strange situation because I saw him open the door and try to close it on the woman, but she apparently pushed her way in. I was more amused than anything, since the sergeant was my neighbor. I was coming home from a night shift after stopping for a couple of drinks. I could never identify the woman or even be sure it was a woman, but it did appear to be so," he said and gave his name and phone number.

Mike went to see the captain as soon as he got back into the office. Mike gave him all the information he'd gathered.

"I saw you talking to her at the wake, Mike. How did she seem to you?" he wondered.

"She seemed to be happy about her new promotion; that much was for sure. She was eating a cannoli and enjoying it immensely," Mike said and then wondered about that too.

"Any news from the coroner, yet?" Mike wondered aloud. Monty nodded. "Do you think it was not by natural causes?"

"I dunno, Monty. I have an awfully suspicious mind from all this police work. You know that."

Monty nodded his head. "I'll let you know if there's anything, Mike."

A little while later, Melville, Lawrence, and Max were sitting in Mike's office going over all the evidence they'd gathered so far, when Monty came in and joined them.

"Mike, the coroner says that Conover died of some kind of glycosins, like digitalis but he believes it is poison, not a medicine. There was a heavy dose of sleeping medicine in her stomach, too. "

"Where was the poison administered? Was it in some food or what?" Mike asked almost angrily.

"Melville, check the place where the pastries

were made and try to find out who else ate the pastries. Max, get the list of all those who attended the wake last night, and Lawrence, you go and help him. I'll look into April's past to see if there's anyone that might want her dead."

"I'll get the crime scene people to the funeral parlor where the wake was held and they can search for any foodstuffs that might have contained the poison."

They all went and did their jobs.

Then that puts Cici right in the middle of possible suspicion of murder. Mike raised his eyebrows and sat back in his chair and thought a lot about it all. *Oh no; not Cici again!* He thought, but decided to dismiss it from his mind at the moment.

The results of the tests on the bottles of medicine in April's room proved to be no help. All the medicine was fine. However, the bottle of sleeping pills was empty so there was no way to test those pills. The consensus of opinion was that the poison was administered in the food.

chapter XVII
the interviews

The interview with the hundred or so people at the wake proved fruitless. Almost fifty percent of the people ate the pastries, and no one saw anything strange. And twenty-five people ate the cannoli too and none got sick.

Max tried to see in his mind where everyone was placed during the time that April Conover was present at the wake, which was all but the first half hour of the six thirty to ten o'clock wake.

After a couple of days of interviews, he and Lawrence put their head together, and they came up empty-handed. No one saw anything suspicious or anyone hanging around the pastry or any of the tables for a long period of time. Many people ate the pastries, including the cannoli.

Mike also came up empty-handed concerning April's private life. She was a good cop, married once long ago, and divorced after only six months no children. She was the fifth daughter of professional parents, both her parents being doctors, and had a normal, upper-middle class upbringing.

Her best friend was Trish Donaldson, another cop. Mike spoke with her, and she said that April was quite excited about her promotion.

"Did she tell you how that came about?" he asked her gently. She looked at him askew.

"What do you mean? She was a good cop. You must know that, Lieutenant. She did have a thing with you a few years ago," Trisha said to put him in his place.

Mike got very official at this juncture. "Miss, your friend is dead, murdered. Anything that you can tell us would be helpful."

"She was close to getting her master's too and was really excited about it and had already decided on her thesis and sent it into her advisor, I think. Anyway, she was really excited, Lieutenant. Yes, it's such a pity," she wailed.

She just sighed and then broke down and began to cry. "She found out something about someone in power, she told me. And there was a promotion in order."

"Did she say who it was?"

Trish shook her head.

"Okay, thank you, Miss, and I'm sorry about your friend."

They all met in Mike's office that afternoon,

along with Monty. After a surprise visitor, the chief of police, they realized that they all wouldn't fit into Mike's office, so they took the conference room.

Mike took over the meeting as planned. "Okay, here's what I've found." After going over the details of the case as he knew them, he continued, "Now Max and Lawrence?"

Max spoke for both of them. "Nothing here. No one saw anything strange, and at least twenty-five people ate the cannoli without getting sick."

Monty sighed. "Melville?"

Alex looked at the group of men in wonder. *Really, why was the chief present of all people? Did he have stake in this thing?* "The pastries were made by Giovanni's Italian Kitchen, who made the biscotti and the pignoli and the fig cookies, and the rest of the pastries were made by Cartellini's family. His sister Rosa made most of them along with his nieces. His sister Anna made the cannoli without any help. I spoke with all of them, and his sister said that she made one hundred cannoli and stuffed them just before the wake, because otherwise the shells would get soggy." He looked up at the masculine faces who were looking at him quite perplexed.

"Anyway, that's what she said. She stuffed half of them herself and put them out and left the other half unstuffed until they needed them, which was about six o'clock. I asked her if there was anyone else in the kitchen, as that's where she stayed most of the time, directing the food preparation and service.

"'Yes, a few women came in from time to time to see the operation, and my sister came in too,' she reported.

"'Who were the women who came in? Did you know them?' I asked her." Looking down at his notes, he read her response word for word.

"'One of them was a beautiful redhead, tall like a model. I think she's well known, Madeline something or other, I think, but that was before the others arrived. She further told me that she had a thing with my brother and wanted to have a few minutes privately without the crowd making a big deal of it. She was very sweet and was quite interested in the cannoli filling and asked if she could help me.'"

Mike breathed in quite sharply. *Was Madeline here, for heaven's sakes?* All eyes turned to Mike, who lowered his and shrugged his shoulders.

"How about the other women?" Mike asked Melville, trying to get their minds off Madeline.

"One of them she thought was the woman running for Senator. She saw her on television one day. She was a cop too. I assumed that was

Cici DeMarco," Melville added. "Anyway, that was it."

"I have something to add, gentlemen, and you're probably wondering why I'm here. I asked Monty to have me come." All eyes turned toward the chief.

"I received an unusual request from the commissioner last month to promote someone whom I wasn't sure was worthy or up for promotion. You know how I hate nepotism. So, I brought it to Monty, who had also received the request that same day. We put our heads together and tried to figure out why the commissioner would ask us to promote detective April Conover to sergeant, actually going two steps up in promotions. She cited some things that April had done for her and showed great aptitude and loyalty, etc., the usual line of bull," he said.

"But, Monty wisely suggested that we do it and not make waves about it all but watch it closely. Now a month later, this same cop is murdered. Any other thoughts on this?"

"Well, now in view of what her best friend said, it sounds like she was holding something over someone's head."

No one in that room looked at McVey, and in fact, if truth were known, none of them wanted to touch that hot potato and mention the name of the commissioner.

"Let's keep our eyes open, men, and someone must interrogate the commissioner again, in view of her being in the kitchen during the wake when the pastries were out on the table."

"You're in charge of homicide, Mike," Max said tongue in cheek. "It's your job." He burst out laughing.

"Thanks, Max, thanks," he answered, rather amused himself. All the men began to laugh.

After the chief left the office, Mike instructed Melville to interrogate Madeline about why she was at the wake and in the kitchen. Melville just looked at him and understood. So, after a few days, Melville was able to track her down and talk with her. She was most uncooperative.

"Listen, Miss O'Reilly, either you answer my question here in your home or at the police station. I don't care which. No one is accusing you of anything. But this is a murder case and you need to cooperate, or I'll take you in and charge you with undermining a murder investigation," he said angrily and adamantly.

"I had a little thing with Cartellini some time ago, and I just wanted to say my goodbyes alone.

That's all. Nothing mysterious about it at all, Lieutenant." Her voice was nasty. "Why didn't Lt. McVey come and talk to me himself?"

chapter XVIII
the self-centered
hedonists

Mike sat down in the upscale Chinese restaurant, which was the only kind that Madeline would dine in. Both of them were very quiet and didn't even seem to want to be together. He'd asked her out one night to talk about their problems. She just looked up at him, having arrived by herself twenty minutes before.

"No one makes me wait, McVey. I hope you haven't forgotten that." She was still steamed at him for having Melville question her instead of himself.

Mike looked at her and wondered about himself. She was extremely beautiful with her big blue-gray eyes and rosy complexion and thick juicy lips and beautiful red hair, a medium auburn, just like Rhonda's had been. Her body was willowy, *almost too thin,* Mike thought, but she had long legs that were shapely. And he loved to hold her and felt he was back with Rhonda when he was in Madeline's arms.

Madeline looked at him with an amused air as he gave her body the "once-over" glance.

"Do I pass muster, Mike?" she asked in a sultry voice.

Mike smiled at her. "Yes, you're almost a perfect creature, Maddy. At least in your body," he said, remembering how mean she could be.

"Oh? Do I not please you in other ways, Mike?" she asked, thinking,

Maybe we could hammer out our differences.

"Well, you're a nasty piece of goods sometimes, baby. You can be a real witch." He sighed.

She laughed out loud at that remark. "Oh? I suppose you're some kind of a choirboy, Michael? You have nasty temper and are way too possessive and even not much of a lover most times. So, don't go throwing rotten tomatoes at me, lover," she said, and her mood was getting dark again. He could feel it.

Mike longed for the loving sweet relationship he had with Conci and wished it were with Madeline instead. He caught himself though. Conci represented responsibility, and Madeline represented freedom and being a young guy again. He knew that well.

"*This is your last chance, Michael McVey, Jr.*" He heard a loud man's voice say. He looked behind him and stood up. There was no one there. He looked down at Maddy, who was staring at him with concern.

"What's wrong with you, McVey?" she asked almost angrily,

"Didn't you hear that guy talking to me?"

"What guy?" she asked, staring at him. *Is he going nuts?* she wondered.

"A man's voice said something to me," he explained, sitting down. "Didn't you hear it?" he asked her, quite annoyed about the whole thing.

"No, you're imagining things again. For heaven's sakes, it's not only your wife that's spooky, McVey, it's you too. Stop it or I'm out of here."

He just sighed, and soon their dinner came and some more drinks. Both of them hardly talked. The mood was spoiled by the voice he thought he'd heard. Then when the fortune cookies came, Madeline insisted that he read his.

"Come on, Mike, have some fun for once."

He opened the cookies and on the little paper was written, "This is your last chance. Repent!" Mike just crumbled it up and told Madeline he was going.

"But what about the bill?"

He cornered the waiter and gave him the money and left. Madeline was quite insulted. Then he returned and apologized for his haste, and they got into his car when his cell phone rang.

It was Melville. "Mike, the doctor that prescribed the sleeping pills for April said they were in capsule form and there should have been six left if she took them as prescribed, which was 'take two at night with water.'"

"That's rather strange," he complained. "I'm on my way right now. Meet you at the station."

Madeline watched him as he drove, wondering what was the great attraction toward him. She did like him herself and was attracted to his machoness, but the big motivator was the encouragement, or was it a command, from Philly Bastriani. For some reason, Philly wanted Mike to be kept concentrating on her rather than his police work. *I wonder why?* she mused but knew it was fruitless to speculate on what Philly wanted. She owed him a lot. That much was for sure, and she did have a passion for him at any rate. Philly was so powerful, like a huge stealthy tiger, a beast that could not be tamed, and she had him purring and eating out of her hand. That made her feel so powerful too. But she knew that she could never turn her back on him, or he would pounce on her. That's why she turned state's evidence against him unbeknownst to him. *He'll be out of my hair for a long while,* she thought, smiling.

Madeline thought back to her childhood with a slight smile. The only child of older parents, who were carnival people. "Carnies" they called them, and early on she learned the family trade. It was dangerous, but her parents showed her the tricks to help keep her safe. But later in life, she denounced all that, realizing how beautiful she was. When she met Philly Bastriani, her whole life changed. She was having trouble getting ahead in modeling, and Philly, who was smitten with her, immediately helped her get ahead. Maddy saw that this was a powerful man who could be a real help to her, and they became friends and then lovers.

Philly was married to a very wealthy woman with a great reputation for business and honesty, and he didn't want to get a divorce. Philly was part of a mob family, and although most people thought he was clean, Madeline knew better. He took care of her and advanced her career to the highest levels. Later, he divorced his wife, and married Madeline.

She was a little afraid of him, that much was for sure, but she had a plan. He said she should never cross him, but she had a few aces up her own sleeve.

Mike and Madeline rode in silence the entire trip to Madeline's place. Refusing to be the one to break it, Madeline just shrugged, got out of Mike's car, and went into her opulent condo and took a nap.

After the guys met in Mike's office at the station, they discussed the implications of the missing sleeping pills.

"We need to go into her computer, too, Al, her friend mentioned that April was working on her master's degree and had sent her thesis to her professor. Maybe there's something in that, too."

Mike suggested. Melville nodded. He was the computer guy among all of them and had been a computer nerd before becoming a cop.

A few hours later, Melville excitedly called Mike.

"We found something here, Mike! Maybe the answer to two of the murders, anyway,"

chapter XIX
the bible class

"We've been studying these deadly sins for about three weeks now, students, and soon we'll be on our Christmas vacation. Timmy, how did the interview with your uncle go? Did he give you any insights into the problem of labeling murder a deadly sin?" she asked in her perky, joyful voice. Mrs. Dooley was a married woman of about sixty-two, but young looking and quite slim and so joyful that everyone wanted her classes. She did in-depth research on different aspects of the Bible and always ended up with faith, which was her strong suit, she admitted.

"Yeah, I interviewed him at his office, and he agreed that pride and greed were often at the root of some of these murders. But he felt that murder was itself a deadly sin and should have been counted as one. To think about killing someone is not a crime, he said. But to do it and actually murder someone is a crime, so he thought it would work like that with a sin too."

"That's very interesting, Timmy. Your uncle must be a clean vessel in order to be around all that crime and not have those sins touch him too," she said admiringly. Timmy looked at her and then at the floor, knowing his uncle wasn't that clean at all.

"How about the Ten Commandments?" Charlie Looper asked. "They spell out some sins that aren't necessarily in the seven-deadly-sin category."

"Like what, Charlie?" Mrs. Dooley was so pleased with this discussion. *The students will never look at sin so lightly anymore,* she thought happily.

"Well, it's very clear in the fifth commandment thou shalt not kill, or murder, as the more modern versions have it," he stated authoritatively.

"Yeah, how about thou shalt not steal? That's another one that's much clearer in the Ten Commandments," Dora Carpenter added.

"I am the Lord thy God. Thou shalt not have strange gods before me. That's another one. It's darn confusing sometimes, to sort them out and wonder why the Pope Gregory and the earlier Christians narrowed it down to only seven deadly sins. There ought to be at least twelve," Jonathan Bowers decided.

As they were calling out these sins, Mrs. Dooley was copying them on the chalkboard.

"So, what we have here is a problem of what constitutes a deadly sin? Anyone?"

They all looked at her. "Raise hands please for this one," she urged them. Three hands went up.

"Timmy?" she deferred to him almost automatically since he'd done such good research on the whole thing.

"I'd like to talk to Sister Mary Concetta Rose, my Aunt Conci's aunt, a missionary nun who raised her on the mission field from the time she was five years old. I'd really like her input on these things," he concluded.

Mrs. Dooley nodded her head. "We'd be glad to hear others' opinions outside the walls of this classroom, students, so feel free to ask your parents or others that you esteem."

But Timmy wasn't finished. "I still have something to say about it myself, though, Mrs. Dooley, if I may?" he asked in his most polite voice. Mrs. Dooley gave him a lot of favor because of this courtesy that he showed to her and everyone. *A real gentleman, a well-brought-up boy*, she said to herself.

"Yes, Timmy, go on please." She encouraged him with a smile.

"I was thinking that the Seven Deadly Sins

seem to be more sins of the heart than actions. For instance envy seems to be more in thinking about something someone else has and wanting it. I guess that if you do something about it, maybe perhaps jealousy becomes envy. I'm not sure. Then there is lust. To lust after something is a sin, but does that mean that it is a feeling and a sin of the heart or what? Then sloth too and pride too are feelings within oneself.

"Gluttony, now that one seems to imply overindulgence, an action. And greed also and covetousness, keeping things to yourself and actually doing something or a state of being as well as a state of mind. And wrath definitely is almost an action word itself. Greed would cause you to be greedy; that would be an action. Envy would cause you to be envious. And covetousness, gluttony, would cause you to be overindulgent or lethargic. Pride would cause you to be proud. And wrath, or anger, would cause you to be angry. So, all these sins are the underlying cause for the action involved because of them. Do you see where I'm going with this?"

Many of the students nodded their heads.

"Yes, I see, Timmy. I see it myself," Mrs. Dooley said frowning. They all sat there quite pensive.

"Then the Ten Commandments name the ten don'ts."

"How about specific sins?" Dora asked again.

"Like what, Dora?" Mrs. Dooley replied.

"Like counterfeiting. My mom said that there's been some fake money being passed around the city. She got some fake bills from the Second Chance book sale the other day, as change for her hundred-dollar bill that she used to pay for our fifty-five dollars worth of purchase. It really riled her good too," she said and almost smiled. Right now, Dora was having a little challenge with her mother over her new prom dress that mother said was too short, too tight and too revealing and ordered her to take it back. "What kind of sin is counterfeiting?" she wondered.

Mrs. Dooley thought about it for a few minutes.

"Well, defrauding the public would be cheating someone, which would really be stealing, and against the Ten Commandments, and so the deadly sin would be what, students?" she asked with a smile.

"Greed!" Almost all of them called it out.

After the class, the conversation bothered Timmy Wiley, and he wondered why. There was something that was said that seemed out of order. *Oh well,* he thought, *I need to see Rosalie and ask her to the school social next week.* His teenaged mind focused on the pleasant thought of talking to his girlfriend, Rosalie Chambers, pushing everything else out of Timmy Wiley's mind as he whistled down the hall.

chapter XX
strange
occurrences

The bank called Lt. Sammy Zurich up and reported some bogus bills that they had received lately.

"Where did you get them? Have you any idea?"

The bank manager just shrugged. "It could have been anywhere, Lieutenant. But they just started to surface in the last two days. At first we didn't spot them, but then one of our tellers was an inspector at one of the mints for several years but retired from the government and wanted to work part time, so he works here. He spotted it by the looks of it. Just felt strange to him, that's all. You know how it is, Lieutenant. Being a cop so long, you probably spot things too that no one else would even notice."

"That's for sure, sir. I'll be right over," Zurich concurred. He knocked on Monty's door before he went out. "A bank called with some bogus bills. Didn't you say that Bartnett spotted some in a recent bank robbery, when the ransom was paid or something like that?"

Monty got up. "I'll go with you, Sam," he said and left the office. They both interrogated the bank manager and talked to his employee who spotted the counterfeits.

"It just didn't feel right to my touch, I guess," he said, and they both nodded their heads in understanding.

"Did you look through all your bills then?"

"We've only just begun."

"But we'll get on it and report to you, sir," he said. They shook hands and thanked him, taking some of bogus bucks with them. "We'll call you if we find anymore," he said as the men exited the bank.

Mike hurried into Monty's office, repeating what Cartellini had told him about their suspecting that someone was smuggling in counterfeit plates and he suspected some models.

"Then this all is starting to fit together."

Suddenly other banks were finding bogus money too.

When Mike went to Conci's to see the children, he told Conci about some of it. Their nephews Mikey and Timmy Wiley were both visiting and playing with the children. Conci was tutoring Timmy for the SAT and the ACT, which he was about to take in a couple of weeks. Mikey, fourteen, watched the twins while Conci and Timmy studied.

Seeing their uncle arrive, they got ready to leave when Timmy overheard his uncle telling about the counterfeit money at the bank. Suddenly the discussion in class about the deadly sins came to Timmy, and he remembered what Dora said about her mother getting counterfeit money from Second Chance.

"Uncle Mike, Dora Carpenter, one of my classmates, said that her mother received counterfeit money back as change from a purchase she made at the book fair at Second Chance a week or so ago," Timmy blurted out.

Mike turned to look at him with interest. "Second Chance? When was this, Timmy?" Mike was instantly interested and questioned Timmy closely. "Thanks, Timmy, for that bit of information. It may prove to be the missing link."

Timmy smiled, kissed Aunt Conci and shook hands with his uncle, and he and Mikey left.

"Really, counterfeit money?" Conci responded. "How interesting. It's amazing to me that someone hasn't already thought about that, what with people coming and going to Europe and other places. Why, they could smuggle in money in their suitcases with impunity. You have money in cash in your suitcase. So what?

"Then there are the people who travel all the time and not even suspect, like the stewardesses themselves and show biz people and certain salespeople and even people in modeling." And Conci went on and on.

Mike's mind began to wander, and he yawned. "I know I almost lose control sometimes," she said and laughed at herself. That made him smile.

That encouraged her to continue. "You know, Mike, a strange thing, now that you mention money and Timmy mentions the Academy of the Second Chance, where they pay their employees in cash."

Mike just stared at her.

"So, if they have two hundred employees and pay them an average of three thousand dollars a month, that's six hundred thousand dollars a month and seven million two hundred thousand a year. Imagine having that much cash on hand to pay salaries," Conci said innocently.

Mike jumped up and grabbed her. "Conci, sometimes you make no sense, and sometimes you are really brilliant." He kissed her and left the house again.

"So which was I senseless or brilliant?" she wondered.

Mike called Zurich up, and he met Mike at the Second Chance Academy.

"This guy only pays his staff, over two hundred people, with cash," Mike told him. He raised his eyebrows.

"That sure is a red flag."

"Another thing, Zurich, my nephew said one of his friends told the class that her mother received change in counterfeit bills at the school book fair a few weeks ago."

Zurich was definitely impressed by these two pieces of news.

They interviewed the new principal, Dr. Harold Green, who seemed to know very little about the inner workings of the school.

"We need to see some of your money and where you get it." The officers thought it was suspiciously interesting that they used three different banks.

They found this dealing suspicious so they got

a court order and confiscated all the money on hand and found that half of it was the counterfeit stuff, very good imitations indeed. It would seem that they cashed the checks they received for tuition at one bank but used their counterfeit money to pay their employees. They were all arrested—including the board—and charged with counterfeiting and passing counterfeit money. The Secret Service was then called in because their agents dealt with counterfeiting.

Monty and the chief knew many of the federal agents and had a good rapport with them, so they called in special agent, Toby Sullivan, one of the top agents that knew about counterfeit bills and how they do it. He and Sam shook hands, and since this tied in with Dr. McMurray's attempted murder in some way (they were sure of it), Mike stayed in on the case too.

chapter XXI
a touch of blarney

Toby Sullivan was a big Irishman with a good heart and a glib tongue that belied his very focused persona as a federal agent. No one would know by his manner that he was a Secret Service agent. He was boisterous, happy-go-lucky, and lots of fun. He liked to flirt with the ladies and was married three times, never was able to be faithful to any of them. *Almost like Joey Bartnett,* Mike thought.

They searched the school building but found nothing, except some hidden drugs in the bottom of some plants. That was a big diversion, but the narcs came out to investigate that anyway. No arrests were made on that basis alone.

Mike mentioned to Sullivan what Cartellini told him about them following some of the models and he suspected them of bringing the plates into the country. But they had no proof, just the word of someone who spotted what looked like a plate.

Mike never mentioned that he suspected Madeline of any of this. *Darn, why do I have to fall for someone like that anyway?* he asked himself. *What if she's involved in this? I need to protect myself. That much is for sure.*

So, he stayed away from her during the whole investigation. In the end, they were not able to find out where the money was being printed, only that the board of directors was not guilty, nor the principal or the director of the school. They were pleading innocence. It was discovered that someone was paying them in cash, and that's how the counterfeit money got into the pot. The police didn't buy this and held the three more suspicious persons on the board of directors responsible. They were all out on bail as the cops scurried to find more evidence to hold and arrest them. The new principal was thought to be just an innocent dupe.

Mike, however, really liked the big Irishman, and they went drinking together and picking up girls.

"You a married guy, McVey?" he asked him one night when both he and Mike were romancing some broads.

"Yeah, but separated. How about you?"

"Not at the moment, but I've been married

three time and three divorces. This your first
marriage?"

"No, my first wife died. This is my second."

"Any children?"

Mike nodded. "Two. You?"

"Six," he said, and they laughed all night
about that. "Two for each wife, cause I'm an equal
opportunity employer." He laughed, and Mike
saw the humor in that too. They were both quite
drunk and anything was funny to them at that
point.

One night Mike asked Conci if he could bring
Sullivan home for dinner. Although she was
still quite upset toward him and didn't want to
reconcile or even have him in her house, she
said okay, feeling that if she was cooperative in
professional things, he would be better to her and
the children.

Conci had prepared her special lasagna for
the occasion and baked her lemon meringue
pies. Toby came into the house and was a perfect
gentleman. Toby had come over at six thirty at
Mike's invitation. Toby kept looking at Conci
and saw right away that she was quite pregnant
and was very sweet, and he loved the sound of
her laughter. He took one look at McVey's wife

and couldn't take his eyes off her. She was just beautiful, and he loved her big, big eyes that seemed to look deep into his soul. Conci was amused by the Irishman, and he made her laugh a lot.

The children were good. And Sonny had to show Toby his toys, and Moira just smiled at him and kept staring at him. Mike so obviously loved his children and was proud of them, a fact that Toby noted.

They didn't eat until the children were in bed around seven o'clock.

"When are you due, Conci?" he asked her in an interested tone.

"In another month and a half, Toby. Do you have children?"

"Oh yes, six of them, four boys and two girls." Then he took out the pictures he always carried in his wallet.

"Oh they're beautiful, Toby. What a nice family you have."

"They're from three different wives, Conci, two a piece." Then he laughed.

"Do you see them often?"

"Oh yes, I drive them to school most days and help them with their studies and take them to their ball games. I have no problem with my children. My only problem is with my ex-wives."

He looked at her and then he laughed again. "I love to see a woman pregnant. I think she's in her best blossoming self. It was what you were born for, Conci. It's a wonderful holy thing. Don't you agree, Mike?" he asked, seeing how Mike loved his children. Mike just shrugged.

"Did you ever ask any of your wives to have an abortion, Toby?" Conci asked him boldly, a question that seemed out of left field to him.

He looked at her quite shocked. "No, never, that would be an ungodly thing for sure," he said and looked over at Mike and knew the truth. No more was said of the subject as they entered the dining room for dinner.

They ate, and he was delighted with the food.

"This is heavenly and delicious, Conci. Yes, it's the best I've ever tasted. You're a lucky man, Mike McVey, not only a beautiful and blossoming pregnant wife, but two gorgeous children and in your middle ages too, man. How lucky can a guy get? Oh wait a minute, you two are getting unhitched aren't you?" he said teasingly and slapped Mike on the back and laughed.

Suddenly Conci saw what Toby was doing. He had a real sensing about Conci's predicament with Mike, and he was trying to help Mike to appreciate his wife and family.

"Your eyes, woman, are so beautiful. Yes, they're lovely and so big and so dark and so piercing. I have the feeling that you're looking right into my soul and knowing all my secrets," he said. "Then your gorgeous hair," he continued. "I don't think any of my wives ever had such beautiful, lustrous black curly hair like yours. You are certainly a beauty, Conci. Yes, too bad you're taken," he said sadly.

"Not for long!" Conci retorted, entering into his playful, flirting mood.

Mike gave him a dirty look. "Are you flirting with my wife, Sullivan?" he asked angrily, finally getting it.

"Perhaps, man, but only because I see that you don't pay her any mind at all. What a waste of a beautiful, compassionate woman."

"Why you old reprobate," Mike attacked him angrily. "You told me yourself that you cheated every chance you got on your wives and that's why they divorced you."

"That's true, Michael, but never when they were pregnant. No, that was always our special time. If I could have kept them pregnant all the time, I'd have never cheated."

Conci was enjoying all the attention that Toby was giving her and his Irish banter. She smiled at Mike with an enigmatic smile one time. And he frowned at her, and she just laughed and laughed. Finally the night was over, and Toby took Conci's hand and opened the palm and kissed it and then closed the palm.

"Keep my kiss under your heart, Concetta. And if things don't improve for you, open your hand, feel my kiss upon your lips, and I'll know it's time to come and get you," he said. Mike barely shook his hand when he left. "Thank you both for a wonderful, enjoyable, entertaining evening." And Toby left on that note.

Mike was angrily helping Conci clear the table.

"What a wonderful man," she said out loud and danced into the kitchen.

"He was just playing with you, Conci. Can't you tell when a guy is just fooling around? He was just giving me the business, that's all," Mike said sourly.

Conci smiled at him. "I don't think so, Mike. I think he was really taken with me. Yes, he really admired me for carrying this baby," she said and put the dishes in the dishwasher and then, leaving him alone in the kitchen, went into the bathroom and took a shower and brushed her teeth.

Mike came in when she was showering and took a good long look at her. She was holding her back and moaning softly.

"Hey, are you all right?" he asked worriedly.

"Yes," she said softly. "I'm better than I was three hours ago," she answered. Mike just stared at her and left the house angrily.

After that, Mike stayed away from Sullivan except when they were working together on the case.

"What's in your craw, McVey?" he asked him one day when Mike was being surly to him.

"You flirted with my wife that night we had you over for dinner. You got her thinking that you were serious about her, and I felt like you were making a fool of both her and me."

"No way, man. I was flirting with her because she's a beautiful woman and obviously was unhappy with you. One thing I never did, Mike, when I was fooling around on my wives, I never was mean to them. In fact I was even better to them. You're a mean guy. I saw you holler at her and in front of me, a stranger. How embarrassing for her. But she obviously loves you no matter. I never did that, Mike. You're not only unfaithful, you're mean to her," he said and walked away.

Mike followed him and pushed him.

"You've got a nerve, Sullivan, mind your own business." Sullivan pushed him back, and soon they were wrestling around on the floor fighting like two teenaged kids.

Finally, Pat broke it up by throwing water into both their faces.

"Now either make up or get out, both of you. Mike, you know better than to act like that," he said disgustedly.

They both got up and went their own way home.

Mike barely made it home with a bloodied nose and an eye that was getting black and blue and some abrasions on his hands and some broken ribs. He was really a mess. And he somehow hurt his arm; it was sore when he moved it. But he drove home and had barely gotten out of the car and to the front door. He rang the bell until Conci saw that it was him and opened the door.

"Mike, come in, for heaven's sakes. You'll wake the children." Then she saw how bloody and hurt he was. "What happened to you?"

"I got into a fight," he said. She had him sit down, and she cleaned his wounds and saw that he was holding his ribs and his arm was hurt too.

"Let me take you to the hospital, Mike, and get your wounds taken care of. Your arm appears broken."

"No, leave me alone."

"Were you brawling over some broad again?" she asked, getting angry.

"Yeah, you're the broad I was fighting over. You're the one," he said and lay down and fell asleep on the sofa. Conci just shook her head. *What a mess he is,* she thought. But she lovingly put a blanket on him and went back to sleep herself.

After she took the children to school and got a sub, Conci came back home to see about Mike. He was moaning and groaning. She woke him up and took him to the hospital, and they put a cast on his arm. It was broken, as were his ribs. They taped him and gave him some medicine.

"What happened to you, Lieutenant," the doctor asked him

"He was hurt in a cockfight," Conci quipped knowingly. Mike just looked at her.

He stayed at Conci's house that night on the recliner, and the next day he left again to stay in his office. It disturbed him though because Conci seemed glad to have him gone.

"You're not staying here for long, Mike. I hope you know that. Wherever that bed you made for yourself lies, that's where you belong, not here with me," she said and just left him sitting in the recliner. But she did take good care of him, giving him his medicine and helping him wash himself and feeding him, making sure he was comfortable.

The children were delighted that he was home but unhappy that he couldn't hold them. So, Conci brought them to him and put the children to sleep after he kissed them goodnight.

"Thanks, Conci, for your kindness." She just looked at him, turned, and walked out of the room.

chapter XXII
lights, camera,
murder solved

Lt. Melville was quite animated, talking a mile a minute while Mike walked slowly to his own office with Melville on his heels and Monty right behind him.

"So, what's up, Al?" he asked as they all sat down in Mike's office.

Immediately they saw that Mike had a cast on his arm, a black eye and some abrasions on his face as well as walking carefully as though he was in pain.

"What the heck happened to you, McVey?" Monty frowned and raised his eyebrows.

Melville stared at Mike, too, as Mike lowered his glance and just took a deep breath.

"It's nothing, guys, I just had a little accident yesterday and don't want to talk about it,"

He said adamantly. "Let's just drop it and get back to this business." He looked at Melville again,

"All right Al, what's going on?"

"We found a curator at the aquarium who had been ill for a couple of months. He'd been fired for sleeping on the job. But, he came forth when he heard about the Australian Wasp Jellyfish being the poison used for Mary Elizabeth's murder."

"How come it took him so long to come forth?" Monty asked suspiciously.

"He was fired from his job the next day and went to Denver to see his brother, who had a construction job for him. Then, he returned this week and got his job back at the aquarium, and his buddies told him that he missed some excitement. Right away he got in touch with the police, and here's his story." He looked down at his notes and then continued.

"Seems he saw a man giving money to one of the sea tank cleaners, one night around three o'clock, when he was doing his rounds. He didn't accost them or anything; in fact he stayed back, watching the scenario unfold. The tank cleaner, Arnold, someone who'd only worked there a few weeks, gave a cooler to the man, and they parted."

"Did he see the man clearly, and can he recognize him?"

"Oh yes!" Melville said and sat back in his

chair, looking at the two men in front of him as they stared at him with anticipation.

"He recognized him all right. It was the actor Sonny Lopelia."

Both Mike and Monty sat up at that bombshell. "So, it was Lopelia all along. I wonder why he'd murder her, though. What was his motive?" Melville smiled at Mike again.

"Remember when we questioned Sister Conci about Lopelia and she gave us this long history about him and afterward we discussed it, thinking that Sister suspected that Lopelia murdered his wife, although she didn't come right out and say that. It was supposed to be a burglar that came in and shot her in the head, robbing some of her expensive jewelry. Suppose he really did do it?" Melville continued.

Mike shook his head. "We don't know that, and if that's true, then why kill Mary Elizabeth?"

"Well, that's where my logic falls down, I'm afraid," he confessed with slumped shoulders. But Melville had nothing to be ashamed of. He had really excited these two men.

"Do we have enough to arrest him?"

"Bring him in for questioning at any rate," Mike said, and Melville got some more cops and arrested Sonny Lopelia on suspicion of murder.

It hit the newspapers the next day. And when

they brought in the witness, he talked to Mike, and they questioned him closely then satisfied, they brought in Lopelia.

"I had nothing to do with her death at all. What a thing to accuse me of. What are your facts, anyway?"

"Do you deny meeting with a Mr. Arnold Duprey at the aquarium on the night of October twelfth and giving him money in exchange for a cooler that contained some Dead Sea wasps?"

Sonny looked at them with a look of shock. Mike thought he was probably a good actor and could carry this off successfully in front of a jury. So, they really had to have the goods on him.

"No way have I ever been to the aquarium for that purpose."

"Aha, so you have been there, then?"

"Yes, I went with my son, Shepherd, a few days before the fundraiser for Commissioner DeMarco. We walked around and had a nice father and son time."

"Did you see the Australian Sea Wasp display at that time?"

"I really don't remember, Lieutenant," he insisted.

Although they had a sworn affidavit from Mr. Allen Duprey, when they went to pick him up for more questioning the next day, he had disappeared.

No one seemed to have seen him after that first day at the job. "Yeah, he came into some big money, he said and left the next day, I guess. We never saw him again. The boss called and was disgusted with him," one of the workers said.

Mike was furious with everyone. They'd put a tail on him and put a guard outside his apartment, but he managed to slip through their surveillance.

The affidavit, however, was enough to hold Sonny Lopelia for a while anyway.

Mike called Conci and was just plain irritated with the whole thing falling through.

"Yeah, this guy ducked out, and I'm so upset. I thought we had Lopelia by the neck," he said, disappointed. "We've got him, but we couldn't find motive anyway."

"What if Mary Elizabeth Morrison was the nurse who was in the house at the time of his wife's murder, Mike? She did say that she worked in many of the Hollywood houses, and she looked at Auntie once with a knowing look. I think she worked for the Lopelias. What if she wasn't gone

like he thought and she saw Sonny shoot his wife
and make it look like a break-in?"

"That's a lot of suppositions, Conci."

"Yes, Mike, but if you tax him on it, he might
break. He is a very weak man after all," she said
definitely.

"Yeah, well, thanks anyway. The reason I
called is that I won't be over tomorrow night to
see the kids. I need to stay on this case," he said,
and Conci wondered about that.

"How's your arm doing?"

"It's all right," he said and hung up.

However, feeling she really was on to
something, Mike called the Los Angeles police
and asked about the nurse on duty taking care of
Lopelia's ex-wife at the time of her death. Yes,
they questioned her, and she was gone that night.
Her name was Mary Elizabeth Morrison. "Thank
you, Sergeant." Mike hung up the phone, and the
light went on in his brain. *So, perhaps what Conci
supposes may be true. I'll surely tax him on it.*

Armed with that knowledge, Mike questioned
Lopelia again. "We know that Mary Elizabeth
Morrison was the nurse on duty the night your
wife was murdered, Lopelia. You'd better come
clean. She didn't go out that night as she claimed,
did she? No, her cousin Luther Boraxo borrowed

her car, so you only thought she was gone at any rate.

She saw you sneak around and take the gun and shoot your wife and make it look like someone broke in and stole some stuff and killed her.

"As we speak, the cops in L.A. are searching your house, having gotten a search warrant, and what will they find, Lopelia? Will they find the jewelry that you swore was stolen from her during the robbery and murder?"

Suddenly, Sonny began to cry. "She was so mean to me; you have no idea. She made my life miserable. It was self-defense. Yes, it was self-defense. But I didn't kill Mary Elizabeth. I did think about it and bought the Australian Wasp stuff from that aquarium guy, but I read up on it, and it said how horrible the death would be. I could never do that to another human being. She did come to me and didn't even ask me for money and said she was in the house that night my wife was killed and she wished I'd turn myself in. 'You'll feel so much better, Sonny,' she warned me. I just denied the whole thing. Then I got so scared I thought about doing something drastic. But I'm not a murderer, anyway, not that kind. I bought the stuff and had it in my pocket, but never used it that night. I was really scared of being found out. Then, too, when I was dancing with Mary Elizabeth, she told me she wasn't going to say anything. 'I thought about it and prayed, Sonny, and I feel that God has to show you, not me. I won't say a word, I promise,' she said sweetly. So, why would I do that to her? I wouldn't! It was a big surprise for Mary Elizabeth to fall over and die like that. When I reached into my pocket, the stuff was gone. But I didn't do it. I swear. I didn't do it." He cried and cried.

Just then his lawyer came running in. "Not another word, Sonny," he advised, turning his attention to Mike. "I need to be here whenever you question my client. Is that clear to you, Lieutenant?" he said angrily.

Mike just shrugged. "I'm finished with him. At least for the moment," he said with an enigmatic smile on his face. Lopelia was watching him with abject fear on his face. "Book him on suspicion of murder," Mike commanded, and the lawyer looked at him and then at Sonny.

"What did you tell him?"

Monty was watching Mike with the interrogation. "Was that for real or just supposition?" he asked.

Mike just shrugged. "Conci figured it out, and I called L.A. and talked to the guys on that murder case of his ex-wife. And sure enough, the nurse on duty was Mary Elizabeth Morrison; the rest I surmised. But, apparently it's a really good guess."

Monty slapped him on the back. "You're like some stealthy tiger, lying in wait for your kill. Then when they least expect it, wham, you jump on them, and they're a goner," Monty said with admiration and pride. Mike smiled a small smile and left the room.

So, at least one mystery was solved: the death of the ex-Mrs. Sonny Lopelia.

Mike had a hunch that Sonny Lopelia's testimony was true and couldn't get out of his mind the things that Conci and Sister told him about the look on Mary Elizabeth's face when the chief of police showed the badge.

Sonny sat there in the interrogation room and talked with his lawyer. When he was finished, he just stared at the walls and thought of what his father told him on his deathbed a few years ago.

"Why do you have to hold onto that much fame for, Sonny? You're a multimillionaire, maybe even a billionaire. You have a gig now and then, a public appearance here and there, but that's not enough for you. You have to be the center of attention and have to be the top banana all the time. Accept the fact that your time has passed. Move over and let the young ones take over; at least yield your so-called position a little. Everyone laughs at you, Sonny, because you're ridiculous in your pursuit of fame. You have it, man. You still have it, but not as much as before. Is that all you are a star flickering in the night sky but giving off no more heat and soon dying out? Or are you a man of honor, doing good deeds and sharing God's bounty that he's given you with others without any fanfare or publicity?"

Yes, Sonny thought *now, I've given everything that I am or ever was up to obtain fame. Now, I'll go to jail and everyone will remember me. Yes, they'll remember me but not with pleasure, but with disdain. I never wanted that. Oh Lord, forgive me for my sins and help me out of this one, now,* he cried within himself.

chapter XXIII
a tiger by the tail

Mike was reluctant to interrogate Cici DeMarco again, and he expressed this reluctance to Monty.

"Look, Monty. Here's the problem. I feel like I'm going into the lion's den by myself over this murder. Please give me your support or at least listen and tell me to stop," Mike complained.

"Sit down, McVey? What's the problem here?" he said in his coldest voice.

"Well, first of all, why are you so upset with me? We've been friends for many years now and have always been able to talk things out. A little while ago you were congratulating me on my interrogation techniques; now, you're upset again."

Monty sighed. "Okay, Mike, that thing the night of the banquet left a really bad taste in my mouth. I forgot it for a little while in admiration of your cop skills, but every so often it surfaces again and bothers me. Here it is: I'm not completely sure what happened. I've talked to Sister

Conci many times about it, and she assures me it wasn't any kind of hocus pocus or hypnotism at all. In fact, she was quite offended that I even mentioned the word *hypnotism*. She says it was an extraordinary gift we all received, the ability to see inside someone else's soul and feelings. 'I myself have only experienced this a couple of times in my life, and this is the first time with Conci.' That's what she told me, Mike, and Conci didn't have any idea how it happened and indeed was astonished that everyone felt her hurt and in fact was quite embarrassed over the whole thing.

"So, regardless, this time I saw and heard what you're doing to your wife, and it's a real sinful thing, McVey. It's a big sin you're committing against her. I would certainly lock you up so fast if it were a real physical thing, but it isn't and I can't do a thing. But I don't have to hang around you when it's not necessary," he said stoutly.

Mike just stared at him. Monty just frowned. "Have you ever thought of just being true to your wife, Mike, like most of the rest of us? It will increase your enjoyment of the marriage, and it can be a very intimate thing, being exclusive with one person. You really try hard, if you know this is it for you," he said like an older brother giving some good advice but also with a little disdain in his voice.

Mike just shrugged. "Okay, Monty, then let's put that aside and listen to my dilemma. I think that somehow Cici DeMarco either has information that could help us or is involved in some of this herself."

Monty just stared at him with big eyes and frowned. "Of course she had a visit from April, who apparently held something over her head, and suddenly, April was promoted. So, are you talking about the possibility that she might have killed April?"

"Well, she did have a motive," he insisted. "Besides, whoever did it must have done it on the spur of the moment, don't you think?"

Monty nodded his head. "It sure looks like that, especially since the coroner has identified the poison as some kind of glycoside called Convallatoxin, which is similar to Digitalis.

They're still trying to figure out exactly what it is. He has a hunch that it's some kind of plant and only a few plants contain that poison. Doc is looking it up." Monty sighed.

He didn't savor the idea of Mike interrogating Cici again, either.

"Okay, I know that. Just listen to me, please. Cici was also one of the people who sent a drink to Mary Elizabeth's table and apparently brought her a dish of cannoli. Then she denied it to me and threatened to have me demoted when I found this out and taxed her on it. I have the testimony of two of the waiters. So that was one suspicious thing."

"Whew!" Monty got up and stood up and stretched and then sat down and pondered the information. "You really do have a tiger by the tail, and you're asking me to milk it, McVey," he said metaphorically. "Why would she murder Mary Elizabeth? Wasn't she one of her stalwart workers?"

Mike nodded. "Two of the women at our table noticed that she had a frozen look on her face when the chief was holding up her badge. That's all I could get from them." He too stood up and stretched and then sat down.

"So what is it that you want me to do for you?"

"I want you to come with me when I interview her again," Mike said hopefully.

Monty shook his head. "I know you have great insight, Mike, and you may be right, but give me more to go on, please," he begged.

"Okay, Monty, but at least you know what's happening, and if I'm murdered, you'll know why," he said and got up and was about to leave the room when the coroner called again.

"Captain, you will probably find this interesting. The plants that contain that glycoside are Foxglove, of course where we get our digitalis from, the Thanghin plant of Madagascar, all the oleanders and Lily of the valley."

Monty sat there and pondered the information. "You're the goods, Doc. Thanks for that information." He hung up and repeated the information to Mike.

"Whew!" Mike breathed out of his mouth. "I wouldn't recognize any of those plants except the Lily of the valley," Then he suddenly stopped. "Let me call Conci. She even commented on the beautiful flowers at the wake."

"Hey, babe," he said in a surprisingly friendly voice. "You remember the flowers at the wake?" He hurried on not giving her a chance to answer. "Did you see any of these plants, the oleander family, some kind of tree from Madagascar, fox-glove, or Lily of the Valley?"

Immediately she answered. "Oh, yes, Mike, there were two arrangements that contained Lily of the Valley among other flowers." Mike took in his breath again.

"Thanks, baby. Thanks a lot," he nodded his head to Monty and hung up.

"Lily of the valley!" he almost shouted. "There were two arrangements with lily of the valley."

Monty almost smiled at that.

Cici was not at the banquet where McVey brought his girlfriend instead of going with his wife. The news traveled to her, however, causing her to just laugh at that. Really, he was so stupid about women and about relationships. *I really don't want him, but I want him to know that I can break him up with that skinny red-haired model any time it suits me,* she thought angrily. She called McVey to come to her house that night.

Mike went but wasn't happy about it. They sat in the kitchen and had some coffee. She was dressed in a beautiful black negligee, looking terrific. She was a great-looking woman for her age, but Mike was quite uncomfortable.

"Okay, McVey, are you finished with questioning me about the murders? For heaven's sakes, I'm the police commissioner," she said adamantly and with a puzzle in her voice. "How could you think that of me?" she continued, acting more hurt than angry.

"Look, Cici, I don't think you had anything to do with it. I can't even imagine what kind of motive you'd have for killing one of your best supporters, Mary Elizabeth Morrison and April too seemed to be guarding you all the time. No, it was just the cop inside me, trying to tie loose ends, honey. I'd never suspect you," he lied.

"Okay, Mike, I believe you," she said as she went over and sat on his lap. Mike felt he should go along with her although he certainly didn't feel much heat with her. She vamped him, and soon they were in bed. But Mike was not able to do anything, and he told her, "I hope you'll understand, baby. It's not you, it's me. And I'm getting some medication for it but just haven't had time to do it. The doctors tell me it's just a temporary problem," he said lovingly. They parted, and Cici felt that what he said was probably true.

Mike doubled his efforts to find the murderer of these two people. *What do they have in common?* But Mike knew that his domestic problems were interfering with his detective work for the first time in his life.

It's that darn Madeline. I'm so hooked on her. Maybe it's an unhealthy situation. Really, he thought, sitting back in his office chair and putting his feet on his desk, then moaning because his ribs still hurt. Carefully he changed positions and thought, *This is where I belong and where I feel the best, like my old self. I don't need a wife or children or even some girlfriend who tries to control me. No, I only need my murder cases and a good mystery to solve.* Once having said that, he ordered some food out and leaned back on his desk chair and tried to figure things out.

chapter XXIV
a deep dark secret

The cops and the FBI had scoured the whole of the Second Chance Academy in their quest to find some evidence of counterfeiting. They had of course found the money, and three of the board of directors were arrested and were now out on bail pending their court date.

But the actual operation was never found. They went into the basement and did a thorough search, and truly, they searched the school from top to bottom. So, they were pretty certain that the operation wasn't on the school grounds at any rate.

The people arrested pleaded not guilty and that they were duped like everyone else. In the end they had to release them for lack of evidence. Dr. McMurray was no longer principal. He and his wife had gone to their ocean-side summer home, and he was resting and recuperating.

Their lives had changed dramatically, and they both had repented of their selfish lives and the error they propagated through the ministry of the Second Chance Academy.

"Who do you think sent that note to Sonny Lopelia or made the phone call, honey?" she asked him now that they were away from the horrors for the moment.

McMurray been in the hospital for a couple of weeks and was doing so well now. "I'm not quite sure, Addy, what the heck was going on. Please don't ask me any questions about the school. I have to keep a low profile and save both our lives, sweetie," he said mysteriously. Addy just shook her head. For a long time now her husband had been keeping secrets from her, and it bothered her a lot. They had been a relatively close couple and had what she considered a good marriage of twenty years. Now, however, her husband, who had been cooling for years about the salvation experience, got on his knees and repented to the Lord.

"I should never have taken that job, Addy. I'm a real sinner and need the Lord's forgiveness and yours too," he said over and over again. He began to read his Bible and opened up a bank box there in Maine, in the little town where they lived right by the ocean.

"Here's the key, honey, but don't open it up unless I'm dead."

"Oh, Albie, you're doing so well, all the doctors are amazed at your progress."

But regardless of their good prognosis, Albert McMurray drowned one morning as he sat by the ocean on the big rocks looking down at the ocean, and it was assume that he fell.

Mrs. McMurray opened the bank box as commanded by her husband. It really wasn't surprising to her, though, having suspected this kind of thing for a long while. After a few prayers, she closed the box and put it back into the vault until she could get a grip on the importance of the information contained therein.

Mrs. McMurray then called the Second Chance Academy to inform them of his death. "My husband was doing so well, but he fell off the cliff outside our home here in Maine and drowned. I just wanted everyone at Second Chance to know that."

Soon, the news trickled down to Conci McVey, and she called Mike right away. "McMurray supposedly drowned, Mike." And she told him the details that had been repeated to her.

"Well, I'll be," he said and then hung up.

But the cops, led by Lawrence, still hung around the school every now and then.

"I'm still suspicious of the place," he explained to Mike, who wondered why he was still sniffing around there. "I tell you, I smell drugs, Mike. I know I'm in homicide, but this may tie in."

"Okay, Fred, but don't make a nuisance of yourself," he suggested. Fred agreed.

chapter XXV
a nose for danger

Conci McVey and Loretta Sterns-Ryan were the two teachers selected to go to the Second Chance Academy to learn about their horticulture program. They grew their own plants for food and for ornamental plants and then rooted them for other schools to buy. They sold the seedlings quite cheaply, and then the other schools could use them in a very lucrative sale for a fundraiser. Other schools had participated and found that with just a little work on the teacher and student's part, they not only learned how to grow things and make them environmentally safe, but then sold these plants for a good dollar. One school had netted over three thousand dollars on one plant sale.

So, the board of directors of Signs and Wonders directed Dr. Leo Halperan to send some of his teachers to learn about this program.

As they entered the building on a day when the Second Chance students were home, as it was an in-service training day for the teachers, Conci and Loretta were glad to do this as opposed to sitting through all that boring stuff they usually served up on in-service days.

It was a beautiful day, and Mrs. Corinne Dowling met them at the front door and escorted them to their immense hothouse on the other side of the building. Both Loretta and Conci had already met and spoken with the charming Mrs. Dowling.

"Nice to see you, ladies. It's a really good day for this too," she noted, and they shook hands and followed her for a long walk across the immense ground of the school.

"This really is a beautiful acreage," Loretta commented. Mrs. Dowling smiled.

"We're so proud of it, Loretta. It's the only program like it in the state," she insisted. Both Loretta and Conci tried to look duly impressed.

"When did the program start?" Conci probed.

"As soon as the school opened last year. I've only been in charge of it this year," she said, and silence ensued.

Loretta was called on her cell phone after a little while during their tour of the horticultural center. It was her mother who lived in Richmond, Virginia; her grandmother had a serious stroke.

"Please come, Loretta; Dad and I really need

you," her mother pleaded. So, Loretta ordered a cab, apologized to both Conci and Mrs. Dowling and left.

Conci continued about a tour of the facilities and looked around at everything, fascinated by the huge greenhouse, with all its hundreds of plants. "Your people really have a green thumb," Conci commented, smiling at her guide.

"Oh, we don't grow all of them here ourselves. Sometimes we import them and then root them. They are lovely, though, aren't they?" Mrs. Dowling said proudly.

After a while, she had to leave temporarily. "Please excuse me, Conci. I'll be back shortly. Just roam around the grounds if you like."

Conci went outside and toward the main building to get a cola from the machine, which was in the basement, as she remembered from her last visit. As she entered the huge cafeteria in the basement, she dropped her purse. One coin in particular fell into a corner, and she went to pick it up. There was a very small crack in the floor and her quarter fell down it.

There must be a subbasement here, she thought and took out her little flashlight that was attached to keychain and shone the light down into the crack and could make out another room below. Since no one was around, she looked in another corner and couldn't see anything. Now her curiosity was piqued, and she went upstairs and out of the building toward the greenhouse again. As she got nearer to it, she looked on the other side of the vast acreage and saw a strange sight. It looked like people were coming out of the ground.

Conci quickly hid in the bushes, not really knowing why she was doing that. After waiting for about a half hour, she ran into the grove of trees that were in back of the property where she thought she saw people coming out of the ground. She got on her knees as she came closer to the sight and moved debris from the ground by swishing her hands and arms back and forth. Unexpectedly, she felt something hard and metallic and brushed the twigs and leaves off it, revealing a trapdoor of sorts. She pulled the handle although it was quite a job and opened it up and shone her flashlight down the dark hole and saw a stairway leading way, way down.

Quickly she closed the trapdoor. There was an odor about the place, and she sniffed it and knew that smell but couldn't readily identify it. Suddenly she felt a pinch like the stick of a needle and turned, seeing three faces, and then passed out.

When Conci came to, she was in another spot, wondering how she got there. She looked around, and the whole place seemed quite unfamiliar to her as she shook herself trying to recall what happened to her. *Why am I lying here on the ground in this forested area?* She wondered, quite perplexed.

She got up and saw the building and started to walk toward it, puzzled as to why she was even here, then realized as she got closer that it was the Second Chance Academy. Conci paused before going in and again wondered why she was here.

In one way she knew Loretta was with her today, because she could remember getting up this morning and talking to Mike about it. Then she beeped in front of Loretta's house and drove to the school. That was the extent of her memory. *What happened after that? Did we arrive at the school? There are plenty of cars in the parking lot.*

Conci stood outside the building for a few moments and noticed a bench by the children's swings. So, she walked there and sat down, still quite puzzled. A look at her watch revealed that it was two thirty. The bench felt good, so Conci stayed on the bench until the teachers came out. Everyone just looked at her curiously.

Finally, Mrs. Dowling came out and sat down,

bawling out Conci. "Where have you been? We've been looking all over for you the whole day, practically. I left you at the greenhouse at eleven this morning, and now it's almost three. How rude and inconsiderate of you to disappear like that," she said, fuming about the whole thing.

Conci began to cry. "The last thing I remember is coming into the parking lot this morning. Then it's all a blank until I find myself out in the woods and lying on the ground. I'm not hurt or anything. What happened to me?"

Mrs. Dowling saw that Conci was looking at her with those big eyes so full of fear and confusion. "Oh my dear, have you had a stroke or something? Did you have a heart attack or did you faint? What on earth happened to you?" Her voice was beginning to sound almost panicked as she looked at Conci's pregnant body. "Let's get you to a hospital right away."

Taking over, the woman called the ambulance, and Conci was taken to the ER at Mercy hospital, where they called her husband. Since they couldn't locate him, they called Dr. Leo Halperan, her principal at Signs and Wonders, who came hastily to the hospital.

"My dear Conci, what in the world happened to you? They called me twice to complain that you had either left the place or disappeared. Are you all right?" he asked in his kind and compassionate voice.

Dr. John Wiley, Conci's brother-in-law, came into the room at that time, greeting Dr. Halperan.

Conci lay there still confused about the whole thing, while they took several tests, and nothing unusual was found. Indeed, if she had a stroke, it was certainly only a mini one. They gave her some medicine and dismissed her, after making sure that the baby was all right. Dr. Halperan drove her home.

Conci lay down for an hour or so feeling very strange indeed. Then she got on her knees and began to pray. Soon it was time to pick up the children, and she did so.

For the rest of the evening she had little time to think about anything except her darling twins. At seven she bathed them and put them to sleep. Then she almost collapsed in her recliner. Being quite large with pregnancy, she could barely sleep in the bed anymore because it was difficult to breathe lying down, so she opted for the recliner which suited her rather well.

Soon, she fell asleep herself and began dreaming. First she saw Lara Connors' face and Lt. Fred Lawrence and Madeline. Then she walked quietly over to a huge box in the ground and opened the box, and there was a bright light that blinded her, then she saw some stairs.

Conci woke up startled when the phone rang. It was Mike. Halperan had called Mike about Conci's condition.

"Hey, what the heck happened to you today, Conci? Halperan said you had a minor stroke or something. What the heck?" he asked. *I sure don't need a sick wife now, that's for sure.*

"It was so strange, Mike. I was in the car and picked Loretta up and we arrived at the Second Chance Academy. The next thing I knew I was laying on the grass in the woods behind the school. I wasn't hurt at all, except for this miserable headache that doesn't want to leave. I got up gingerly and walked over to the building and realized it was the school. I had no recollection of how I got into the woods. When I looked at my watch it was two thirty. My last memory was of us arriving at eight thirty this morning. Anyway, Mrs. Dowling insisted that I go to the hospital for tests, and I did so. There was no indication of a stroke or anything, Mike. So, now I'm home and just dozed off and had some weird dreams. I don't know what's happening to me, Mike," she said, quite alarmed and worried.

Mike felt her fear and knew he had to protect her. "I'll be there in a little while, Conci," he said.

But she'd heard that story many times before, and he wouldn't show up. This time was apparently different, because ten minutes later he was knocking softly on the door so as not to awaken the children. Conci was busily making some coffee in case he really did show up and also to have one forbidden cup in hopes it would take the headache away.

"Hey, baby." He took her in his arms and held her close to him after he came in. Conci sighed and felt protected and safe again.

They sat down, and she poured him the coffee and had a cup herself.

"How come?" he asked looking at her cup.

"I have the terrible headache, Mike, and this sore arm too. Maybe I fell. I don't know." And then she began to cry.

"Okay, honey, now listen to me. I called the hospital and the doc there, and Dr. Oliver said you were doing fine, so don't worry about it."

"Okay, Mike," she said and stopped crying. That was the end of it for a while. He stayed for a short time that evening then left.

Conci, however, was determined to find out the truth of why she lost her memory. So, after school the next two days she drove to Second Chance and walked around the school and stopped where she found herself in the woods. *Was there any telltale sign of anyone being with her?* She looked again and again but with no results. Still, her memory eluded her.

Every night for a week, she had some disturbing dreams. She would be kneeling down and opening up a huge box, and in the box was a great light and that was it. Then she was seeing faces on the flowers, as though they were people.

"She won't remember anything," one flower said to the other. The faces looked familiar on the flowers. One looked like Madeline, and the other looked like Lara Connors and one like Fred Lawrence.

"Maybe we should just kill her and then be completely safe. She's such a buttinsky," the Lara flower said, but the other two flowers fluttered.

The Fred flower said, "Absolutely not. I'm not a killer, and neither is Madeline. No way are you going to kill her. For heaven's sakes, she's pregnant. You'd be killing two people. No way."

The Fred flower was adamant about it all. "Just give her the shot, and she won't remember a thing."

Then Conci would awaken. "Why Lara Connors for heaven's sakes," she thought out loud. "For goodness sakes I barely know the woman, and she was very pleasant to me always. Madeline, I could understand. She would be in my private nightmares for a long while, I think. Lt. Fred Lawrence is another curious person to have dreams about. Oh well, maybe they're all just dreams," she concluded.

Finally, her headache left her, but she went back to the doctor a couple of days after the event to talk to him about it, just to be safe.

Dr. Oliver looked at her swollen upper arm and examined it closely.

"It looks like you were given some kind of a shot, Conci, and it's infected and irritated." He looked at her rather curiously.

"Did you give me a shot recently, Ollie?"

"No way, Conci. No way," he exclaimed as he continued his examination.

chapter XXVI
christmas

Christmas vacation time came, and Conci was off work for two weeks and loved it, and so did the children love having her home and being home with her.

Maureen Wiley was over almost every day to help Conci, and so was Loretta. Sister Conci was coming the day before Christmas Eve, and everyone was excited to see her.

Conci was a little blue at times because Mike was making himself scarce instead of coming over to see the children as the holidays approached. But, she bucked up for the children's sake.

Conci and the children were at the airport to pick up Auntie in the afternoon on December 23. Mike was at the airport too, and there was Conci standing there waiting for a plane to land with Sonny sitting in the stroller and Moira standing by the stroller holding onto the handlebars.

Moira looked over at Mike who hadn't been to see them in almost a month and just stared at him. Then she pulled on her mother's skirt and whispered something to her.

"Yes, that's Daddy, Moira. Yes, that's him," Conci said.

Moira got his attention and waved to him. "Hi, Daddy," she screamed across the room. Mike just smiled at her and waved back.

The people were alighting from the plane, and Auntie came off first and purposely looked at Mike, stared at him then smiled at her niece and grandchildren. They were smiling happily.

"Grams, Grams!" Both children ran to her at once, screaming her name. Conci took the luggage, and they left the airport.

Mike felt badly about being out of that loop and wondered why he felt that way.

This was what he wanted, Maddy and this free and easy life. But it wasn't very free at all. It cost him almost all his money to keep her happy, and he'd become quite impotent and knew he was about to lose her. The thought, rather than upset him, almost made him sigh with relief. *Maybe this madness will be all over soon too, and I can become a real person again.* Mike waited and she never came. He felt like a complete fool.

He called her on her cell. "Where the heck are you, Maddy? I've been waiting for you here at the airport for over an hour, and you're not here. Where the heck are you?"

"Oh Mikey, I was going to call you, I decided to stay in New York for the holidays with my best girlfriends. I'll call you on Christmas," she said, trying to hang up quickly.

"But, I thought we were going to have Christmas together like a family and go to church and have some of our friends over. Oh, Maddy," he said in a heartbroken tone.

"Oh Mikey, now don't go giving me a guilt trip. I'll see you when I see you," she said lightly. Mike was furious with her and drove to the Daffodil and got really snockered and had to spend the night in Pat's back room because he was so very drunk.

He was lonely though and disappointed, so he went to his sister's house on Christmas Eve as they were about to go over to Conci's.

"Come with us, Mike. You know the children would be so happy to see you."

"I'm embarrassed in front of Sister. What if she says something to me, Maureen? I don't want to have to deal with her."

"Wait, I'll call her right now." Maureen did so and explained to Sister about Mike's reluctance. Maureen smiled. "I knew you'd say that. We'll be there shortly. It's all right." She said turning to

Mike, "Both of them promised they wouldn't say one thing to make you feel strange. Okay?" They loaded the car. And Mike followed them, and they all went to Conci's house.

Mike walked in after the Wileys, and Moira screamed and clapped her hands. "It's Daddy, Mommy. It's Daddy," she screeched. Mike had to laugh at her as she jumped into his arms. "I knew you'd come for Christmas, Daddy. I prayed that you would," she said.

He almost cried at her little three-year-old voice and held her very close to him then put her down as Sonny pulled on his pants.

"Me too, Daddy," he said, and Mike picked him up too.

"They are so precious, aren't they, Mike?" Sister said. And they all went into the kitchen, and the women prepared the food as Mike and John and the boys played on the floor with the children.

They ate the fantastic ravioli, and Mike just sighed. He felt better here than he'd felt in the last three months. Maybe this was where he belonged. Then they had their dessert and sang Christmas carols as the children opened up the packages that Uncle John and Aunt Maureen brought, and they were so happy.

Everyone prayed, and the children went to

bed. Mike tucked them in and heard their prayers, which pleased Conci. The adults sat down and had some more coffee and talked and told jokes, and it was very jolly.

Just then, Mike's cell phone rang. He took it in the kitchen. "Mike, I just wanted to wish you a Merry Christmas, honey."

"Look, Maddy, you've disappointed me for the last time. I'm here with my family, and it's the best Christmas without you." And he hung up.

The next day was Christmas Day, and Mike spent it at his sister's house. Conci and Auntie and the children came over in the afternoon, and they had a wonderful Christmas Day too.

Too soon it was all over, and everything was back to the way it was before. Nothing had changed as far as they could see. Everyone said their goodbyes, and Conci and company left.

Mike just sighed. "Thanks for everything, you guys. That was the best two days I've had for over three months and maybe before that."

He was about to get up when his brother-in-law stopped him. "Then why are you not back with your family, Mike? You see how much they love you and they need you, buddy. More to the point, you need them, Mike, and you know it," he said man-to-man.

Mike looked down at the floor. "I'm so confused, John. I know I'm doing them wrong, but I'll try to do better by all of them," he said. And that was the end of that little talk, and he left but on a good note.

While the children were home from preschool for the holiday vacation, Mike came over every day to play with them, and once he and Conci took them to the movies. They had a ball. He bought them popcorn and took them out for hamburgers at the place where they had an indoor gym.

Conci was so pleased with him. Sister had gone on some exploration excursions with Maureen during those times. But Mike got along with sister quite well too, since nothing was mentioned about him coming back or anything.

One day, Conci had gone to the store, and Mike was there with the children and looked through the Christmas cards that were openly displayed, hanging on a big wire tree. He stopped and took one off the tree, when he realized it was from Toby Sullivan, the Secret Service agent that flirted with Conci.

He read the inscription,

Dear Conci,

You're in my thoughts almost all the time. When you're ready to give McVey the shaft forever, I'm your man. That's no blarney either, my girl. No, it's the honest truth. I think of you almost all the time and daydream of how it could be, married to the one woman who could make a difference in my life. You're the only clean vessel I've met for many years.

Your crazy-about-you-fool, Toby.

Mike looked at it again and put it into his coat pocket lying on the chair. He was in a bad mood from that time on, and when Conci came home, he barely spoke to her and left.

However, New Year's Eve came, and Mike asked Conci if she'd like to go the captain's party with him. She just jumped at the chance to get out as an adult. "Oh yes, Mike. Thank you. I'd love to be with just adults for once," she said and laughed.

They were quiet in the car, but he was a real gentleman and helped her out of the car. Everyone was quite surprised to see them together, although Conci asked Auntie to call Colleen to give her a heads up on it.

Although most everyone was shocked to see

them together, they were quite happy about it. They sat together now and then, but mostly the guys went with the guys and the women with the women.

Madeline called after they'd been there for almost an hour. "Hello, lover, I rushed back to town just to be able to spend New Year's Eve with you, darling. I'm at the airport right now. Come and get me, and I'm all yours." Mike got a little excited, but his anger was stronger than his lust this time.

"No, Maddy, I waited for you at the airport like a fool, and now I'm at a party with my wife and if she'll have me, I'm going back to her. You've shown me how little you care for me, so bug off, woman," he said nastily and hung up, feeling quite good about himself, and that surprised him.

With his chest stuck out, he went back into the party room and found his wife and grabbed her and danced with her, holding her as close as her very big stomach would permit. He laughed at the increased girth of her stomach and kissed her softly on the lips. "I love you, Conci," he said. "I realized tonight that I really do love you." He said it more to convince himself than her, but she took it as a peace offering and really she needed him with her, at least for now.

Conci smiled, and they kissed. Monty saw

them and began to clap, and that was followed by a thunderous applause as everyone in the room clapped for them. Both of them stopped and stared and then burst out laughing. It was a very joyful time for all of them.

chapter XXVII
a new lease on life

Mike took Conci home that night, and they spoke about the evening. "I want to come back, Conci. I want to come back," he said humbly. "I know I hurt you this time worse that the other times, but this is the last time, believe me."

"I still love you, Mike, but I'm too hurt this time to start over again. I'm just too hurt and scared. This is the pattern of our married life, and it really is tearing me apart. When you brought Madeline on your arm that night at the roast for the chief, I was so broken. I can't even explain it to you. This time the deep went too far, Mike, and I'm still not healed from it." She began to sob and cry.

Mike stopped the car and pulled over to the side of the road and began to cry too. "I can't make it without you, Conci. Please give me this one last chance."

"If I do, Mike, we have to go to a counselor, and you're only here on probation. Will you agree to that?" He nodded his ahead, and she began to hold onto her back. Conci began to have some really good labor pains. As they arrived home, she was still holding her back.

"Are you all right, sweetheart?" he asked, concerned.

"I must be going into labor, Mike. It's about a month early, but that's still within the parameters of all right," she said. As she took off her beautiful outfit, her water broke, and she stood there quite upset.

"Mike, Mikey, I'm really getting some hard pains. Call Ollie, please," she pleaded. He ran into the room and saw the mess on the floor and helped her into the shower, and as she washed up, he called the doctor.

"How close are they, Conci? Ollie wants to know."

"They are coming together very fast. Tell him there are only a few minutes between them."

She heard Mike on the phone.

"Okay, I'll hurry her up."

"Get out of there, Conci." He insisted then hurriedly dried her off and helped her into her clothes and took her suitcase. He knocked on Sister's door, and she got up sleepily. "Conci is in labor, Auntie. Call Maureen, and she'll come and help you. We'll call you from the hospital."

Sister quickly got her holy oil and anointed Conci and kissed her. Just then Conci screamed and lay down on the sofa, and Mike just watched her.

"We have to go, honey."

"No, Mike, the baby is coming now." She took off the necessary items, and he helped her and then saw that the baby was crowning.

"Auntie," he said, his voice aquiver, "get me some clean towels quickly. Okay, honey, now just try to relax." Mike helped her as she grunted and whimpered, trying not to yell too loud and awaken the children.

Sister was mesmerized by the process and galvanized into action, getting the towels and holding Conci's hand as she labored.

"Don't panic, sweetheart," Mike said, his heart racing. As he prayed out loud for guidance from the Lord, Sister joined him and slowly, he delivered his baby daughter and tied the cord with his hands sweating and covered with blood and shaking and then kissed his wife.

As he gently put his finger into the baby's mouth to pull out a plug of mucous, she began to cry loudly and turned all red.

"Mike you did it. You delivered our little girl."

"You're a real policeman, Mike, able to take

care of any emergency," Sister said and kissed him on the cheek.

Mike smiled proudly and gave the baby to Sister who wrapped her in a clean towel and put her into Conci's arms, after he tied and cut the cord.

Mike called the doctor, "She gave birth already, Ollie, and I delivered the baby and tied the cord, but you need to send someone to help us. I'm exhausted, and so is she. I didn't have any gloves on or anything." He sighed and then looked at his wife's beatific face and knew they were going to be all right.

In fifteen minutes Ollie arrived with a nurse and an ambulance and looked at Mike's handiwork and shook his hand. "Good job, McVey. You're a true cop," he said and smiled.

Mike left the room at this time and took the baby with him. He rocked her while the nurse and Ollie took care of Conci.

"Let's take them to the hospital and see that they're all right, and if so, they can probably come back home tonight, or stay the night, whichever they prefer," Dr. Oliver continued as he leaned over and kissed Conci on the cheek. "You're a real Hebrew woman, Conci."

She thanked him and smiled. So, that's how it was, and Mike stayed all night with Conci and the baby. "Mike, I have a special gift for you, honey."

"What is it, baby? You gave me a sweet little girl. That's all I want, that and your love."

"This baby is very special to you, Mike, because you delivered her. I know you won't put her above Moira and Sonny, though. They're special to you too."

"Oh, honey, I would never favor her over them. No way!"

"Okay, then my gift is that you get to name this baby whatever you want, even Rhonda if that's your choice," she said sweetly.

Mike closed his eyes, knowing he didn't deserve this gift at all, repenting in his heart for even thinking about not wanting this child. *Oh Lord*, he said within himself, *please forgive me for that bad evil attitude.*

"No, honey, thank you. If I get to name her, I'll name her Concetta Maureen the way you wanted and call her Little Mo."

Conci just stared at him, completely confused. Mike looked her directly in the eyes and smiled at her, having nothing to hide. Conci saw that and returned his smile. "Really? That amazes me. I thought you'd want that above everything else."

He shook his head.

"No, this is our baby, yours and mine, and

Rhonda's time is over. What I had with her is private to her and me, and what I have with you is private to us alone too, sweetheart. I'm sorry I got them all mixed up," he explained lovingly. Mike put his arms around her. "Thank you. I won't goof this time."

chapter XXVIII
what are you
doing, conci?

Conci recuperated at home with the new baby, and Mike was right there helping her. Sister was reluctant to believe he was as serious as he claimed and reserved her wholehearted support of him until he proved himself to her. It annoyed her that Conci immediately not only forgave him but reinstated him as head of the household and gave him all the honor she felt was due to him while telling her aunt he was there only on probation and that they would go to a counselor very soon.

But Sister kept her own counsel and only shared it once with Maureen, who had her reservations too.

"I feel the same way, Sister, but I don't want to put doubt in Conci's mind and burst her bubble. It's not as though this was the first time he's done this. I'm vacillating between seeing her as a real fool or admiring her for her tenacity and beautiful forgiving spirit."

Sister nodded. "It's so difficult for me, Maureen, to act like this is a new day and the slate is wiped clean as though it never happened. I know that's the way the Lord sees it, but I sometimes disdain Conci for seeing it that way. It's wrong of me, of course."

They both prayed about it, feeling guilty within themselves for even feeling this way and even more for discussing it openly. But once it was aired and spoken, Sister could take a good look at it and wonder not about her niece's propensity for forgiveness, but her own lack.

After the baby was a month old, Sister left for the convent again. Conci was now on her own, but she had the baby on a nice schedule at any rate. She slept for eight hours at a stretch during the night and two and three hours twice a day and sometimes more. Little Mo was a darling baby, and Moira and Sonny were crazy about her.

Loretta couldn't stay away from the baby, and neither could their aunt Maureen.

The McVey household was filled with peace and love again, for Mike seemed to be relishing his role as daddy and husband. Conci still put the twins in the nursery at Signs and Wonders and put the baby in for four hours one day, in anticipation of her returning to work in another two weeks, when her six weeks were up.

So, that day when Mike came home from work at noon unannounced, he was upset that Conci had put all the children into the nursery.

"When I come home, Conci, I want to see my children. Why did you put them into the nursery? So you could run around all day, shopping and playing bridge and following me around?" he asked accusingly.

Conci shook her head.

"I needed to do a dry run, Mike, to get the baby used to being at the nursery, so when I return to work in a couple of weeks, she'll be all right with being there all day long," she explained.

"Oh yeah, I forgot. You're about over your maternity leave. Are you anxious to go back?" he tried to smooth it over.

"No, I'm not looking forward to it at all, Mike. It will be physically more difficult. You know my wish is that I get to stay home and take care of you and the children," she reiterated.

Mike sat down and drank his coffee as she prepared his leftover lasagna for lunch. "Put that on the back burner, babe. I have some other things to talk to you about."

So that is it then, he is upset about something else, not really the babies being gone. Conci obediently sat down at the table and looked at him expectantly as he chowed down on the lasagna.

"Let me enjoy my lasagna first," he insisted. Conci sat there quietly while he scarfed down two platefuls. Then as she poured him another cup of coffee, he explained his agitation.

"Madeline was picked up by the U.S. officials in Florida for passing counterfeit money. She claimed that she was duped, but unfortunately for her, they also found some special paper that is only made in a remote area of France in her luggage. She denied knowing it was there."

He didn't look at Conci while he told her this tale. She tried to discern his feelings about it all, then just took a sip of her coffee and looked at him expectantly, waiting for more information.

"So, she was in on the smuggling operation after all," Conci finally noted.

Mike nodded his head. "I was really surprised about it all, never really believing Cartellini's story that they thought the model that got away was her," Mike continued and sighed as though the weight of the whole world was upon his shoulders. He was quiet for a long while, sipping on his coffee and refreshing both his and her cups. Finally, he got up from the table.

"So, Mike, how does this affect you, personally or professionally?" Conci finally asked.

He sat down again.

"I don't know, Conci. It just irks me that I was so duped by her, and it reflects badly on my judgment."

Conci was relieved that he was thinking about it negatively in that way.

"She called me this morning wanting my help," he continued, frowning at her.

"She had a real nerve to do that, Mike." Conci was getting a little upset about now.

Mike heard the inflection in her voice. "No, it's not like that at all. I have no more feelings for her and really am upset that she hasn't left me alone and wants to pull me into her quagmire again, not for my benefit but entirely for her own." His voice was filled with anger and resentment.

Conci remembered the faces she saw in her dreams. One of them was Madeline's. Was she involved in Conci's little adventure at Second Chance? Conci just sighed.

"What did she want from you, Mike?" Conci finally asked the question that was now bugging her.

"She wanted me to post bail for her and to help her out of her troubles. She swears that she's innocent and someone else put that paper in her luggage."

"What happened to her relationship with

Fred Lawrence? Why would she call you instead? I thought they were having the affair of the century," Conci insisted.

Mike just looked up at her, surprised. "Lawrence? How do you figure that?"

Conci didn't know how she knew about it, but indeed she did know. She shrugged. "I just know it, Mike. I just know it. That's all."

"You're way off base, Conci. I never heard nor ever saw anything between them," he insisted, getting a little annoyed at her accusations. He got up and stretched and yawned. "I'm going to take a nap. I'm really beat, honey. Forget about what I said about Madeline. It has nothing to do with us personally or our relationship. I'm completely over her and only feel angry and upset that she'd bother me like that," he said honestly, and Conci discerned he was telling the truth.

Then he looked at her with that special look in his eyes. "If you're a little tired, why don't you join me?" Conci smiled and thought that was a good idea.

As it turned out, Madeline jumped bail, fled the city, and no one could find her.

"Good thing you stayed away from her, McVey," Monty congratulated him.

"Listen, Monty, I even told Conci about it all. Believe me I didn't want to get involved with that mess again." His voice and manner were sincere, and Monty noted that with a sigh of relief.

"You two back together for good this time, McVey?" Monty asked him roughly.

He nodded his head. "Conci has me on probation and said I hurt her more this time than at any other time, and she's afraid to just accept me back like before. We're going to a counselor here starting in another month too, Monty, after the baby is at a better age and Conci feels all right about leaving her with a baby sitter."

"Good man, Mike. Good man." He slapped Mike on the back proudly.

Conci, however, decided to not return to school until her eight weeks that she was allotted were up instead of going back in six weeks as she originally planned. She really needed the time alone for a while. Then after she'd drop off the children and get them safely and comfortably ensconced in their nursery room, she would go to the Second Chance Academy and look around, retracing her steps, along the path that she saw in her dreams. After some searching, she finally found the tree that had a really gnarled branch that she saw in her dreams. But, she could find nothing else.

So, this was the third day she'd done that and finally left after a few hours, not wanting to be seen by anyone. She did her shopping and went to a huge copy center to get some copies for the classroom. When she entered the store, a smell assailed her nose, and she suddenly knew what the smell was that she'd noted in the woods or somewhere. Printing—it was the smell of printer's ink. Suddenly all the memory returned, and she saw herself finding the trapdoor in the woods, opening it up, putting on her very bright flashlight, and seeing the stairs that went way, way down, then feeling a sting and seeing the faces in front of her momentarily: Lara Connors, Madeline, and Lt. Fred Lawrence.

She hurriedly did her copying and drove straight to the Second Chance Academy and called her husband on her cell.

"Yeah, Conci, what's up?" His voice held his usual surly undertones.

"Mike, I remembered what happened to me," she said very excitedly.

"What are you talking about, woman? I don't have any time for this, Conci. Say it quickly and spare me the never-ending background stories," he growled.

"Remember when I lost my memory at Second Chance?"

"Yeah, so what?"

"I just remembered everything, Mike. I found a trapdoor on the ground in the woods by Second Chance and opened it up and flashed my flashlight in it and saw stairs that went down, down, down. Then I felt a sting and turned and saw momentarily, three faces. The three faces I've been dreaming about: Madeline, Lawrence, and Lara." She was out of breath now, and Mike was barely listening to her.

"Yeah, yeah, yeah, so what?"

"Did you hear me, Mike? There's a subterranean place below the basement at Second Chance."

"So what, Conci? Zurich's the one on that case. Now leave me alone, will you. I'm so darn busy," he said and hung up.

Conci just stared at the phone. "What a jerk," she said out loud to relieve her feelings.

Just then Mike called back. "I'm sorry, baby, to be so crabby. I love you, honey, please believe me. I'm just so darn busy. Where do all these murders come from? Is that the only crime people are committing these days? Joey and them aren't near as busy with burglary. Everyone's killing each other. It's really distressing. So please excuse me, sweetheart. Please," he emphasized.

Conci was so pleased he'd called back. "Okay,

Mike, I'll try to understand, and I'm so glad you called me back. It means a lot to me. I love you too, sweetheart." She prayed for a few minutes, asking the Lord for protection and also for direction on whom to contact about this.

In the end, she called the big Irishman, the Secret Service agent, Toby Sullivan, who had already gone back to Dallas, the guy who'd sent her that beautiful Christmas card that she couldn't find and wondered if Mike had taken it.

"Hey Conci. How are you, darlin'?" he asked, sounding delighted to hear from her.

"I'm just great, Toby. I had a little girl, and Mike delivered her. Can you imagine that?"

"Wow, that's really something? You still living with him? I heard you were going to get a divorce. In fact I was looking forward to it," he said, rather disappointed. "I said as much in my Christmas card to you, honey," he said sweetly.

"I know, Toby, and I appreciated it more than you can possibly know. I think Mike must have found the card and read it because he has been so very nice to me and wants to reconcile. But I will do it only if we go to a counselor on a regular basis. I'm really tired of living walking on eggshells, Toby. Your love and support has been invaluable in helping me to be strong about it all. I do thank you."

"I wish it could be different, Conci. You know that."

"I need to talk to you about something professional, agent Sullivan," she said and laughed.

"Oh?"

They talked for a while and Conci told him about the subterranean rooms below the basement of Second Chance Academy.

"No kidding? So, there is something strange going on there. Call Zurich up, and I'm on my way. Thanks, doll. Thanks a lot."

So she called Lt. Sammy Zurich. He was quite polite to her on the phone and asked her to come into his office. Conci wanted to avoid the police station so she met Lt. Zurich at a coffee shop.

Conci was already ensconced in the booth when Zurich arrived. She motioned for him to come over to the booth, and he complied.

"Hello, Conci. How nice to see you," he said in his best polite voice.

Conci passed on the niceties and cut right to the chase. "The reason I wanted to meet you here, Sammy, is because I told this whole thing to my husband a little earlier on the phone and he said you're the one to call about it. This is really important, Lieutenant," she said and began right away without any preamble to tell him her tale.

Sammy listened wide-eyed and wondered

about this lovely woman sitting across from him. When she finished, she studied his face for a full two minutes.

"I see that you have your doubts about me, Lieutenant. So, if you wish, let's go right now to the place, and I'll show you exactly where it is," she insisted. "By the way, I called Secret Service agent Toby Sullivan, and he's coming back here today or tomorrow to work with you," she said casually. He turned to look at her.

Sammy nodded his head and followed her to the Second Chance Academy, then into the woods, and sure enough just where she indicated, there was a trapdoor. He looked at her rather astonished.

"You didn't believe me, did you?" she asked him softly.

He opened the trapdoor and flashed his own light down there and saw the stairs. He called for backup, and within five minutes three cop cars drove up to the spot, driving right on the grass of the field.

They got out quietly and knelt behind Lt. Zurich. Conci just stood back and watched them do their stuff. He had already forgotten all about her in his haste to get the other police there with him. They went down into the cavern quietly and cautiously, with Zurich leading the pack. A few of the officers were standing nearby and spotted Conci but saw that she was with Zurich.

After a long period of time, an hour or so, Zurich surfaced. "There's a whole operation of printing going on down there," he reported. Soon, more cops and the crime scene investigators came to get fingerprints.

Conci had already gone to her own car and driven home, knowing that they had found the counterfeiting equipment.

Arrests were made and the stuff confiscated by the police, and never was there ever a mention made of Conci McVey's involvement. And she was gratified but still perplexed because Zurich never got in touch with her again about it all, not even to thank her.

"It never fails to surprise me, Auntie," she told her aunt after a few days, "how arrogant the police are about their own sometimes inept discernment about things. I was grateful that Zurich never mentioned me but surprised that he didn't even thank me. But that's the way it is with them," she said. Sister agreed.

Although Conci told Zurich about Fred Lawrence and Lara Connors and Madeline O'Reilly being there and giving her the shot and what she remembered them saying, none of the three were arrested. Indeed, she didn't even hear that they were interrogated. There were, however, many arrests made of the board of directors at Second Chance.

Conci wondered about all that. *Why didn't they move on that information? Were they waiting for something or someone? Maybe none of these were the brains behind the operation.*

Was Toby Sullivan here in town, and what was his part in the arrests? *He didn't get in touch with me if he was, and all his blarney was just that,* she thought, *just blarney.* Then she chastised herself for those thoughts. *You're a married woman, and those thoughts are beneath you, girl. Straighten up and rebuke any thoughts of him.*

Two weeks had passed since the operation was discovered, and although some arrests were made, none were of the three people that Conci saw.

So, she carefully and cautiously approached Mike one night about it all. "I need to talk to you, Mike, about something important." She told him what she'd done after he ignored her information that one day.

"So you're saying that Zurich met you and even followed you and you showed him where to look? Really, Conci, is that the truth? Of course it is because you told me about it first. Sorry, babe, I forgot all about it. So you're telling me that Zurich never even mentioned you or even called you and thanked you or even followed up on your information about the three people you saw?" He looked at Conci searchingly and saw only a sweet-natured, very honest and very astute person who was perplexed about the whole thing.

"I never wanted any kudos, you know that, Mike. But I just wondered why he never moved on my information. They never even questioned me again or anything. It was as though I was out of it completely. What an ego he must have." She sighed for the fourth time.

Mike just shook his head. "That really surprises me, Conci. What exactly do you want me to do?"

"I'd like you to find out if they even questioned Lawrence, Lara, and Madeline about the whole thing. I promise I won't do or say anything to anyone. Just find out for me so I'll know what they're doing and how to feel about Sammy Zurich," she said.

Mike agreed and got a hold of the files and studied them. Sure enough there were no questions toward those three people, and Mike also thought it was darned odd. So, he ventured into Monty's office and told him the whole tale.

Monty just shook his head. "Maybe we should put her on the payroll, Mike. Yes, that would be to our advantage," he said, believing the whole story because he knew Conci very well.

Monty went right over to Conci's house and interviewed her. "Why didn't you call me, Conci?" He wanted to know right up front.

"I didn't want to go over Mike's head, Monty. You can understand that. He all but ignored me, and I was up a tree and thought that he would be livid with rage against me if I called on you for help. So I called the Secret Service agent first, even though it could be trouble for the McVeys, then called Lt. Zurich."

"Really?" Monty asked, perplexed. Then he got it. *So that's why Sullivan only stayed a few hours this time and seemed to want to wrap his part up right away. Does he have a little crush on Conci? Why not, she is a beautiful woman, and a clean, sweet woman with a lot of class and a stupid husband who doesn't appreciate her enough.*

"Okay, Conci, you're off the hook; now you tell me the whole story. Mike already told me what he knows; now you tell me the rest, please," he said sweetly.

Conci told the whole thing and was almost breathless at the end.

"You're really something, Conci. Yes, you're really something."

Monty called Zurich in later and talked with him and asked for full details about the case. "How did you know to look for the hidden trapdoor, Sam?" he asked like a tiger getting ready to pounce on his victim.

"I just had a hunch."

"Oh, a hunch given to you by Conci McVey? What's going on, Zurich, and how come you didn't interview the three people she told you were there when she got drugged?"

"Oh, Captain, I thought that was a figment of her imagination and she saw that after she got the shot," he said nonchalantly, hoping it would fly. It didn't.

"I want those people interviewed, and as of right now, you're off the case."

"Why, Captain, why am I off the case?"

"Because this sounds like some kind of collusion between you and these people that you failed to interview. You know, Sammy, that it would be policy to follow any lead." He stared angrily at Zurich, who sat down and closed his eyes.

"I thought she was trying to get publicity for

herself, and I was the one who worked on this case for a long time and got nowhere. Then this woman comes up to me and gives me the answer," he said in a pouty voice.

"Okay, Zurich, if you apologize to her and go after these three people, I'll reinstate you," Monty said really not wanting to lose one of his good men.

The first thing Zurich did was to get a hold of Conci McVey. "Conci, I need to see you right away," he said in his most professional voice.

Conci just sighed. "Look, Lieutenant, I have about two hours free at noon. That's the only time for me. I'll meet you at school."

"No, I want to see you at the Razor Sharp Coffee house. At twelve then," he commanded.

"Sorry, Lieutenant, I can't leave the premises of the school. It's either here or nowhere," she said just as adamantly.

He decided to go to the school and interview her. He gingerly walked into the classroom and looked around. Conci was sitting at her desk working on the computer.

She got up and smiled at him when he entered the room.

"Hello, Lieutenant," she said softly.

"I need to apologize to you, Conci, on the one hand, and on the other hand, I really resent that you found the entrance to the underground counterfeiting room when I worked on the case for so long."

"Sorry, Sammy, but I was the one who was given some shot to make me forget things. It bothered me for a long time. I had to know the answer. Actually I called my husband first when my memory came back." She told him the story.

"Oh, so it was the smell of ink. Isn't that something? I'll put it into the file that you were the one who gave me the tip. All right?"

"I am sincere in not wanting the credit, Sammy. You can have it all. I just wanted a decent thank you or at least to have interviewed me again on the basis of the other information I had about the three faces I saw before I blacked out," she said, staring at him.

He lowered his eyes. "Sorry, Conci. Really. It was rude of me and very childish. Can we just forget it and you forgive me and go on with their investigation? Any information that you have or can dig up to help me would be appreciated."

"Thank you," she sighed.

"Monty almost took me off the case, because it seemed like some kind of collusion to him. I'm really upset about that part of it. Does Mike get upset with you when you're involved in a case?" he asked, suddenly getting an insight.

She nodded. "Unfortunately, yes. So it really behooves me to keep it quiet anyway, Sammy. So you see my desire is heartfelt." She smiled at him, and he loved the look of her smile.

McVey is a really lucky guy, he thought. His own marriage was humdrum now, and although he wasn't a skirt chaser, he was involved at the moment.

Conci looked up at him as though she heard his thoughts. "Your marriage will never get better if you have someone else, Sammy. Believe me from a person who's looking at it from the other side, the side of the injured wife. It hurts me so much when Mike cheats on me and then gets angry with me too. Monty says that there's a certain excitement and challenge in knowing this wife is it and this is as good or as bad as you make it yourself. It can even be intimately stimulating, having the one lover. He's told Mike that a few times, and Mike told me."

Sammy just stared at Conci. "How did you know?"

"I don't know, Sammy, I just did. I'm not judging you, believe me. We all have fallen short of the glory of God and are sinners saved by grace."

Sammy just kept looking at her.

Suddenly, he saw his wife, Dora, on her knees

praying about him and their relationship. "I love him so, Lord, please bring him back to me. Show me how to make our life more exciting for him."

Just as suddenly as it started, the vision stopped.

Sammy was in his car driving, thinking about it, after leaving Conci's house in a tizzy. He just got up and left without saying another word.

In his office, he sat and twiddled his thumbs as he thought about his marriage. He and Dora had been married for fifteen years and had three children. Lucy was fourteen and the reason they got married in the first place. Dora was three months pregnant. He was just about ready to break up with her too, as he found another woman that he had started to date. But now he was trapped.

For the most part, Dora was a good wife, and he really did love her. And they had two more children, Sammy, Jr., age twelve and Nancy Louise, age six, who was the apple of her father's eye.

Their relationship had never been a wild abandoned thing, except at the beginning. Now, it was a calm, serious affair with ups and downs. He thought about what he saw and wondered if that was a vision or what. Conci McVey seemed to know a lot about his situation, and it bothered him.

Sammy went to a florist and bought some roses, which his wife liked, and brought them home. She was busily ironing some clothes when he got home. She looked droopy to him and her hair was getting gray and she had put on some weight, but he tried to see her when they first got involved. He had been so crazy about her.

"Hi sweetheart. These are for the exciting woman that I love," he said and took her into the bedroom, and they rekindled their love. He held her afterward, and she was delighted with him.

After he left, she went to the beauty shop and had the gray in her hair washed away and got some new clothes. When he came home that night, he was greeted by a lovely looking woman who looked ten years younger. They had their close passionate affair after that. She lost weight and exercised with him. Soon, peace and joy reigned in their household. Sammy dropped his little girlfriend, and that was that.

Later, when he saw Conci McVey at the police station, he went up to her and kissed her on the cheek and held onto her. "Thank you. Thank you.

Thank you," he said, and she smiled at him. They were great friends after that.

chapter XXIX
lt. zurich

As for now, the next day Zurich began to question the three people whose faces Conci remembered. Lara Connor was out of town and, in fact, ministering in Africa with her husband. So that would have to wait.

Madeline O'Reilly had jumped bail, and no one seemed to know where she was hiding. However, Zurich passed by her opulent condo one day and saw a red Cadillac convertible parked in the driveway next to her Mercedes.

He decided to just drop in, and he rang the bell. Finally after the fifth ring, she answered the door. "Ms. Madeline O'Reilly." He showed her his badge. "I tried to call but no one answered," he lied.

"I can't talk to you now, Lieutenant," she said and held her jaw as though it hurt.

"Sorry, ma'am, but this is in regard to an attempted murder and to a counterfeiting scam, and you were found to have some counterfeit bills a few months ago in your possession. Also, you jumped bail, and that is an arrestable offense.

"I already have an officer here questioning me, Lieutenant, so I really don't need to have two." He forcefully walked into the house, pushing open the door, and she had to let him in. She showed him into the living room where Lt. Fred Lawrence was sitting and making notes.

"All right, Lieutenant, but make it brief," she said angrily.

"Hello, Fred, what are you doing here?"

"I'm questioning her on the attempted murder of Conci McVey. That's what I'm doing here. How about you?"

"About the same incident but in so far as it relates to the counterfeiting operation," he said and wondered about Lawrence. *Why is he here? Isn't he involved?* Zurich asked himself.

Conversation with her proved almost fruitless, and she was quite upset that she was being questioned in this way.

"I was on a plane on the way to Sweden during that time," she angrily told him in answer to the question of where she was on the day Conci was attacked.

"Oh? Give me the particulars on that, please," he insisted.

Finally, she capitulated.

"I'll call the airlines, Zurich," Lawrence said helpfully and found out she wasn't on that plane at all.

"Well, maybe it was another day. You've confused me, Lieutenant," she said, pouting.

"I have witnesses that you were there, Ms. O'Reilly," Zurich bluffed.

He was a good poker player, Lawrence noted.

Finally, she began to cry. "All right, I was there giving some kind of workshop to those ugly teachers. None of them even know how to dress most of the time. Really, what a bunch of droopy women," she said with real disdain.

"All right, ma'am, I'm bringing you down to the police department for more questioning and for jumping bail."

Madeline looked hopefully to Fred, who was into protecting himself at this juncture of the game.

"You'd better go, Miss," he said with authority.

She lowered her head, and Zurich brought her in for questioning, wondering why and how Lawrence had so much control over her. He soon got a writ to search her house for any counterfeit money, after she was taken to jail. Her lawyer came quickly.

Fred Lawrence then left, relieved that Madeline had gone along with his lie to Zurich. *I need to be more careful for sure,* he thought. In reality he hadn't been passionate to her at all, only kissing her once when he came into the house. He really did want to see her, but more for professional reasons. *I need to leave her alone. If only I could,* he lamented.

Monty was the one who called Lawrence in after talking to Zurich.

Yes, I'll question him. It's very strange him turning up here and there, at the carnival, at Ms. O'Reilly's condo, and in Conci's recollection of her being attacked.

"Sit down, Lawrence, and let's chat for a while." Lawrence sat as instructed. "Were you on the premises of the Second Chance Academy at any time in recent weeks?" Monty asked him bluntly.

Fred looked at him with surprise. "Yes, I was there at the carnival, and you know about that. No other time was I at or near there."

"Well, Conci McVey says she saw you and Lara Connor and Madeline O'Reilly together when she was given the shot at the school."

Fred looked at him with surprise. "Well, she's wrong, Captain. She's wrong. I wasn't there, and why would I be hanging around with Madeline O'Reilly? And who the heck is the other woman anyway?" he asked sounding quite innocent, yet slightly defensive.

"She's the wife of a famous minister, Rev. Johnny Bob Connors, and is a minister in her own right. Do you know her?"

He shook his head. "No, of course not. How would I know her? I'm not a church-going kind of guy, Captain. What is all this anyway? You're taking the word of a woman who was *supposedly* given a shot and lost her memory? Now it's come back and you're accusing me of giving her the shot? Is that it?" Fred was sounding outraged at the suggestion.

Monty just looked at him closely and stared at him for a good two minutes. "Okay, Fred, you can go," he said, and Fred just sat there.

"No, Captain, I'm really not satisfied with this interrogation. Is the woman maligning me and casting aspersions on my professional life? I don't like that at all. I only met the woman once, and I don't even remember where or when. Why would she be so malicious about me? I never hurt her in any way." Fred acted indignant and outraged at Monty's suggestions.

"Well, if you're innocent, Fred, then I

apologize, but if you're guilty, I'll throw the book at you," Monty said, and they shook hands.

Zurich was not one to be put off. He devised a plan to get Connors back into town so he could question her properly. First, he needed the cooperation of a few of the teachers and the principal at the Academy of Signs and Wonders.

"Pave the way for me, will you, Conci?" Zurich asked her in a friendly way. She agreed and talked to Halperan about Zurich and his desire to question Lara Connors.

"Laura had a strange feeling about her too, Conci. I'm sorry to say that I just dismissed her ideas. Now I think it was Holy Spirit inspiration, and she gets an apology from me tonight." Leo confided in Conci.

So, the next day Zurich went to see Leo Halperan. They hit it off right away. "Any friend of Conci's has to be a valuable person, Lieutenant. Yes, I'm very glad to meet you."

Sammy Zurich liked the man in front of him and felt to tell him about how Conci helped his marriage.

"Are you saved, Lieutenant? Do you believe that Jesus is Lord?" Leo asked boldly. Sammy was taken back and stared at Leo and then for some reason answered him.

"Well, I was brought up as a Christian, but being a cop for many years has jaded me, Dr. Halperan."

"Leo! Please call me, Leo," he asked and took Zurich's hand, and before he could protest, Leo was leading the man in a confession of faith.

Suddenly Zurich felt good from his head to his toes. Those headaches that plagued him were instantly gone, and he was able to breathe better and actually felt the desire to quit smoking. It was almost like a physical thing.

"Thank you, Leo, thank you," he said over and over again.

"It's not me, Lieutenant. It's the Lord," Leo kept saying.

Finally, they got to the reason Zurich was in Leo's office.

Leo nodded his head in agreement. "Yes, a little subterfuge for a good cause is all right, especially to help the police. We have a yearly women's conference coming up in a couple of weeks or so. Although we already have some speakers planned, we can ask Mrs. Connors to be our main speaker, asking her to fill in at the last minute. Let's see if that will fly." However, he had some second thoughts but then justified it in his own mind. *It won't really be subterfuge because we do have speakers every now and then and the women would be delighted to have her speak here.*

Within a couple of weeks, Rev. Johnny Bob and Lara Connors came back into the city. Both Zurich and Sullivan were on hand to greet her at the airport and question her about her whereabouts the day that Conci was attacked.

"Well, isn't that the most ridiculous thing you ever heard of? I for one will not stand for the brutality of the police." She was enraged and wouldn't even sit down for them to talk to her.

"Call our lawyer, Johnny Bob," she commanded her husband. He did so right away.

"Listen, Mrs. Connors, this is just an interview, and we would appreciate your cooperation. Were you on the premises of the Second Chance Academy on the day indicated to you?"

"No, I was not. I was out of town with my husband."

The Reverend Connors had just returned from his phone call to the lawyer and looked rather perplexed at his wife. Sullivan caught it right away.

"Is that incorrect, sir?" Sullivan asked him quickly.

The reverend got upset and confused and just shook his head. "Nothing, Officer, nothing. I just can't imagine you asking my wife these questions. She was with me, of course."

"Where?" Zurich rushed in with his question.

"Oh, in Zimbabwe, I think. It was so long ago."

"Only a month or so ago, sir," Zurich answered and eyed the reverend with a suspicious look at him now. Johnny Bob got quite concerned and moved about. "Give us a contact person, and we'll check it out, sir," Zurich said.

Lara just stared at him. Reverend Connors was the one who broke first. "Look, sir, my wife is a little confused about things, and so am I. The date you mentioned, I was in Zimbabwe, but my wife was in the states. Remember, Lara, you wanted to stay here in fact to visit with your cousin for a while?" He turned to his wife.

She just shook her head violently. "You've got the wrong date, Johnny Bob. You're the one that's confused. Now shut up," she said angrily.

Johnny Bob sat up straight in his chair and frowned at her. "I know I should have stopped you when you went on those shopping sprees and going to those expensive jewelers and coming home with bracelets encrusted with diamonds and rubies. For heaven's sakes, Lara. Where did you ever get the money to buy those? Your daddy wouldn't have sent you those kinds of things. He has been flat broke for a long while. Now tell these gentlemen what's going on. I certainly have no idea."

"You, you hypocrite, you heretic. That's all you ever thought about was yourself and your fame. When was it ever going to be enough fame for you? Popularity, being seen with the best people. You didn't care about the Gospel. No, your gospel was one of riches and being in power and fame. That's all you cared about was if people knew you and adulated you. Fame, fame, fame. That's all I ever wanted too was to be famous with you, but you always overshadowed me. I was the one who brought you into a famous preaching family, and then you took it all away from my daddy. You coveted his fame too.

"You convicted everyone else of their sins, and yet you were the biggest one of all. Fame was your sin, yes; your search for fame was one of the deadly sins, maybe the biggest of all. So shut your mouth about anything having to do with me," she said hatefully and to the surprise of both officers present. Zurich thought to step in but thought better of it when he realized they might be getting somewhere.

Johnny Bob began to cry. "It's not true. I

always loved the Lord. I wanted to stop, but she's right. The fame was so great, and I didn't want to give it up. But I never defrauded anyone. No, I was always sincere in my love of the Lord. I did and do love Him. I just got greedy and wanted to be known and loved and to be first on the airplanes and given the best suites in the hotel and the best cars. I was first class all the way, and didn't want to give that up. Everyone knew me by sight. 'There's Rev. Johnny Bob; Oh, Johnny Bob, we love you,' they'd shout. Oh God, forgive me," he cried and got on his knees in front of everyone and crawled over to his wife and put his head on her lap and cried like a baby with his shoulders heaving up and down. Zurich looked with alarm at Sullivan, who just shrugged his shoulders.

Lara Connors patted her husband on his head. "You see, gentlemen, I have nothing to do with your counterfeiting ring. You can prove nothing, and I'm innocent of everything. We are both staying completely quiet until our lawyer arrives," Lara said very poised and cool.

Just then the phone rang. "Your lawyer has arrived," Zurich said, and they let Mr. Angelo Dukakis into the room.

"Do you have any proof about this, Lieutenant, or are you just fishing?" the lawyer asked in his usual pedantic, lawyer way after hearing the reason for the inquiry.

"I just want them to stay in town for a couple of days while we clear this matter up," Zurich said with authority. They all agreed and everyone left.

Afterward Lt. Zurich went to Monty's office, and he called Mike in too and also Melville and Max.

"Looks like Mrs. McVey's report could very well be true, because at least two of the suspects were actually at the school and on the premises between eight a.m. and two thirty p.m. or thereabouts. Lawrence was quite upset and angry that we would accuse him of something like that. Ms. O'Reilly was cool as a cucumber. Mrs. Connors was also quite cool and hateful and then her husband completely broke down though we didn't get anything out of him," Zurich explained.

Mike went home that night still upset at his feelings for Madeline. Conci could tell there was something wrong, but the children were so happy to see their daddy. He had been coming home late for the last few weeks and missing them because they were already in bed.

"Daddy, daddy, I was missing you." Moira jumped into his arms. She was crazy about her daddy, and Mike felt the same way about all three children. Sonny just tapped him on the leg and then hugged his leg. Mike was moved and picked him up too. Little Mo, now three months old, just got all excited to see him and her little arms and legs moved up and down. Mike held her for a long time.

"Wow, what a greeting from my family."

"We all love you with all our hearts, Mike," Conci said lovingly. Mike put the children down and held onto her too. She felt some kind of the need inside him, and she prayed for him.

"Are you all right, sweetheart?" she asked him.

chapter XXX
temptation

He nodded but sadly. "I'm so tired tonight. I just don't feel like talking, Conci," he said in that same depressed voice.

They both put the children to bed, and then he got into his recliner and fell asleep. A little later, he was awakened by the sound of his cell phone. "Yeah, McVey here," he said, a little more surly because he'd been sleeping.

"Mikey, I wish I could have talked to you for a while today. It was so good to see you at the police station. How are you, sweetheart?" she asked him in a saucy voice. Mike took a deep breath. Conci watched him from the kitchen where she was folding baby clothes. She observed his body language, and suddenly, he looked up and saw her staring at him, almost studying him. He got up and took the phone into the bedroom.

"Police business," he explained and closed the door.

Feeling something was wrong, Conci went

upstairs in the attic area that was right above their bedroom and knelt down and listened through the cracks in the ceiling downstairs.

"Yeah, I miss you too, Maddy. But I'm back with my wife, and I can't see you at all anymore. I still have feelings for you too, baby, but it just can't be right now. Maybe someday, but not right now. I'm committed to Conci and the children, and I have to keep my promise. Please, Maddy, don't tempt me like that." Then he laughed. "Well, we'll see if I can even get out tonight without Conci getting suspicious." Then he hung up, feeling that someone was watching him.

Conci was very quiet and waited until he left the bedroom before she crawled out of the attic.

"Conci, where are you?" he called, wondering where she'd gone. Somehow he felt she was watching him and heard him talking to Madeline. *Darn*, he thought. *I wish I didn't have these feelings for her. Please, Lord, take away these yearnings, please,* he begged and pleaded.

Conci came downstairs with some of her spring clothes in her arms.

"Did you call me, honey?"

"Yeah, where were you?"

"In the extra bedroom closet getting my clothes. Why?" She looked at him innocently.

"Oh. Okay," he said and went back to the recliner.

"That was Max. I may have to go out again tonight," his voice didn't sound convincing at all. Conci looked at him.

"Oh?" she said and stared right into his eyes. He saw the look she gave him.

"I had an interesting phone call today too, Mike. It was from Toby Sullivan, and he wanted to come and see me. Wasn't that lovely? But, I knew that if I gave in to my desire to flirt a little that it not only would hurt you, but hurt our marriage and our chance to get together again."

Mike looked up at her, shocked. "What? That darn Irishman full of blarney? He was trying to get with you again? No way, Conci. You and I are together, and we're going to stay that way. I don't even want you to speak to him. No, not ever again," Mike said angrily.

"I feel the same way, Mike. Yes, I feel that if Madeline called you and if you gave in to your baser instincts to see her, our chances of getting together would be null and void. I just wanted you to know that I have temptations too, Mike." She looked directly into his eyes, and fear suddenly filled his mind. *How could she know? Does she know or does she just suspect?*

So, Mike sat in his chair, and he really was so

tired that he fell asleep again. He always had his cell phone out of his pocket and on the chair arm, and Conci quietly and quickly took it off the chair and brought it into their bedroom, so that when it rang about an hour later, she answered it.

"Hello," she said sweetly. Whoever it was hung up, but Conci saw the number and wrote it down. It rang again and again and Conci answered it each time, until it finally stopped several minutes later. Then she put it on the floor by the chair as though it had fallen.

Two hours passed then three hours, and still Mike was asleep. By now it was midnight, and Conci got ready for bed.

Sometime later, Mike got up and had some more coffee and then decided to just go back to bed. Conci made her moves toward him. And they were bonded once again, and she managed to tire him out some more. He fell into a very satisfied sleep and slept all night long until six o'clock when he heard Conci padding around the bedroom.

"You up so soon, baby? What time is it?" he asked sleepily.

"It's six, honey. I have to get ready for school," she said.

"Wait, baby, get back into bed with me and

call in sick. I'll stay home for the day too. I'm just plain tired and need to be with you, honey."

Conci was surprised but pleased and got into bed with him. He held her and loved on her. And he felt so good to be in her arms, and she felt the same.

"I love you, Conci. I hope you know that. It's not like the love I've felt for other women, it's much stronger and deeper and seems to almost make me a physical part of you. It's strange to me. I never felt that with anyone else ever, not even Rhonda." He sighed, and they cuddled and were together again.

Conci felt so good about him and being in his arms.

"Thank you for telling me that, Mike. I love you like that too." Quickly she called in for a sub, then went back to bed.

They stayed in bed until the children got up, and surprisingly they slept until eight o'clock. Conci got up and let her husband sleep some more while she took care of the children, then got them dressed and was going to take them to school when Mike got up.

"No, baby, let them stay home with us, and we'll spend a family day together. I never get to spend a lot of time with them either." Conci smiled at that.

Conci made Mike a big breakfast then took a shower as he watched the children, and then he showered and they all went to the zoo, which the children just loved.

"It's great to be out in the warm air. It's quite balmy today," he commented. They laughed and joked and had a great time that day. Mike was like a young guy with his family. He never let Conci get away from him, though, and held onto her the whole day, either holding her hand or walking with his arm around her.

The day passed pleasantly, and then it was over and life continued as before, except Conci noticed a difference in Mike, a desire to be close to her most of the time. He even called her from work every day and wasn't surly, but sweet most of the time.

Unfortunately, there was no more evidence to hold Rev. and Mrs. Connors, so they were let go with a warning that they might be called back at any time.

Since it was April, it was time for the contracts to be signed for the next year. Conci brought hers home to show Mike that she was getting a raise, which was long in coming.

"Look, honey, I'm getting a raise this year: five

thousand dollars. Isn't that great?" she asked him. Mike looked at her and saw a beautiful woman who was tired and overworked. He knew life was hard for her with a husband who was demanding and sometimes unfaithful and three little children and a full-time job with challenging students and parents and administration. Suddenly he felt her tiredness and went to her and put his arms around her.

"Don't sign it, baby. Stay home for a couple of years and be a full-time mother and wife. Please, I'd love for you to be home when I come for lunch now and then," he said with a smirky smile on his face.

"Take the children to the nursery anyway, but just not as often, maybe twice a week or something like that." Conci just stared at him.

"Oh, Mikey, I'd love to do that. Really, oh honey, that would be my heart's desire," she said and loved on him again.

So Conci talked to Halperan and told him why she wasn't signing the contract.

"I'll miss you, Conci, but I do understand, and I'll make it possible for you to bring the children only two or three times a week. Okay? Then when you're ready to come back to teach, you let me know and I'll make a position for you," he said and they hugged.

chapter XXXI
easter

They had to let the Connors go out of town again because they couldn't get enough evidence against Lara Connor to make any accusation stick. Conci's memory of seeing her at the sight of the counterfeiting setup at Second Chance wasn't enough for them to hold her for any length of time.

Easter was right around the corner, and the McVeys went to the Wileys' house to celebrate the resurrection of Jesus. Sister Conci came on Holy Saturday, and the children were delighted to see her. They colored Easter eggs on Saturday and then went on an Easter egg hunt on Sunday at their aunt Maureen and uncle John's after everyone went to church and ate their dinner.

Mike got to talking with Timmy, curious about his discussion on the Seven Deadly Sins. "Whatever happened to that, Timmy? Did anyone come up with a satisfactory eighth one?" he asked laughingly.

"Yeah, Uncle Mike, almost everyone had an

eighth one, and some even said as many as fifteen. Mrs. Dooley was pleased with our discussions and our research. I told her what you'd said about murder. She said you must really be a clean vessel to be among these great sins and not let any of it come upon you personally." Timmy looked at his uncle with meaning. Mike lowered his gaze.

Conci joined in the conversation. "In Proverbs 6:16–19, it mentions 'these six things doth the Lord hate: yea seven are an abomination unto Him: a proud look, a lying tongue and hands that shed innocent blood, an heart that deviseth wicked imaginations, feet that be swift in running to mischief, a false witness that speaketh lies, and he that soweth discord among brethren.'"

Timmy nodded his head. "Yeah, we saw that and discussed it from every angle, dividing them into categories of sins of commission, involving an action and sins of the heart and the thoughts and the mind," he continued, very pleased with how knowledgeable he was on this subject. Everyone, even his parents and Sister Conci were listening to him with rapt attention.

"That was very clever of you and your class, Timmy," Sister said with admiration.

"The underlying sin in almost every case is pride, Sister. Would you agree with that?" Timmy surprised everyone by taxing Sister on this. His mother looked at him with awe.

Sister nodded ignoring Maureen's gaze. "That's what most theologians think, Timmy. Yes, I would agree with that," she said, smiling at him.

Timmy felt great that Sister admired him and agreed with him.

"I've seen many murders that have been committed, and not all of them have been because of pride," Mike disagreed.

"Tell us about them, Mike, and we'll give you our opinion," Sister offered that challenge to him.

"Oh? So you can show me up in an area of Christian philosophy that I'm not familiar with?" he asked in a hostile manner.

Sister raised her eyebrows. "Really, Michael McVey, what a thing to say. Okay, right there, your reason for saying that was pride, wasn't it?" Sister pressed on. Conci closed her eyes. Maureen saw the gesture and patted her hand.

"All right, how about what's going on now at Second Chance Academy? The first incident was an outright murder and could have hurt more than one person, I might add. How do you figure that was pride?" Mike took up the challenge.

Sister shrugged. "When you capture the murderer then we can discern the proper motive,

Mike. I have some ideas, but I know your pride is so prevalent as to not allow me to do that," her voice was tinged with sarcasm.

"All right, how about the counterfeiting operation? How can that be pride? It's probably greed if anything," he stated assuredly.

Sister nodded her head. "Yes, I do agree with that, Mike. Yes, the underlying sin is greed." She suddenly realized that her niece was sitting there uncomfortably watching her, so Sister just dropped the ball back to Mike.

"All right, then. How about Johnny Cartellini?" he continued to probe.

"Someone wanted him dead because he was getting too close to their counterfeiting operation, or perhaps it wasn't them at all but someone else whose pride wouldn't let Johnny Cartellini live to tell an interesting tale about her," Sister spoke up and raised her one eyebrow, watching Mike closely.

He looked at her and nodded. "It's hard to slip one by you, Auntie. That's for sure. Yes, I've had my doubts in that area too. Thanks for confirming them."

Suddenly Mike was finished with the discussion. "You did a good job, Timmy. Let's continue this another day, though, and not use all our Easter fellowship time discussing it. I for one am ready for some more coffee and pie," he said, getting up and touching his stomach.

Everyone dispersed as though Mike was in charge of the discussions. Timmy just stared at his uncle. Sister took him by the arm and led him onto the patio and he went obediently. Once out of the earshot of everyone else, she explained some things to Timmy.

Conci was discussing the whole case with her aunt a few days after Easter, as they were having their nighttime coffee. Sister loved to have some good dessert with her coffee. Conci made some ricotta Easter pie, which sister loved, and some cannoli, which were a real treat for her. Mike too, loved these pastries.

"Oh, Conci, these cannoli are so delicious. Remember the last time we had cannoli was at the commissioner's fundraiser?"

Conci nodded her head and smiled too. Just then Mike came home, and after greeting them, Conci invited him to join them for coffee and cannoli or pie or whatever he liked.

"That sounds wonderful, Ladies, just let me change into my jeans and sweatshirt." Soon he was sitting down in his recliner and enjoying the dessert and coffee. "You are the best cook and baker, sweetheart. Yes, you are," he said, sighing over his food.

"The last time I had this was at the fundraiser for the commissioner, Mike. I was just telling Conci about that."

"Yeah, that was really something. Bad ending, though."

Conci sat back and saw the whole thing played out in her mind again as though she were seeing a movie. *The chief was holding up the Cici's badge upside down and the gasp from Mary Elizabeth... Wait, that was before he put it right-side up. She was staring at someone at the head table.* "Yes, she was staring at someone and let out a gasp when the chief held up the badge upside down, not when he righted it. What was the badge number, Mike? What was Cici's badge number?" Conci asked, saying her thought aloud, her eyes glassy with excitement.

Mike just stared at her.

"It was 606, Conci. I remembered because it was 909 when he had it upside down, and I thought that was strange," Sister offered.

"Oh my goodness, Mike. We've overlooked something. Please find out whose badge number is 909. That's what Mary Elizabeth was trying to tell us. It was nine something. Nine oh...She just said nine, oh, and stopped and then passed out."

Mike almost jumped up from his chair and called the police station. When he returned, he said, "They're looking it up right now and will call back. You think this is something important?"

"Oh yes, Mike. This will tell us who Mary Elizabeth's killer was. Yes, the poison must have been in the cannoli. Yes, the cannoli. Cici gave her some cannoli, but someone else did too and also knew that Sonny Lopelia had the vial of poison in his pocket."

The phone rang. It was Officer Martinez. "It's an old badge number, never used again, Lieutenant. Only four precincts even used that number. Here are the names: Bertha Dials, Memphis; Darlene Moroney, Hatchehootchie, Texas; Martha Hines, Fueltown, Pennsylvania; and Lara Lawrence, Petersmarket, Alabama."

"Thank you, Officer. Thank you very much."

Mike turned to Conci and Sister and told them. Both were startled.

"Any relation to Fred Lawrence?" Conci wondered.

Mike shrugged.

"Is there a picture of her?" Sister asked excitedly.

Mike got up and put on his jacket. "Can you watch the children for us, Auntie, while I take Conci to the station with me?"

She nodded her head and smiled at him. Conci got ready in five minutes, and they were off.

chapter XXXII
the truth will out

In his office, they went over the old records, and all the pictures were faxed to them. The face looking back at them on the file of Lara Lawrence was that of a much younger Lara Connors. They both pored over it.

> Age: 23—fresh out of the academy two years before.
> Married—to Officer Fred Lawrence

"There it is, Conci, the connection between those two. Married! They were married, for heaven's sakes."

"Look at this, Mike. There was an incident whereby she shot and killed a robber who had killed a little boy and an innocent bystander. She shot and killed the robber, but the bystander lived for a while and was operated on but died before he regained consciousness. There was a complaint from several nurses at the hospital and two doctors that the policewoman would not leave the side of the bystander, and they had to evict her from the operating suite although she pulled a gun on them. They called her supervisor who had to talk to her on the phone, and she finally left the place. They never saw her again. She quit the force after this incident. Now, isn't that interesting? Mary Elizabeth said she'd worked in hospitals in Alabama for four years. Isn't that quite a coincidence?" Conci said as though it was a fact.

"That's enough to arrest her, and we'll see where we go from there," he said and smiled at

Conci, then called Melville and Monty into his office. Max was out of the office on a case.

"Well, gentlemen, look at this," Mike sat back in his chair like the cat who swallowed the canary as they carefully perused the information he'd gleaned.

"So, then she must have been the one that killed April Conover, too. I'll get right on it and see if anyone noticed them talking together at the wake. For heaven's sakes, Lara Connor; a murderer!" Monty sighed. Everyone left the office, but feeling good about unraveling the mystery.

"You want to join me in my office while I talk to Fred Lawrence?" he turned to Conci.

Conci looked quite pleased about it all. "Yes, I'd like to, Mike. Thanks."

"You can't say anything at all, though. Okay?"

"Of course," she said and waited in the office until Mike brought Lawrence in. It was after ten, but Fred happened to be in his office.

"Hello, Conci," he said and sat down tiredly.

"Fred, it's come to our attention that you were married to the former Lara Connors at one time. How was it that you didn't bring that up to us at any time during this investigation?"

"Yes, it's true, and I never thought it was important. She wasn't under any suspicion of anything as far as I could see. We were married quite young and divorced within a year. We were both too young, and we realized it right away. It was nothing, Mike. Believe me," he said, and Conci felt to believe him.

"She left the police force after an incident whereby she killed a robber who had killed a little boy and an innocent bystander. Did you know that? Apparently you were married at the time."

"Yeah, so what? It had nothing to do with me, and she was just doing her job."

"The police received reports that she was a real pest and wouldn't leave the side of the bystander, and they had to almost physically evict her from the operating suite. Were you aware of that incident?"

He just sighed. "Yeah, I knew about it. She was a real nut about some things. That's one of the reasons we parted. She was so devoted to her police work that she all but ignored me," Fred said disgustedly.

"Is that why she left you and married Johnny Bob Connors?" Mike asked in a derogatory way.

Fred just cringed at that question. "For your information, I left her; she didn't leave me." His voice was surly and agitated now.

"Fred, we have reason to believe that she killed Mary Elizabeth Morrison at the commissioner's fundraiser, and perhaps even Sgt. April Conover after the wake," Mike said, watching Fred's face the whole time.

"No kidding? Lara a murderer? No way!"

"But, she could have changed in the years since you've seen her. Or have you kept in contact with her?" Mike pounced on him. Conci admired his style.

"No, I never saw her after our divorce. You're right, maybe she changed. I don't know, Mike. Why involve me in the whole thing?"

Fred turned to look at Conci. "Why is she here, Mike? Why would you have your wife sit in when you're interrogating me about these things?"

"Conci says you were with Lara Connors and Madeline O'Reilly when she discovered the trap-door to the underground area where the counter-feiting ring was located at Second Chance Academy, and someone gave her a shot in her arm, making her unconscious. That's why she's here."

Fred stood up. "You think I'm going to sit here and listen to your wife lie about me. You said yourself that someone gave her a shot and that put her out. So she's confused. Of course she is. She forgot the whole thing. She's confused, Mike."

"Please sit down, Fred. Okay, now what about your being at the carnival when the water moccasin bit McMurray? You seem to be on the spot here and there when something unusual is taking place. Also, Zurich found you at Madeline O'Reilly's condo after she'd jumped bail and he was trying to find her for questioning on another matter, and there you were in her condo, supposedly interviewing her about the attack on Conci," Mike said again. By this time, Mike was in Fred's face.

"I did ask her about it, yes. I did," he said.

"Why didn't you bring her in for jumping bail?"

Mike asked him again. "Too many coincidences, Fred. Yes, too many."

Fred's eyes threw daggers at Conci, and he left the room. Mike just sighed then turned to Conci, "What do you think?"

"You hit a nerve when you talked about her marriage to Johnny Bob Connors. That's the guy she left the lieutenant for. I'll bet on it, Mike, and if you tax the reverend, he'll tell you as much. By the way, Mike. I heard that the two of them have separated. Did you hear that?"

"Who, you mean Johnny Bob and Lara?"

Conci nodded. "Yes, he's in a retreat house repenting to the Lord, and she's gone off somewhere, probably hiding from the law," Conci reported.

"Well, there's a warrant out for her arrest on suspicion of murder, now. We'll have to get her back from there somehow." He sighed in frustration.

"Let's go, baby, you've been a darn good helper today," he said and took her hand and led her out of the station.

They were both quiet on the way home. No more was said about any of it, and both of them fell into bed quite tired.

The next day after Mike had gone to work, Conci and Auntie sat around discussing the preceding evenings events.

"So you think what, Conci?"

"I think that Lara Connors must have killed Mary Elizabeth because Mary Elizabeth suddenly recognized her on the stage when she saw the badge number 909 and knew Lara was the one who'd killed the little boy by accident and then shot and killed the bystander because he saw the whole thing. What happened in their marriage, I have no idea, but he must have loved her a lot or something for her to get him involved in the counterfeiting," Conci thought aloud.

"Wait, Conci what if it's the other way around, and he got her to do this for him because he knew her secret and threatened to reveal it to her husband and she would be ruined."

Conci stared at her aunt.

"Auntie, you've got it. Yes, you've got it. Of course, he was the head of the whole thing. But he couldn't have done this all himself, even with Madeline and Lara helping him. There were too many loose ends. He had to have a partner who had money and clout too."

"Bastriani?"

"Yes, Bastriani. They might have met during

some crime caper or when Lawrence was on narcotics and got together. Perhaps Bastriani held something on Lawrence and persuaded him to help him with this big operation. Then he met the beautiful Madeline, the perfect siren, and she and he fell in love or at least he did and wanted to get enough money to get her away from Bastriani and so he went along with this operation. Then Bastriani warned Fred to leave his wife alone. About that time, Mike met Madeline and they became an item. Although she never seemed to really love him at all, nor he her, but he did find her fascinating. Fred Lawrence must have been quite jealous, and Philly Bastriani wasn't too happy about it either."

They both were quite excited. "But this is all speculation, Auntie. That's what Mike and the other cops would say. How can we find some evidence to that effect?" Both ladies began to pray and cast it over onto the Lord and asked him for a word of knowledge regarding this matter.

As it turned out, Fred Lawrence got in touch with Lara, and soon he was picked up and held there pending further investigation. "Hey, what's this?" he asked, quite upset about the whole thing when

Monty and Mike both took his arm and brought him into Monty's office.

"What's going on here?" Lawrence was livid with rage.

"Did you not know or even think that we might tap your phone, Lawrence? Here you were under suspicion of being an accomplice in this scheme, and you go and call Lara Connors. No one else knows where she is, but you call her on some private line and get a hold of her. What's going on? Quit being angry at us and get angry at your own stupidity," Monty said in his most professional surly cop's voice, which he hardly used anymore.

"You guys got nothing on me. So, I made a phone call to a possible suspect. So what?"

"She was listed not as a possible suspect, Fred, but as a suspect. Now, you'd better come clean or you're in more hot water than just losing your badge and suspension. We're talking hard time here." Monty continued.

Fred just sat there for a while thinking.

"The only thing I'm guilty of is trying to get my ex-wife and the woman that I love out of trouble. That's it, guys. Please believe me. I had nothing to do with the counterfeiting operation and didn't even know about it until that day when Conci McVey went snooping around the grounds of Second Chance Academy. I followed Lara when she left her condo that morning and confronted Lara and Madeline as they quietly walked toward the secret entrance to the subbasement. I saw them go down the secret passageway in the ground and found them halfway down, and they were about to hit me with a bat.

"'Okay, ladies, what's going on?' I flashed my badge at them, and they began to cry. I know it was a woman's bag of tricks, and it didn't sway me. They both assured me they were innocent pawns and that Bastriani had forced them to help him. I bought it because I wanted to believe it. I know that now. So, then we surfaced, and as we left the woods, we saw Conci McVey walking toward the hidden trapdoor to the basement. We doubled back and followed her at a safe distance. Then as she shut the door, Lara quickly injected her in the arm with an instant, yet harmless narcotic, and we dragged her down the stairs. And one of the doctors that was a junkie that I'd help rehabilitate came and gave her a shot of pentathol or something to make her forget.

"Then we brought her back up and put her in another part of the woods. We weren't going to hurt her. I'm amazed the woman found the trapdoor again. What a sleuth she is," he said in grudging admiration. "But that's it, guys. I had no idea that Lara, especially, was so involved in the whole thing."

"How about Madeline?" Mike asked, looking at him straight in the eye.

"Listen, McVey. I wasn't the only one mesmerized with the beautiful Madeline, was I? She told me all about you, too," he said and turned away from Mike.

Monty and Zurich looked at both these men, Zurich thankful that he'd been pulled out of the den of sin and restored and now breathing a sigh of relief, and Monty, who wondered about these two guys. *Both of them are under the spell of Madeline O'Reilly. Is she some kind of witch or a siren or what?* He mulled it over in his mind.

"Turn over state's evidence on the counterfeiting ring, Lawrence, and things will go much easier for you," Zurich counseled him.

"Didn't you hear what I said? I had no part in nor was I privy to any information of that nature. I stayed away from not only the place, but also the women," he said in an angry, surly voice.

"If that's the case, why didn't you inform us somehow about the counterfeiting operation?"

"I wanted to, but first I was trying to extricate Madeline and Lara from the clutches of the Bastriani clam," he grumbled.

Everyone was quiet for a while.

"Is there nothing that you can tell us now?" Monty asked him softly.

He shook his head sadly.

"Then I have no alternative than to take your badge and your gun and suspend you pending a hearing, Fred, and caution you to stay in the city and stay away from the others. You will be under surveillance, and we have a writ to tap your phone. I'm sorry, Fred. I'm so very sorry," Monty said and left the room.

The other two men left hurriedly, with Mike looking at Lawrence with pity in his eyes. *There but for the grace of God, go I,* Mike thought and sighed. "Thank you, Lord, for your tender mercies toward me. Have mercy on Fred, please."

Fred Lawrence left the police station seemingly a broken man, without his badge and without the woman he loved. It was irony. He'd played a dangerous game, and now he had to pay if not at the hands of the cops, then at the hands of the Bastriani who wouldn't like the idea of his being interrogated. *I'm bloodied but unbowed,* he thought. *Yes, I'm still standing.*

Instead of leaving by the main entrance to the police station, he went to the second floor, made a few cell phone calls, and climbed out a window and shimmied down a drainpipe, a huge round gutter type of thing, and hid in the heavily treed area behind the station and waited until dark, and then left. Earlier he'd heard the sound of an explosion and knew it was his car.

"How stupid do they think I am?" he wondered talking softly to himself while walking away from the station. "Pretty stupid, that's for sure, and a real fool, but not that big a fool." He smirked, thankful that he'd called her and told her to come and get his car, and he would call to give further instructions later.

He left by cover of night and joined some of his old informers, a bevy of bums on the edge, and sometimes used as drug runner. They all knew Lawrence and liked him. He got them food and kept them out of jail many a time. He would be safe until it was clear to leave the city.

Mike stood by the ambulance as they put the body of Madeline O'Reilly on a stretcher, covered her, and placed her in the ambulance.

He lifted the cover off her face for a moment just to make sure of a positive ID and then saw that she was almost beyond recognition. Steeling himself against the pain and the gruesomeness, he lifted the cover slowly and took a good long look. She was in terrible shape, all burnt. But he saw a tattoo on her upper left leg, or what was left of it and he knew it was Madeline. Her red hair was there too, all right.

He got into his car and drove off. That was all he could stand of it. *What happened? How was it that she was in Lawrence's car? Were the Bastriani's upset because we called him in for interrogation. Did they think he'd talk? So, then how or why did Madeline get into Lawrence's car?* Mike wondered about this as he drove around.

He did something he seldom did anymore; stopped at the cemetery and sat by the grave of his first wife, Rhonda. He knelt down and prayed, then sat there and talked to her. Next, he walked a couple of blocks down and knelt before his parents' graves and cried like a baby.

After a few hours of this, he got into his car and drove off, feeling a lot better, becoming his stoical, hard-in-the-face-of-death cop again and took over the investigation of the obvious murder of Madeline O'Reilly.

They tried to get in touch with Lawrence, but he had successfully flown the coop. "Well, in a way you can't blame him, guys," Zurich explained. "After all, the bomb was probably meant for him. He's probably running scared now."

The funeral was held a few days later. Mike and a few other cops were there. Mike insisted on taking Conci with him.

"Why do I want to go, Mike?" she asked him suspiciously.

"I just want you to go with me, Conci. Can't you do that for me?" She just shrugged and got dressed and went with him. He sat very close to her and held her hand throughout the whole proceedings.

At one point, she felt his hand shaking and wondered about that. *Does he still have a thing for her?* Conci hoped that Madeline had repented of her life before she died, and she prayed that the Lord would forgive her for harboring such anger at the very dead Madeline.

Surprisingly, Conci spotted Toby Sullivan at the church briefly and just caught him walking away swiftly at the cemetery. *So that's the way it is,* she thought. *Was he giving me more blarney? He and Madeline? How is it that I never thought about them together? Of course, Toby is the missing link,* she thought excitedly.

Mike looked at Conci's face and saw her staring at someone and followed her stare. He was surprised too that Toby Sullivan was at the funeral. He leaned over and whispered to Conci. "What do you make of that?"

"I never caught it, Mike. Toby and Madeline. Of course. That's why it never made any sense." He held her hand harder and pulled her away from the cemetery scene and put her into his car, and they drove off, trying to follow Sullivan. But he had successfully disappeared.

"How do you figure this?" Mike stared at her, finally picking up from the conversation from the church."

"Toby and Madeline, Mike. They were lovers. Of course that was the one she always loved." Mike opened his eyes really wide and was about to protest, then thought better of it.

"You thought it was you, and Lawrence thought it was himself. But in reality it was always Toby whom she loved. Yes, now things will begin to happen, Mike. It will all play into your hands so neatly," she said cryptically. Mike stopped the car. He'd had enough of her suppositions.

"What in the world are you talking about, woman? First of all, how do you know it was Sullivan that she loved? Maybe it was Lawrence, or even me," he said almost in a whisper. Conci shook her head.

"Believe whatever your great pride wants you to believe, Mike, but I'm a realist. Although you think you're one and that I'm a dreamer, actually it's the other way around. I can accept that someone doesn't love me. It hurts me oh so badly, but I won't deny it, for heaven's sakes. That's life. Rejection is a part of life. It won't kill you. Well, maybe in this instance it did kill Madeline," she said almost lightly as though she'd made a joke.

Mike slapped her across the face, and it almost wrenched her neck it was such a hard blow, causing her head to hit the car window. Conci sat there and just stared at Mike as the tears ran down her face. Then she fished in her purse and took her small can of mace and sprayed it right in his eyes. "Don't you ever touch me in anger again. No, not ever!" she screamed at him.

His rubbed his eyes and grabbed her and held her close to him and he began to cry too. "I'm sorry, baby. I didn't mean to hit you that hard. I just wanted you to come to your senses, because you were talking crazy." Conci just sobbed and sobbed. They stayed like that for a few minutes, and then, once he could see clearly, although his eyes still burned, Mike started the car and drove off.

Conci was quiet now and had stopped sobbing; instead she just stared out the window as her face became swollen and her eye became black and blue where it had hit the side of the window.

When they got home, she got out of the car and went into the house. He just sat there not knowing what to do. He was hurting so very badly, partly because of her words that Madeline never loved him, only Toby, and then the violent way that Madeline had died. He started up his motor and drove off toward the Daffodil Bar.

Conci sat in the house waiting for the call from Toby, feeling he'd check in with her. Then it came. "Conci? Oh, baby, how are you? I know you saw me at the church," he said, probing now to see if she did.

"Yes, and at the cemetery too. Why were you there, Toby? Did you know Madeline… intimately?" She almost hesitated to ask that.

"Yes, I did. Does that hurt you?"

"Well, a little, until I figured it out. So you were the man who was the love of her life that she talked about. I can surely understand that, Toby," Conci said honestly.

Toby sighed.

"I didn't love her like that, though, Conci. No, not for a long time. At one time, she was what I thought was an innocent person, but she was never that. No, she was always on the make and always desiring to be famous, no matter the cost. She used me, and she used the other guys too. But, I know that she really did love me. Yes, she did love me."

"But you haven't said how you felt about her, Toby."

"She wasn't a clean vessel, Conci. No, she

never was, and I was so deceived by her. And she was willing to trade in what we had together in order to get with Bastriani, who could and did make her famous. You're the only clean vessel I've ever met, Conci. I love only you, my darling, now and forever." There was a pause. "Here's a little bone for your very prideful husband. Lawrence set her up, knowing that the Bastriani would be trying to kill him. A car bomb was the most likely method. So, he called her and asked her to get his car for him and he'd meet her somewhere. Yes, he set her up, and she was so stupid herself, never realizing that these were killers she was dealing with. No, she was prideful too thinking that her charms would make a difference to these killers. It didn't." Then he hung up.

Conci stared at the phone. She got on her knees and repented of falling for the charm of Toby Sullivan. "Lord, I've been so hungry for the love of my husband and for his faithfulness. You know I can't bear any more treachery on his part or his rejection. Please help Mike and me, Lord, and Toby too, and forgive me for flirting with him and enjoying his attentions to me."

Conci picked up the children from school and enjoyed their three-year-old chatter. Little Mo just stared at them and tried to join them by chattering in baby talk too.

Mike didn't come home that night, and indeed Conci didn't expect it.

Conci got ready for school the next day with the children. The twins were sitting in their booster seats eating their breakfast and Conci was feeding the little one in the highchair. They were always in a good mood, and Conci was singing to them, a really cute song, "This Little Light of Mine."

It was only six thirty, and Conci had taken her shower and had her hair fixed and her makeup on and her underclothes, waiting for the last minute to put on her good clothes so that she wouldn't get all stained by the baby.

Just then Mike came in the door, looking very bad indeed. He was still a little drunk, she could see and tried to stay out of his way and not start any altercations.

"Daddy, Daddy!" Moira screamed with excitement.

Sonny looked up at Mike and smiled. "Daddy home!" Conci had to laugh at that. Mike just looked at all three of them and smiled at them, then crossed over and kissed Conci softly on the lips. She smelled the liquor on his breath and tried not to respond.

"I called Halperan up at home and asked

him to get you a sub today, Conci. Then I called Loretta, and she's going to pick up the kids," he said and had to sit down, feeling a little dizzy.

"Oh? Why did you do that, Mike?" she asked sweetly.

"I need to see you and talk with you. That's why," he said now getting a little surly.

"That's fine, honey," she said, and that seemed to placate him.

"I'm going to take a shower first, though." He went into the bedroom, and Conci continued her chores. At seven Loretta Sterns-Ryan, her best friend and fellow teacher, came to the door.

"Come in, Loretta. I hope this doesn't inconvenience you, my friend. I didn't put him up to it at all," Conci quickly explained, sensing that Loretta was a little irritated by it.

"I wish you'd given me a call last night, Conci, It would have made it easier for me," she said in a complaining voice. Conci got her a cup of coffee and a piece of pie, and soon she was feeling better. Loretta had low blood sugar, hypoglycemia, and was in bad sorts unless she got her breakfast.

Now, she was brightening up a lot and talking to her godson, Sonny, and Moira. Little Mo always smiled in a special way for Loretta, and the children called her Aunt Loretta and her husband, Uncle Billy.

Conci helped her put the children into the car seats.

"Shall I bring them home too?" she asked happily now.

"Thanks, Lor. You certainly are my best friend. I don't know what the old crab has planned or even why he got me a sub and called you. But, I'll plan on picking them up myself unless I call you, okay?" she asked and hugged Loretta. Conci kissed and hugged the children, and they were off.

Mike was still in the shower, which was suspicious to Conci. She peeked in the bedroom and there he was on the bed sound asleep with the shower running, and he hadn't even taken off his clothes.

She turned off the shower and put on her clothes and made some breakfast for herself and read the Bible. She had several chores to complete and did so, and then around twelve Mike got up and had some coffee again and looked at her, bleary-eyed. The first thing he noticed was her swollen face and the big bruise above her eyebrow and the darkness under the eye.

"I'm sorry, honey. I really didn't mean to hurt you, just get you to stop talking nonsense. That's all. My eyes are still irritated from the mace you sprayed into them if that's any consolation to you." Conci didn't say a word, just watched him.

"I went to the Daffodil and got snockered as you can see. I'm sorry about that too," he said humbly. Conci just looked at him waiting for more.

"It's not that I loved her, Conci. It was just a shock that she was killed in such a violent way. It must have been Lawrence who set it up. Don't you think?"

Conci nodded. "Absolutely. He probably called her and asked her to bring his car somewhere, and when she got into it, he knew she'd be killed. Yes, he did set her up. I'm almost sure of it too," Conci concurred, not mentioning her conversation with Toby the day before.

Mike poured himself and her some more coffee. "I felt like when Rhonda died, baby. I'm sorry. I felt so bereft," he explained to her. Conci just looked at him, feeling nothing.

"So where did you go then?"

"Well, first I went to the cemetery and sat by Rhonda's and my parents' graves then went to the Daffodil and got drunk."

"Where did you sleep last night?" she asked as though it was immaterial to her.

He looked down at the floor. "I was a good boy, Conci. I was so drunk that Pat had to practically carry me into his back room. He was really upset with me too," Mike confessed.

Conci gave out a big deep sigh, and Mike looked over at her. They were both quiet for a while, and then she got up and was about to leave the kitchen.

"No, wait, I'm not finished. I need to apologize to you more, I know that. Why do you think that Fred Lawrence wanted to kill her?" he asked, staring at her.

"He was upset that she really loved Toby more than you or him, and he was in a jam himself. She had betrayed him no doubt, probably more than once. So, when the chance arose for him to get his revenge on her or to at least stop her from dragging him down to her level, he got rid of her, only let Bastriani be the bad guy."

"You think it was Bastriani who rigged the bomb?"

"Or one of his flunkies. He is a very dangerous man. She, on the other hand, always thought that her looks and her body and her fame would keep her safe and keep Bastriani dangling, but he must have gotten wind of her affair with you and with Lawrence. So, he undoubtedly knew about Sullivan. Bastriani is a killer, and it was no surprise that he wanted Lawrence dead, maybe even you, Mike. But at least you dropped her, and that saved your life. Perhaps my and the children's lives too," she said and closed her eyes.

"Where do you think Lawrence has gone to?"

"You'll never find him, Mike. It's convenient to have friends in high places, but Lawrence has a better group of friends to hide with, friends in low places. He probably has a half dozen guys that would hide him. Maybe even families that he's helped. He was probably a really popular man among the low life," she said and smiled at that.

"You're probably right."

"Besides, Mike, you would have a hard time proving that he purposely told Madeline to take his car because he knew there was a bomb planted in the motor. How could you prove that?"

Mike just shrugged. He already felt better talking to his wife about things.

"So, we have two murders solved. Lara Connors most likely killed Mary Elizabeth, and Sonny Lopelia killed his wife. Who do you see as the killer of April Conover? Cici? Do you think Cici did it, Conci?"

She just shrugged. "I don't know for sure yet, Mike. So I'd rather not say," she hedged.

"What? You have an idea. Let's hear it?"

Conci shook her head. "No, it's not even an idea, just a random thought."

Mike took his shower. And she napped with

him, and both of them felt better when they got up. In fact, Mike was whistling.

"Let's go get the children early," he suggested, "and take them to the park and have a nice old-fashioned family day. How about that, honey?"

Conci smiled. "I'd like that a lot, Mike." So, that's what they did.

A few days later, upon hearing about Lawrence disappearing and Madeline being killed, Mrs. Addy McMurray sent a letter to Lt. McVey at the police station.

Curiously, he opened it right away, while Max and Melville were sitting in his office, jawing over the murder of Madeline O'Reilly and the disappearance of Fred Lawrence. Mike read it and then looked at the guys and the reread it again. It was in a large manila envelope, and another piece of paper fell out and a key to a bank box in town.

I'm on my way to Africa to work with the nuns in an orphanage that Mac and I started in our youth when we were both missionaries. But I need to set the record straight for all those that are innocent and those that are guilty, of which, I'm afraid my

*husband was one of the latter ones. I do swear to you
that I never thought he was involved with this kind
of stuff. I really thought he was having an affair. I
want you to know that he repented before he died and
regretted the harm and hurt he caused by his greed.
The drowning was always bogus to me, but I have
no proof and don't want to pursue it. But he made
me promise that when he died I would look in this
bank box and give anything that I felt necessary to
the police. So, here is the key to the bank box in town,
which is where I sent the box a week ago. May God
have mercy on all our souls.*

Addy McMurray

Mike showed the letter around to the other guys,
and Max read it aloud as Mike called Monty into
the office.

"Well, I'll be."

"Let's go guys, and we'll get the proof."

"Be careful, Mike. This might be a trap,"
Monty said, and Mike looked over at him.

"Thanks, Monty."

So, they got everyone to go home from the
bank and closed it and got the bomb squad to
carefully go into the vault. There was no bomb,
and it really perplexed Monty, although he was
relieved.

They took the box out and went through it, and to their shock and surprise it was empty.

"What the heck? Is this some kind of joke?" Mike's voice was full of anger and incredulity. All the cops just stared at him.

"We've been had, Lieutenant," one of them offered.

Mike talked to the bank manager.

"Let's see if anyone has been to the box since it arrived by special messenger a couple of days ago," Mrs. Collins, the bank manager, suggested.

After much interrogation and talking, she found that no one had touched the box, and it was put into the bank-box area as soon as it arrived and was under lock and key.

All the guys were quite discouraged by this disappointment and went their separate ways to work on other investigations that were pending.

Mike angrily told Conci the whole deal, and she tried to soothe him as best she could, wondering all the time what Addy McMurray was thinking.

When Conci arrived at school the next day, she found a package on her desk. She looked at the returned address, and it was from Addy McMurray. Conci opened it up immediately and saw a large cigar box and stared at it.

"What in the world?" she said out loud. Then

she opened up the cigar box, and there was a note from Addy explaining the subterfuge and how she thought it was necessary and several other pieces of paper and a handwritten confession from her husband. Conci put the box under her desk and put her sweater on top of it and took the wrapping and folded it neatly and placed it in one of her drawers then called Mike.

"Yeah! What do you want, Conci?" he asked in his surliest voice.

"I received a package, and it was on my desk this morning, Mike. When I opened it, there was a cigar box with a lot of stuff in it." She paused.

"Yeah, why do I care about that?"

"It was from Addy McMurray, Mike."

"I'll be right over."

True to his word he was there in approximately seven minutes, using his siren to get there quicker. He came walking briskly into her room, and she pointed to the box under her desk as she pushed her chair away.

He leaned over and looked inside.

"Well, I'll be," he grunted. "Well, so that's what she did. Good girl." His voice was full of admiration now.

He took the box and completely ignored Conci and got as far as the door and turned around and came back and kissed her. "Thanks, baby. You did good." Conci smiled at the whole thing. The smile remained the rest of the day.

In Monty's office, three men were assembled waiting for Mike as he waltzed in with the cigar box under his arm.

"Well, guys, here it is." His voice was triumphant as he placed the cigar box on the Monty's desk, who opened it immediately and looked through it and read the note to the other two guys.

"So, she felt that someone was watching her, and that's why she sent the one box to the bank and this box to Conci. Good thinking on her part." Monty nodded his head.

The information was invaluable. There were receipts and snapshots of people paying for the money and others that were part of the operation. The Bastrianis' pictures and name were all over the place, specifically Philly and his younger brother Stevie.

Then there were agreements between Mc-Murray and Bastriani and Berger and Bastriani. In fact, Berger wasn't even an educator but was one of the Bastriani gang, an educated one, and he got the job from Bastriani. McMurray always hated Berger according to the letter explaining everything in the bank box. The plot became clear then.

As you probably have figured out by now, the big operation was the counterfeiting money. What a great racket that was. We had the best counterfeit artist in the business. He did all the plates in Europe, and then the girls smuggled them in, the models mostly, and Madeline O'Reilly was the head of all that too. She was, among other things, Philly Bastriani's wife and the best known model in the world. Another partner was Lara Connors, wife of Rev. Johnny Bob Connors. She got in and out of the country with no problem over and over again because of her missionary status. So she smuggled a lot and then also brought money in and out.

We paid the employees of the school with cash, first putting our counterfeit bills in the bank along with our checks and money orders, etc from the parents. Thus, every week, we put in a certain amount and got back a certain amount of good bills. It was a great scam. We had that great operation going on right in front of the cop's noses. Only a few of the board of directors knew what was going on, and they had a piece of the action. They were Smalley, Martinez, and Sonia Valentine. The cops really were stymied because of the façade of holiness and Christianity in the school, but in fact, it was never intended to be, nor was it a Christian institution. We offered all types of religions and even some anti-religions like witchcraft. We did offer Bible classes and hired Christians to staff that, and they were all completely innocent of the clandestine doings. In fact, most of the Christians eventually left, so we had to only get ones that had some deep hidden sin that perhaps they had confessed but had not paid the penalty.

This is the way I figured it. Berger wanted to get out of the situation with Bastriani, so he tried to fix it so he would be pronounced dead. But it had to look like someone killed him. So he stole this black mamba that had its poison glands and its fangs removed to fake the death bite, but unfortunately someone else got wind of it and put in a real mamba and that one killed him. He knew someone who had a connection at some kind of snake farm, or so he said one day, when we were talking about something else. Someone had to know about his plan, so although he didn't confide in me, he did drop hints. I was pressed into service, because unbeknownst to Berger, Bastriani must have sent someone to watch him and tail him and saw him steal the disabled snake and then got someone of his group to obtain another one and some guy gave it to me to take care of and put it into the right place. I was quite scared about the whole thing, but the snake was already heavily drugged. And while it was still in the *cage and apparently sleeping, I gave it another shot of morphine that a seedy doc that I knew supplied. Then I brought the thing in its cage to Berger's office at night and carefully opened the cage and ran out of there so fast. I was shaking the whole way.*

When Berger went into his office the next morning, he apparently didn't see the poisonous snake but opened the desk drawer where the non-poisonous snake was. However, it was still quite aggressive and reared up and bit him in the face and the neck. Berger was probably taken aback and must have tripped over the sleeping mamba, which woke up and chased him into the hallway and struck him in the face again and again. He fell over, dead.

Berger was probably in on the operation from the start, being a greedy man, and then tried to keep more money than he agreed upon. So, they killed him. They thought this would keep me away from the coffers, but they were wrong. I was too far in to get out anyway and thought I could sneak away without them noticing. So, I made my plans carefully, but they must have known something was up, because then at the carnival the water moccasin bit me in the dunk tank. Now I know for a fact that the students would never have the guts to do that, so it had to be someone on the spot who was a snake handler too. I was really scared now and decided to spend my last days with my beautiful, wonderful wife, and then whenever the end would come, it would come. I made my peace with the Lord and repented of my sins. I'm not sure who put the snake into the tank, but I have my hunch that it was the person who worked at a circus and for her parents who were snake handlers.

It was signed Dr. Albert McMurray. And dated. He also had it notarized. The four men sat there in the office and pondered the information given to them. "So who do you think put the moccasin in the dunk tank?" Monty asked his men.

"Was it Philly Bastriani?" Max suggested.

All of them just shrugged, trying to digest this new information.

"Who of his gang was familiar with handling poisonous snakes? That's the question I'd like answered," Mike forged ahead.

Melville nodded his head too. "Maybe we need to go through all the histories of any of the people involved in the counterfeiting: Lara Connors, Madeline O'Reilly, Dr. Berger, Dr. McMurray, Mrs. Berger, and Mrs. McMurray, and whomever else was involved and Lt. Lawrence too, although McMurray didn't mention him. I wonder if he didn't know about Lawrence's part in the whole scheme."

They all dispersed to their own offices. Mike

was still bummed out about Madeline's death. He went to the Daffodil, had some late lunch, since it was almost two o'clock and his stomach was rumbling with hunger. This place had the best drip beef in town, and he ordered two of them and coffee and a double scotch.

"Mike." It was Pat who approached him with a perplexed look on his face.

"Yeah?" he looked at Pat with interest.

"I thought that red-haired model you went with was killed in a car bomb incident or something like that." He looked at Mike with a frown.

"Yeah, that's right. What's bothering you, Pat?"

"Either she or her twin was here earlier asking about you." Mike almost fell off the barstool.

"Did she leave me a message?"

Pat nodded his head. "Said something like, 'nothing is as it seems,' then left. That's it," he insisted.

Mike wondered about that and went back to the office to see if he had received any e-mails from Madeline. *So, it wasn't her in the bombing. Then who was it? I swear I saw the butterfly tattoo on her upper left thigh. But then anyone could have had one there too.* He looked through his e-mails. There was nothing from her.

He then called Conci at home. She was out of breath when she answered. "Why are you panting? Chasing after the little ones?" That always made him smile.

"I'm on the treadmill while they're napping, honey," she said sweetly.

"Did I get any phone calls where someone hung up when you answered?"

Conci stopped what she was doing and concentrated on what her husband was asking her.

"Yes, all morning long, Mike. What's it all about?" she wondered.

"I'll let you know later." Then he hung up. Conci just shrugged and got her Bible and began to pray.

Mike decided to play a lone hand for a little while in case the woman got in touch with him again. First of all he went to her former apartment and saw that it was still empty. He hung around the bank for a little while unobtrusively, sitting in his car across the street.

After a few hours, he realized there was no action there. *Where else would she be? I'd better call Conci and confess this whole thing stymies me. Maybe she'll have a few guesses.* Then he had to smile at that thought. *She'll have more than a few, McVey. Do you want to put yourself through all that still another time?* But in the end, he knew it was the right thing to do.

"Conci, Pat at the Daffodil says a woman who he thinks is Madeline came into the bar last night or yesterday afternoon, asking for me. Is it possible that it's Madeline? I guess it's possible, and the woman who was killed in the bombing was someone else."

He answered his own question. Conci was a good sounding board. And he could put forth some crazy ideas himself, and she always thought they were so clever. He needed to respect her ideas like that too, he cautioned himself.

"So you think that's who has been calling and hanging up when I answer the phone? Could be, I guess," she said without much enthusiasm.

Mike heard the tone of her voice. "Help me here, honey. It has nothing to do with romance, believe me. You're all I ever want and need from now on. But, you're really good at extrapolating some information out of a tiny scrap of knowledge."

Conci opened her eyes really wide. "Thank you, Mike. Yes, thanks so much," she said sincerely, and that brought out a barrage of ideas.

"It's odd your saying that, Mike, because the last few days I've spotted someone who appears to be following me, and I hesitated to mention it to you, for fear you'd think I was making it up or something," she admitted.

"Go on," he urged her.

"It's a woman, and I've only seen the side of her as she hides her face. Maybe I'm getting paranoid, Mike. I hope not." Then she had another thought. "Did the dental records check out for Madeline's body?"

"Yes, they did, but we didn't do a DNA test because it seemed to be her."

"Did you see her body and identify her, Mike?" Conci continued to probe.

"Yeah, I did. So what?"

"Did she have the butterfly tattoo on her leg like Madeline?" Conci asked almost in a whisper.

"Yeah, I guess she did. Stay on the subject, Conci. That's why you annoy me so much," he said and hung up. Then he called her back. "Sorry, that's the old Mike talking. I was just embarrassed that I could identify that about her, honey. That's all. But go on with your speculations."

"If Lawrence loved Madeline so much, he could have called Lara instead of Madeline and had her to get his car, telling her to wear her disguise. Perhaps she already had a tattoo on her left thigh too. Maybe this was some kind of scam they were both going to pull. Of course she didn't know that it would mean her death. No, maybe it was to be getting rid of Madeline, and he double crossed Lara instead."

Conci chatted on with her ideas. "It looks like Lara was one of the people involved in the murder, Mike, but who was the person who supplied all the snakes then? That's what I'd like to know. Have you been able to really delve into everyone's background again?" she asked, feeling that somehow Madeline was responsible for some of this stuff. But then she thought, *Maybe I'm just prejudiced because she almost broke up my family.*

Having said everything to him, they hung up amicably. Mike sat back in his desk chair again and thought about things. His cell phone rang, and he answered it not identifying the number of the caller ID. "Hello, lover," the sexy voice spoke softly and in a sultry way.

"Maddy, is that you?" Mike asked excitedly.

"Yes, lover, it's me. I need to see you, Mike. You're the only one that can help me."

"What's going on, Madeline? I saw your body in the morgue, or at least I saw the pitiful remains of someone that had a tattoo just like you on her left upper leg and red hair like you too. What's going on, Maddy?" Mike was all cop now, and she felt it and shook her head, feeling that he was going to be difficult to convince.

"I don't know, Mike. I heard about it too. Just

like other people. It alarmed me when they said it was me. Of course it wasn't me. But it seemed like a good time to pretend it was me, and so I'd be out of the clutches of Philly. I don't know who it was in the car, Mike, and that's the truth," she reiterated.

Mike wasn't taken in by it at all, but wanted to find out where she'd been and why she was calling him now.

"Oh Mike, I still love you. Don't you love me anymore?" she asked in a little girl's voice. Mike felt a strong temptation but knew it was the wrong thing to do, so he ignored it and decided to be a stalwart guy, an immoveable object.

"It's not a matter of love or no love, Maddy. It's a matter of the law. You've broken the law, and you have to clear it up before we can ever be together again. You're not dead; therefore, you're living a lie, and I can't be a party to it." With that, she hung up.

At first Mike pressed the recall button to call back the last number, but stopped himself. He was almost shaking and wondered why he was in such a state about her being alive. *So then, who was in the car? Probably Lara Connors.* As late as it was, he still called the coroner and asked him about a DNA test.

"We need to do it, Willie, because the woman

whom we identified is now alive and I haven't seen her but it sure sounds like her. I can only assume that someone switched the dental records."

"Okay, Mike, another curious thing that I was going to call you about, her hair isn't a real auburn but has been bleached and dyed that color. I thought you said she was a real redhead, but then I thought you probably didn't know. Most of us guys would be fooled," he said in a jovial way.

"I know for a fact that she's a real redhead, Willie. Please do a DNA test on the body, and I will get something from another woman, a Lara Connor, and take the DNA from this item, if I can find any, and see if it belongs to the corpse."

Dr. Willie Chalmers agreed and they hung up. Mike was still quite upset about the whole thing and wished he hadn't been so curt to her. His arms ached to hold her, and then he stopped himself. "Is that how you are, McVey, a liar, an unfaithful bum who has no class and whose word is worth nothing? If you go for her now, your life with Conci will end, and your worth as a cop will go out the door too. In fact, you will have to turn in your badge because this woman is bad news." He talked to himself out loud, but in a low tone.

Mike bowed his head and prayed, "Please take away this temptation, Lord. I want to be with Maddy so much."

Suddenly, he heard the audial voice he had heard the night at the restaurant. "You've got the first part of repentance down pat, Michael, the part that you're sorry, but you never follow through on the second part, the go and sin no more—the don't do it again part. That's the part you have to work on, otherwise it's not a true repentance. That's why you're tempted so often. You need to do a complete repentance." The voice sounded like his father's, but Mike knew it was the Spirit of the Lord speaking to him. He got out of his chair and fell to his knees and began to cry and humbled himself like he'd never done before.

"I'm so sorry, Lord for all my sins. I won't do it again, but I need your grace to stick to that, Lord. I can't do it alone. I desire not to sin again," He continued to cry and sob, his shoulders heaving up and down.

Finally, after some time on the floor, he stopped, got up and blew his nose. It felt like a weight had been taken off his shoulders.

Mike looked up Madeline's record and looked thoroughly through her file. She had filled out a form telling about her early life and how she was brought up, naming her parents as Edward and Charlene O'Reilly, circus performers, a high-wire act. He decided to pursue that further for some reason.

He called several circuses and found a few people that knew of these performers, the O'Reillys. But they weren't high-wire acts, they were snake handlers. Mike stopped and closed his eyes. *So that was it,* he thought with a heavy sigh. *So Madeline was involved up to her pretty ears,* He thought. *Yes, she was the one who supplied the snakes for the kill. How little I know about this woman for whom I wanted to give up my wife and children and even my career.* Mike was disgusted with himself and his emotion. *Please keep me strong, Lord. Please keep me clean and safe,* he prayed fervently again.

Mike knew that he had to be the one to bring her to justice. Yes, he had to do this for himself, for the Lord and for his family. Conci would then know that he was aware of his own foolishness without any words being spoken, and he himself would know what kind of strong mettle he was made of too. Madeline was still a fugitive from the law; therefore, he got another warrant for her arrest.

Toward that end, he looked at his cell phone and found the number of where the call from Maddy came from. He dialed it as he made a note of it. "Hello," he almost sighed at the sound of her sweet, sexy voice.

"Baby, it's me. Where can we meet? I have to see you and hold you in my arms. I've missed you so," he said lustily and with conviction. It was no lie, that much was for sure, and she sensed the truth of it.

"Are you going to arrest me, Mikey?" she asked, and he could see her in his mind's eye, so beautiful with her dark auburn long, full, curly hair and her tall, lithe body with fabulous legs. Yes, he could see her and had to close his eyes and shake himself into reality again. How he wished he could just pursue her and stay with her and they could live happily ever after.

Yeah, McVey, you don't believe in happy endings, remember? He chastised himself. *We'd be on the run from the police and from Bastriani. I would have let everyone down, and they would all view me as a weak man.* The thought really irked him.

He remembered Melville's words to him regarding cheating. "I don't cheat, because I know who I am, Mike. Sometimes I don't even love Marily and she's a pain in the foot, but I stay and am sweet to her because I know I'm a macho guy, a promise keeper. Then we survive the bad days of marriage, and soon, we're honeymooners again." Mike wanted that. Yes, he wanted to be that kind of strong man, a promise keeper, and a big man to his family, especially his wife and children. Suddenly, he felt an infusion of strength and faith and saw into the spirit. Madeline's voice didn't sound sweet and saucy at all, but was almost a hiss, like a serpent. Mike had to physically restrain himself from hanging up. He tried to make his voice sound excited like before.

"Baby, I've missed you so much that all I want is to be with you for a while, and then whatever happens, happens," he said with difficulty. But she didn't buy it.

"I can't take that chance, Mike."

"Then why did you call me in the first place, Madeline? Why get me all riled up again about you?" His voice was stern and yet held a modicum of poignancy, which she detected, and it made her lower her defenses.

"I had to hear your voice, Mike, and let you know that I still love you, no matter what I'm forced to do to you or your family."

"Whoa, what does that mean, Madeline? Why bring my family into it?"

"Ask your wife, Mike. She knows. Goodbye, my love," she said and hung up. Mike instantly phoned in the number and tried to trace the whereabouts of the phone, but it was impossible since it was turned off.

Mike went home immediately and paced nervously because Conci wasn't home yet. In five minutes she was driving into the driveway immediately ran out and got the children out of their car seats, and they kissed him and were excited that he was home. Conci was herself a little surprised.

"Come in and let's get these children fed or something, Conci. I need to talk to you pronto," His voice was commanding, quite professional.

"Okay, honey. Will you help me?"

"Of course," his voice was angry. And he took one of the children and put her in her high chair, and Conci dealt with the other two.

Once they had some food before them, they settled down. While she was doing this, Mike made some coffee and poured both of theirs.

"What's up, honey?" He looked quite tired and worried she noted.

"I talked to Madeline today, and she said something about what she had to do to my family. And when I questioned her, she said to ask you why she had to kill you or hurt you or something? What the heck is this all about? You been talking with her?"

Conci raised her eyebrows. "What are you insinuating, McVey? Why would I talk to her? Of course not. I never heard from her. What's her gripe against me? I'd like to know."

"Yeah, me too. Okay, she said that you'd know. Why does she want to kill you, Conci?"

Conci just stared at him. "I have no idea, Mike. Perhaps because she wants you to herself?" she ventured.

"You told me that she didn't love me or Lawrence, remember. You said she loved Sullivan," he said nastily and got another cup of coffee for himself.

Conci suddenly got it. "Oh!" She looked down at her coffee cup.

"Yeah, oh what?"

"Maybe because she thinks that Toby cares for me, Mike. Remember the Christmas card he sent to me? Perhaps she's jealous and thinks he wants me and not her," Conci said softly.

Mike got up and threw his cup in the sink and then threw hers in too, breaking both of them. "Okay, I see it, now!" His voice was angry, and he just frowned at her. "Well, you got yourself into this, Concetta Marie. Now you find your own way out and protect yourself. I'm out of this whole thing. Let your precious 'Toby' come to your rescue." With that he slammed the door, ran out of the house and sped away.

Conci called her aunt, and she was about to come back into town anyway, having a feeling that things weren't quite right between the

McVeys. "I'm scheduled to come there tomorrow anyway, sweetie. Hang in there," she said, and they prayed.

Conci went to school the next day and talked to Halperan about the whole thing, struggling the whole time over the decision of whether to put the children into the nursery or not. "Wow, I'm wondering where she'll strike, Leo. I can't really believe that Mike would leave the children and me hanging on a limb by ourselves. I know he's hanging around, either trying to find her or somewhere around here."

Leo nodded his head in agreement. "I know him too well too, Conci. He may be livid with rage against you, but he'll protect you nonetheless."

Conci concurred. And in the end she and Leo prayed, and Loretta came in and she joined them. They decided to take the children to the nursery all right and gave the workers there a warning about someone trying to take them out. Everyone loved Conci and her children and vowed to keep them safe.

That done, Conci returned to her classroom. Suddenly there was an unexpected fire drill. Conci wondered about that and gave her students to Loretta next door.

"I have to make sure the kids are all right, Lor."

"Go on, Conci. I'll take care of these guys," she said helpfully.

Conci ran to the nursery, but they were already outside. She quickly found them and saw that one of the workers had all three of her children standing down by the trees, talking to someone. Conci moved quickly and grabbed her children.

"Thanks, Mildred," she said and looked directly into Madeline O'Reilly's face.

"You witch!" she shouted at Conci and tried to grab one of the children. Mildred Halstedt pushed Conci onto the ground and tried to wrestle her. Quickly, Conci got the mace from her pocket and sprayed Mildred. While Conci was screaming, Madeline took Moira and ran with her.

Conci blew her whistle, and her senior boys as well as her nephew Timmy Wiley went running after Madeline. Suddenly, she put a gun right up to Moira's head, and everyone moved slowly toward her.

"Conci, stop these boys, or I'll shoot your daughter's brains out," she screamed, with the gun pressed right against Moira's head. "I have nothing to lose," Madeline shouted to them.

"Can I come with you, Madeline? You can have my life for the childrens.' I'm the one who you hate, not them," she pleaded.

Madeline motioned for Conci to come closer

to her, and she put Moira down and grabbed Conci.

"Run to Timmy, Moira," Conci shouted, and she did so. Timmy grabbed her and brought her back to the school along with the other children. They all watched in horror and fear as Conci was escorted away with a gun to her head.

"Okay, you witch. Now don't give me any trouble, or I'll kill you right off and then go after your children too." Conci nodded in assent and moved along with Madeline.

Soon, the cop cars came, and they approached the scene prudently. Mike wasn't with them, though, and that surprised Halperan.

He told them what happened. Madeline pushed Conci into the car and got inside herself, still pointing the gun at Conci. Just then someone in the back seat sat up and grabbed her around the throat. "Let her go, Maddy, or I swear I'll kill you right here and now."

Madeline still held the gun and shot at Conci. It hit her in the arm, and she fell across the seat passed out. Mike tightened his grip on Madeline's neck, and she passed out too. But taking no chances, he took the gun from her and called for backup, which was only a block away. In minutes other cops were coming. Mike called for an ambulance.

"Get a bus here for my wife. She's badly hurt," he said in a calm hard voice. Madeline in the meantime had awakened and managed to escape, as Mike turned to hold his wife's hand while they put her into the ambulance. Madeline ran out of the car and was so fast that no one saw her until she was a bit ahead of them, and then she ducked behind some trees and they lost her.

"Darn, now she's on the loose again," Mike complained. But in minutes they heard the sound of just one shot. The officers ran to the trees with their own guns unholstered, and there they found Madeline with a bullet in her head, dead. That was the end of Madeline.

"Who killed her?" Mike asked almost in a stony voice.

"Not one of us, sir," the officer answered with a perplexed look on his face.

"I'm going in the ambulance with my wife," Mike said and left the scene to the other officers.

Much later in the day, Conci awoke to the sound of some machines that she noticed were attached to her, and her arms had needles in them.

"Oh pooh!" she said out loud. "I'm in a hospital, for heaven's sakes."

Mike heard her voice and awoke and approached her and kissed her softly on the lips. "How do you feel?" he asked in a low, gravelly voice, as though it hurt him to talk. Conci just stared at him.

"I feel like crud but good enough to go home, Mike. Have them take all this stuff off me, will you, honey? I'll get up and we can go home. I think Auntie should be at the house by now."

Mike had to laugh at that. "Sorry, baby, you have a bullet wound in your shoulder, and they had to do surgery on it. You'll be all right, but you'll probably have to go for therapy to regain full use of it," he stated in an emotionless voice.

"The children, Mike. Are they all right?" She was worried now.

He nodded. "Yes, you saved Moira by offering Madeline your own self, honey. You're a real mother," he said proudly.

"How are you, Mike? Did anyone catch Madeline?"

Mike nodded. "She tried to get away, and someone shot and killed her, Conci, though we don't know who yet," he said softly, not wanting to look at her.

"I knew you'd be around, Mike and would rescue us. Now I remember. You were in the backseat of her car and put your hands around her neck to choke her and force her to leave me alone, but she shot me, I guess. That's all I remember," Conci explained and then moaned as she tried to move her arm.

Mike immediately called the nurse. "My wife's awake and in pain. Please come and give her a shot," he said in his most professional police voice. Conci just looked at him with love. He saw the look and sighed himself.

chapter XXXIII
explanation

Later in the week, Mike was telling his nephew Timmy, and indeed the whole family, including Sister Conci how it all played out as they sat having coffee at the Wileys.'

"So, in view of your great research on the Seven Deadly Sins after I've told you this whole story and identified the killers and their motivations, which ones committed murder as a deadly sin, or who committed the murder as a result of a sin of the heart?" he asked, feeling good about his own suppositions.

Timmy looked over at his Aunt Conci and then at Sister, who was staring at him with apt interest. His mother, dad, and brother were sitting there quietly interested too.

"The first murder and the attempted murder were committed for a profit motive, for greed, and to get rid of the weak links in their chain. These two guys, Berger and McMurray, were greedy too, and their pride prevented them from seeing Bastriani as a very dangerous person. They only saw the counterfeiting crook Bastriani, not the cold-blooded murderer that he was, so sloth could be part of their sins too. But the motive for the murders was greed, I think."

Mike just shrugged his shoulders.

"The poisonings of the nurse Mary Elizabeth Morrison and that of Sgt. Conover were terrible murders and committed because the person didn't want to be found out in their very serious error of killing two people, one on the spur of the moment, but a very painful one, but both to shut someone up. So, the murderer was Lara Connors, Rev. Connors' wife of twenty-five years. That was a shock. She wanted fame and fortune and wanted to be right beside her husband and even faked some things to give the illusion of spirituality. But in the end, it was her desire to be famous that led her to commit the murders. Ms. Morrison recognized her as the cop from long ago that shot and killed the little boy and the witness, and Sgt. Conover recognized her from the research she was doing for her masters in criminal justice. She came upon this unusual case and studied it further and approached Lara Connors probably at the wake. Quickly, she must have improvised, and from what Uncle Mike tells me, somehow she got into Sgt. Conover's purse and put some Lily of the Valley stems or something into her sleeping capsules. Those murders were out of fear but also to keep her fame. Maybe that's one of the deadly sins, fame." Timmy looked over at his audience and sighed in satisfaction, seeing that they were listening carefully to him. He continued, "Then, of course going back to Sonny Lopelia. His crime was not one of passion, but a cold-blooded thoughtful enterprise, killing the one thing that stood in the way of his being adored again by his public, his ex-wife, who knew all his secrets and had this love/hate relationship with him. In the end, he justified it as saving his own life and his reputation. I guess he's being prosecuted for that murder in California, I think." He looked at his uncle, who nodded to him, then continued.

"That was pride too, but he also wanted fame and would do anything for it. He even talked about what his father told him on his deathbed about fame. Yes, he would and did anything to obtain and keep his fame. He already had more money than he could ever use in a lifetime, but he wanted the fame that went with it.

"Madeline, the model, was a real number, though, a cold calculating icy woman who fell in love with one man, and that colored how she would live the rest of her life. It must have been Fred Lawrence, and indeed they did have a relationship for a while. But he was a dupe, but not a murderer. He just liked two things: easy money and Madeline. So lust definitely entered into the picture, but Madeline had only one goal in her mind from the time she was little until now. That was to be famous, to be the most famous and sought after model in the world. Indeed, she did attain that. So, again fame certainly should be somewhere in that mix of deadly sins." He looked at his audience to see if they agreed.

All nodded their heads except Aunt Conci. "Just one correction, Timmy. You've done an exemplary job of research, and your suppositions are very apt. Just like the love of money is the sin, not money itself, so also is the search for fame the sin, not fame itself. Do you see where I'm coming from?"

They all nodded their heads in agreement. "Thanks, Aunt Conci. That did bother me."

"Timmy, you have really done a great and thorough job of identifying the deadly sins behind each of these crimes. We still don't know who the person is that was in charge of the whole operation. Everyone says it was Philly Bastriani and Madeline and Lara, but who was the brains behind the whole deal and probably killed Madeline when she was running away from her attempt to kill Aunt Conci? None of the cops. How odd," Conci continued.

Everyone in the room had their own thoughts about that but kept their silence.

"How did you find out about Lara's studying the old cases for her master's thesis?" John Wiley asked, fascinated with this whole explanation.

"That was a real fluke, too, John," Mike explained. "For a while it looked like we were getting nowhere and then while Melville was getting all the information off her computer, you know, looking for clues, there was an e-mail from a professor Martin Colton, congratulating her on the research she'd done on the cold case files and referring to an attachment of the files. We hit pay dirt! There were some other files, but the one that was highlighted in yellow was the one concerning the cop who'd shot a guy who shot a kid and a bystander. That was of course, Lara. In fact, her name was mentioned in the file—Lara Lawrence. I then followed logically that April had somehow gotten in touch with Lara and tried to shake her down or something."

Everyone looked at Mike with respect and admiration.

After a lovely time with family, Mike and Conci left to go home.

chapter XXXIV
the greatest of
these is love

As they drove home, Mike thought about who was the leader of the group. Was it one of the Bastrianis'? Then it suddenly occurred to him like a bolt of lightning.

He looked over at Conci, and she looked at him with sadness in her eyes. Then he knew. *Of course, it was Sullivan. Who was on the scene and then not on the scene off and on and who could move with impunity? We all assumed it was Fred Lawrence. But he confessed to his part in the crimes, and they certainly didn't involve murder. In fact he was in the dark about that part of it. He did love Madeline, even I fell into her trap too. I can only feel sorry for him because of that. Thank you, Lord, for pulling me out of the snake pit and setting me in high places.* Mike stopped himself, feeling as though he'd said something profound from a psalm or something. Maybe he heard his wife say it, but it certainly applied here. *Anyway, thanks, Lord. Thanks.*

"So, Madeline always loved him, not me," Mike said as though it really hurt him.

"She loved you and Fred too, Mike, but her great love was always Toby, whom she couldn't have. He wasn't a faithful man, and she knew it. But he was far more powerful than even Bastriani, and she loved that about him. When she realized that I was one of the people that he admired, she tried to get rid of me too, Mike. That's when he moved on her. He did care for me even though you always thought it was blarney. I knew better, but neither of us ever acted on it," Conci confessed to him. Mike stopped the car and pulled over onto the side of the road and pulled her over to him.

"If I ever lost you, I'd kill myself, Conci. Oh baby, forgive me for being such a jerk. I thank Sullivan for opening my eyes about your specialness and the motivations of Madeline. I will never betray you ever again," he promised, and this time, for some reason, Conci knew the promise was forever and true.

She reminisced silently about her last conversation with Toby Sullivan, when he confessed his love for her. "Oh Toby, I'm a married woman, and I can't fool around or love you the way you deserve to be loved, although I am so tempted. We live in two different worlds. I can't go into yours, and it would be so difficult for you to come back into mine."

"Oh Conci, you're the love of my life. I always knew that when the right woman came along that I would give everything up for her, and I have and I will, my darling," he said and held her in his arms, but they didn't kiss. They dared not touch their lips to one another, knowing it would be a betrayal to Mike, and Conci couldn't do that and be straight with the Lord. Somehow he knew that as much as Conci loved Mike and her children and loved him too, she loved the Lord more than all of them. Yes, he'd found a perfect vessel, the pearl of great price he'd been seeking all his life. Conci heard the thought and pulled away from him.

"No, Toby, I'm not the pearl of great price, the Lord Jesus is. If I left my husband to go with you, then I would have sinned, and you wouldn't think of me as a perfect vessel anymore. You see our dilemma? You can only give your whole heart to the person who won't sin. But if and when she does, then she won't be the perfect one anymore," Conci reasoned. Toby looked at her in awe.

"You hit it on the nail, Conci. But at least let me have my daydreams of having found the perfect woman and let my life be changed because of loving you."

"Okay, Toby, you told me that at one time in your life you were an altar boy."

"Oh yes, it was a wonderful time in my life, Conci. I felt so close to the Lord, then. Yes, I did love the Lord at one time."

"Well, why not make that commitment to him right now, Toby, and your life will have been changed because you knew me and loved me and I loved you too, so much to share the greatest gift that I have, a knowledge of the Lord Jesus and his salvation in your life and mine."

She took a hold of Toby's hand, and he repeated the confession of faith after her and then held her for one last time.

They said their goodbyes, and he left her house.

"Don't try to find me, Conci. Someday I'll come back, and you'll see what a changed life I have because of you."

That was the last time any of them saw Toby Sullivan in person. It was as though he disappeared off the face of the earth.

Deep in her heart she knew that someday she would see him again not as a lover, but as a brother and sister in the Lord.

Mike dropped her off, and she went inside to relieve the babysitter. It was only six in the evening. But they wanted to have a good conversation with the Wileys without the children, so they hired a couple of neighborhood teenagers to watch them for a couple of hours. Conci loved on them, fed them, bathed them, and put them to bed.

Alone now in her prayer closet, Conci felt the tears in the back of her eyes, and she began to cry copious amounts of tears for Toby Sullivan and a life so wasted and a love so lost. But the knowledge of his salvation at the end of their beautiful, holy, innocent relationship was reward enough for having their paths cross.

After a good cry, she wiped her face and took a shower and put away her memories and her daydreams of Toby Sullivan. *Forgive me, Lord, for that flirtation and for almost falling into the trap. Thank you for saving him and for saving me.*

Mike came home late that night and just fell into bed. Conci was already sleeping. The next day, however, Mike stopped at the school and got her released early and took her out for the rest of the afternoon. The whole thing about Madeline and Toby and Lara bothered him a lot, and he felt somehow lost. Conci greeted him with her usual exuberance. And he felt the door was opened again for him, but this time he was going to do it differently.

When they got home, they hugged, and he held onto her and then got on his knees and begged for her forgiveness. "I know it went too far this time, Conci. I almost couldn't get back again, and I don't want that at all anymore. Last night I had a dream that Rhonda got healed and we lived our life together again and I was so happy, but after a while, she began to stray again. And this time, I was upset and angry about all of it and decided to get free of it. In the meantime I met you at Everlasting Life, and we fell in love. And then you found out that I had a wife that I was trying to get divorced from and you left me. I was bereft, and Rhonda wouldn't give me a divorce. I was a very unhappy man, Conci. I knew the dream was from the Lord, and I've been looking at things upside down, always trying to find the perfect redhead that had been Rhonda. But she wasn't so perfect after all. She never loved me the way that you do. And I hurt so much of the time, but you came along and soothed that hurt. Forgive me, baby and give me this one last chance. I know I've said it before, but this time I'm a changed man saying it to you."

He got up and went upstairs into the attic and brought down a covered urn. "This is where I hid her ashes, baby. You know I placed half of them in her grave and half in this urn, which I've been hiding from you all this time."

He took them outside, where it was storming

and there was a north wind blowing so hard that he could barely hold onto the jar. He was getting soaked, with lightning striking all around him, as though the very heavens knew what he was about to do.

He opened up the urn and let the wind take all the ashes, and then they were all gone. He felt the sudden pressure of a hand on his shoulder and turned to see Auntie standing there staring at him with compassion in her eyes. She'd come home from Maureen's, knowing in her spirit that this was a special time.

"Now, Mike, the healing has begun." She closed her eyes and put her hand on his head.

Mike went toward the brick house and hit the house with the urn, over and over again, and it broke into little chards.

Suddenly the storm stopped, and the sun peaked out from the clouds as Mike went inside and down into the basement and opened up a trunk and took out pictures and newspaper clippings and memorabilia, even little wisps of red hair on a card enveloped in plastic and brought them into the backyard, put them into a huge green plastic lawn bag and dumped them into the trash. Conci just watched him in awe.

"That's it, baby. Wait! One other thing!"

He took out his wallet, and behind her and

the children's pictures were pictures of other women and mostly of Rhonda. He tore them into little bits and tore all the little notes and phone numbers he had accrued.

Finally finished, he sat down and just stared at Conci. "There, all gone. My past life without you is all gone," he said and looked so pleased with himself. Conci started to smile and went up to him and hugged him, and he held onto her.

"Do you forgive me, baby? The Lord pointed out to me that I did well with part of the repentance, the sorry part, but not the I-won't-do-it-again part. But that's all gone. Now I've done a full total repentance. Do you accept that from me, Conci?" he asked with a look of fear on his face.

Conci held onto him. "I do forgive you, Mike, with all my heart and soul and spirit too."

Surprisingly, a few weeks later a letter came in the mail addressed to both Conci and Mike. For the writer's own protection, it was left it unsigned, but they both knew who it was from. Inside was a confession of sorts which told the tale of how the counterfeiting ring got started and Bastriani's part in it and the writer's part too.

Dear Conci and Mike,

Madeline was the runner, and she and three other models smuggled in the plates and the papers for the counterfeiting machines. Fred Lawrence really played a minor role and gave us police protection, but really we had the operation set up so carefully that we didn't need any help. Unfortunately, he fell head over heels in love with Madeline, which was always a bad deal for everyone.

Lara still loved Lawrence, since she married him in her early career when she

was a cop but left him to marry the Reverend Connolly, which pleased her family no end. She told me once that she'd been a really wild young woman and rebelled against her pious parents and joined the police academy because they were pacifists

and didn't believe in violence of any kind, so she married Lawrence who was already a cop. Because of these actions her parents were about to disown her and there was a huge amount of money involved, so she divorced Lawrence and married Rev. Connors whom they introduced to her. She described him as a sweet innocent on fire for the Lord. She certainly helped to corrupt him. But, I believe she always had a hankering for Lawrence and he fro her, even though he was now crazy about Madeline, too.

Lara smuggled money in and out of the country

and to different parts of the country. It was foolproof until we started to make mistakes, primarily of the heart.

Madeline was so jealous of anything I did and anyone I spoke to. She was married to Bastriani, who didn't like me at all, but knew I was a big man to deal with. Lara was the greediest of all of us and also a hard-hearted murderer. We really didn't know that until the nurse Ms. Morrison was murdered in that violent hurtful way, and then Sgt. Conover was killed when she told Lara she recognized her from some cold case Conover was working on. Lara told me about it and she was quite upset. "The little bimbo had the nerve to hint that I might be generous in my gratefulness."

"Just leave it, Lara. You'll be swimming in money very soon and can go out of the country again," Lawrence advised her, or so Madeline reported to me. Somehow, though, all of them thought that Lara killed Conover, probably with some kind of drug put into her cannoli that night at the wake.

He went on and on giving details and places and names of people involved. It was a full confession, not whitewashing himself or his part in it at all.

McMurray and Berger were weak links in the chain. I was against putting them in the picture, but Lawrence was sure he could handle them. However, they both got greedy and kept part of the money back from us, and that really irritated the Bastrianis. Surprisingly, it wasn't Philly who killed Berger, but McMurray himself, wanting to get himself off the hook. Madeline was the one who supplied the snakes. After that, McMurray himself got careless and wanted more money too, not taking Berger's death as a warning. He had to be taken care of that was Madeline's job.

But Madeline got screwy and wanted me all to herself and hated Conci because of my feelings for her. Her jealousy prompted her to try to kill Conci and the children. She was half out of her mind by this time with fear as well as jealousy. Bastriani was in jail awaiting trial on murder charges, but Stevie Bastriani was bothering her.

I followed her that day when she tried to kidnap the McVey children, and when she put Conci in the car and then ran off, I killed her in the forest. She was a bad seed. Believe me, I've seen a lot of evil people in my life, but she takes the cake. Sorry about everything but glad to have met you, Concetta Marie D'Amato McVey. Yes, I'm saved because of you. Mike, give her a break. You've got the best woman in the world; treat her like it, would you?

P.S. I have no idea where Captain Cartellini came into the picture. None of our people killed him. Maybe he just had a heart attack. Have you ever thought about that?"

Life went on for the McVeys. As per his agreement with Conci, Mike and she went to a counselor to make their marriage better and to insure that Mike wouldn't cheat again.

Dr. Marty Bukachek was a man in his late forties, with graying blond hair and black, beady eyes and a gray and black goatee. He was short and quite slim. He'd been a detective in his day and then went on to school and got his PhD in psychology. Many of the cops went to see him because he had a greater understanding of their problems in marriage, since he'd been one himself for ten years.

They both liked Dr. Bukachek and went to see him for over six months together and sometimes alone. It was helpful, and they began to enjoy being together and relax with each other. Mike recommitted himself to the Lord.

"I feel that the Lord is leading me to get more involved in the Word and to get more Bible training," he told Monty one day.

"There's a night course that you can take,

Mike, at Everlasting Life Church, and if you're not able to attend, you can do that lesson on the computer."

"That sounds great," Mike agreed.

"And two of the other guys are going to do it too, Mike," Monty continued happily.

Mike talked to Conci about it. "Honey, I feel the Lord leading me to get closer and press in. What do you think?" Conci was quite delighted with him and told him so.

Cici DeMarco didn't get the nomination of her party at all. She lost to the other side and blamed everyone that she knew, especially Mike McVey. She called Conci one day after a big story about her and her lurid past came to the fore. "It was Mike who goofed it up for me, Conci, what with him questioning me about everything. I never killed anyone ever in my life, Conci. He ruined my reputation, and he's going to pay for that."

"Calm down, Cici. That had nothing to do with it. The newspaper said someone called in to them and gave that horrible story about you. It wasn't Mike, for heaven's sakes. It makes him look quite stupid, too."

"Okay, then who did it?"

"Probably someone from the other side, of

course. All your friends know it's not true. We'll go to bat for you if we have to, Cici," Conci said sincerely. "Sister said the same thing," Conci lied. What Sister said couldn't be repeated to Cici, that much was for sure.

Mike was grateful to Conci for calming Cici down. "So, who do you think put that story in the paper, honey?" he asked her one night as they were sitting down spooning on the sofa, with the children crawling on them and them ending up wrestling on the floor. Their home lives were so much better now that Mike knew without a doubt that Conci was the one that God had for him.

"I think it was the general, Mike. He always loved her but really disdained her methods. He was and is a straight-down-the-middle guy. Very conservative. He seldom saw her on the campaign trail, and he complained to us ladies one night at some kind of affair. Yes, I think this will keep her home, and he liked it that way."

"Really, that seems kind of underhanded, doesn't it?" Mike commented, frowning.

Conci just shrugged. "All's fair in love and war, Mike," she said and stared at him to see his reaction. He laughed at that.

Now that those murders were cleared up, the Bastrianis were also arrested on the basis of McMurray's confession. Philly, however, was still awaiting his trial for murder anyway. When they asked him about this, he just shrugged. His brother Stevie in the meantime was apprehended and sang like a canary.

Fred Lawrence turned up dead in the woods behind the Second Chance Academy, which had closed for good now. He'd been shot in the head.

"I'm so sorry about all that, Mike. I think he wasn't as innocent as everyone painted him out to be. After all he did let Lara get killed instead of himself," Conci said in disdain. Mike nodded his head.

Both Conci and Mike knew that Toby Sullivan was the head of the counterfeiting ring, but not a murderer, feeling that he had to kill Madeline to save Conci and her children's lives. Once in a while both of them wondered where he'd gone.

Then one night they were in a theater watching a short subject film about a group of monks that were building two orphanages after having received a huge influx of money from an anonymous donor. There was a shot of over two hundred monks, and Conci sat up straight, not believing what she was seeing. Mike had gone to get some snacks, and she was glad.

There, before her very eyes, was Toby Sullivan with his hair shorn and his head down, and then he looked up at the camera and smiled that big Irish grin. Conci smiled back at him.

"Oh, Toby, you really are serving the Lord," she whispered. Then she began to think. *Who was the anonymous donor? Was it Toby himself?* And then an incredible thought *was it real money they were using or counterfeit?* "Oh Lord, let him be on the straight and narrow and have a happy life serving you." Then she had to smile knowing in her heart that God was in control of Toby's life as well as hers and Mike's.

Mike came back and sat down. And they had their popcorn and diet colas, and he reached over and kissed her.

Conci had to smile. "Yes, the Lord is good."

The End.

bibliography

Stevens, Serita Deborah, R.N., B.S.N. with Klarner, Anne, *Deadly Doses,* Writer's Digest books

An imprint of F & W Publications, Inc., Cincinnatti, Ohio, 1991

Wikipedia, Wikipedia Foundation, Inc., *Seven Deadly Sins, April 14, 2008*

listen|imagine|view|experience

AUDIO BOOK DOWNLOAD INCLUDED WITH THIS BOOK!

In your hands you hold a complete digital entertainment package. Besides purchasing the paper version of this book, this book includes a free download of the audio version of this book. Simply use the code listed below when visiting our website. Once downloaded to your computer, you can listen to the book through your computer's speakers, burn it to an audio CD or save the file to your portable music device (such as Apple's popular iPod) and listen on the go!

How to get your free audio book digital download:

1. Visit www.tatepublishing.com and click on the e|LIVE logo on the home page.
2. Enter the following coupon code:
   19ec-9a5b-eb8e-c814-ccb1-bacd-332e-01cc
3. Download the audio book from your e|LIVE digital locker and begin enjoying your new digital entertainment package today!